THE

TEMPLAR'S RELIC

A James Acton Thriller

By
J. Robert Kennedy

Detective Shakespeare Mysteries
Depraved Difference
Tick Tock

James Acton Thrillers
The Protocol
Brass Monkey
Broken Dove
The Templar's Relic

Zander Varga, Vampire Detective
The Turned

THE
TEMPLAR'S RELIC

A James Acton Thriller

J. ROBERT KENNEDY

Copyright © 2012 J. Robert Kennedy

CreateSpace

All rights reserved. No part of this publication may be reproduced, stored in or introduced into a retrieval system, or transmitted in any form, or by any means (electronic. mechanical, photocopying, recording or otherwise) without the prior written permission of the publisher.

This is a work of fiction. Names, characters, places, and incidents are products of the author's imagination. Any resemblance to actual persons, living or dead, is entirely coincidental.

ISBN: 1479194735
ISBN-13: 978-1479194735

First Edition

10 9 8 7 6 5 4 3 2

For the moderates who died speaking out, for they are the true martyrs.

THE
TEMPLAR'S RELIC

A James Acton Thriller

FORWARD

The bulk of the events in this book take place after those in *Broken Dove*, Book #3 in the *James Acton Thrillers* series. Reading the earlier novels is not necessary to enjoy *The Templar's Relic* as it is a wholly self-contained novel, however it is recommended to fully understand how many of the characters met and those relationships developed.

"And when the sacred months have passed, then kill the polytheists wherever you find them and capture them and besiege them and sit in wait for them at every place of ambush. But if they should repent, establish prayer, and give zakah, let them [go] on their way. Indeed, Allah is Forgiving and Merciful."

Koran 9:5

"The Jews say, "Ezra is the son of Allah"; and the Christians say, "The Messiah is the son of Allah." That is their statement from their mouths; they imitate the saying of those who disbelieved [before them]. May Allah destroy them; how are they deluded?"

Koran 9:30

Port of Acre, Dominion of Saladin
July 12, 1191

"We are defeated."

Malik nodded, his chest tight with the shame of it. It was a statement nobody could dispute. The infidel hordes had broken through the gates about an hour ago and continued to pour in, despite the valiant effort put up by the starving defenders. Malik had tended to the wounded, stacked and burned the dead, distributed the rations to the hungry civilians. He had done it all. And it was all in vain. *Why had this happened?* If they had just surrendered at the start, when it was obvious there was no way to win, this all could have been avoided. *Pride.* It was pride that made the elders decide to fight, to weather the siege.

And for what?

It was over.

The last stand of Acre was over. Tens of thousands were dead. The rest were dying. And after holding out so long, could they expect any restraint from the angry Christian soldiers now pouring through the once mighty gates?

We're all doomed.

Malik looked at Ali, his Imam since he was a little boy. "What are we to do, Imam Ali?"

"Besides pray to Allah?"

Allah hadn't come through so far, so why continue?

"Yes, sir, besides pray."

"Nothing."

Malik opened his mouth to object, when Imam Ali held a boney finger up to stop him.

"*We* shall do nothing, as *I* am too old." He put his arm over Malik's shoulder, guiding him deeper into the mosque. "But *you, you* are young, and still fit. You shall take our holiest of possessions, and save it from the infidels."

Malik's heart pounded against his chest. He stumbled, Ali catching him.

"Are you alright, my son?"

Malik nodded. "Yes, Imam, just overwhelmed with the—" Malik wasn't sure what to say. Honor? Responsibility? Death warrant? "Honor."

Imam Ali smiled.

I guess I chose the right word. But he wasn't sure he wanted the honor. Right now, after almost two years of constant battle, he simply wanted to sit in a corner somewhere and wait for the blade of a Christian Knight to end his suffering. The last thing he wanted was the responsibility of saving the parchment.

"But how, Imam? How can *I* save it?"

"You shall be provisioned for two weeks of travel, disguised as a poor laborer"—he stopped and looked at Malik—"which shouldn't be a problem," he said, smiling. Malik was about to open his mouth to protest some more, when the aged Imam spoke again. "You will be sent out of the city by way of the ancient tunnels."

Malik stopped. *Ancient tunnels?* "What ancient tunnels?"

"Tunnels carved long ago by Allah's will, and the labor of his devotees. They lead out, past the city walls, and under the camps of the infidels. When you reach the end, head south to Jaffa, and seek the Imam there."

Tunnels? Under the city? Suddenly he felt like he might just make it. But then a question begged to be asked. "If there are tunnels, Imam, why haven't we used them to save our people?"

Imam Ali patted the young man on the top of his head. "You are a good boy. Allah would be pleased. If we evacuated our population through these tunnels, there would be so many spread across the desert, that the infidels would surely capture some, then find the source, and enter our city that much sooner." He paused and sighed, his eyes looking into the distance. "Why Saladin hasn't come this time, we'll never know. We had held out hope that he would save us, but he hasn't." He looked back at Malik, a sad smile on his face. "We were foolish. We thought Allah would protect us from the infidel hordes, but Allah obviously had other plans for his children. If only the great Prophet Mohammed, peace be upon him, were here. Such a warrior! He, he would have found a way to save us, and push the infidels back into the sea. Especially that deviant Richard the Lionheart." Ali spat on the ground, as did Malik. It was just something that was done.

"When do I leave?"

Suddenly shouting erupted from the street, the strange tongue of the infidel echoing off the ancient walls. Imam Ali grabbed Malik by his robes and hurried him into the sacred chamber containing the ancient scroll that was so revered. He lifted it off its pedestal and carefully rolled it, placing it into a tube-shaped case sitting under the display. Giving the case a hug while looking up to the heavens, Imam Ali handed it over to his young student.

"Come, we must hurry!"

The shouts from outside sounded closer. Screams of the defenders violated the stillness of the mosque as they were slaughtered; their weakened state no match for the well-fed Christian army. Imam Ali pulled Malik toward the entrance to the cellars, grabbing a torch off the wall. Malik had enough presence of mind to do the same.

They wound their way down a spiral stair case, and eventually emerged into a room filled with scrolls and artifacts collected over the years, by the Imam, who considered himself a scholar, and indeed was renowned throughout the region, taking great pride in his collection, and his writings. This was their history. This was their knowledge. And today, it could all be lost.

Imam Ali stopped at a desk, grabbed a piece of parchment and a quilled pen, then began writing rapidly. When done, he carefully folded it and placed his seal upon it. He handed it to Malik.

"Keep this with you. Should you be faced with a situation where you think a word or two from me might help, break the seal and let them read it. If not, when you reach Jaffa, show it to the Imam."

Malik nodded, tucking the letter away inside his robes.

The sound of the outer doors to the mosque crashing open echoed down the staircase, startling both of them.

"Come, quickly!" hissed Imam Ali. "There's no more time!"

He rushed over to the far wall and pushed aside a tapestry that appeared from the dust to not have been moved in years. Malik bent over and looked under the old cloth, expecting to find a hidden door, but instead found his Imam saying a prayer.

In front of a wall.

A wall no different than any other wall in the room. Imam Ali, finished with his prayer, placed his right hand on a stone, a stone that appeared like all the others in every way. Then he placed his left hand on another stone. Malik wasn't sure what was going on. *Has the old man gone mad?*

Suddenly, with a grunt, the elderly Imam pushed forward with both hands. Malik gasped as the two stones receded into the wall, sounds echoing from behind the stone betraying the presence of some sort of mechanism activating. Moments later the sounds stopped, and Imam Ali looked at Malik with a smile.

"Have faith in Allah." He shoved against the wall, but nothing happened. "And help an old man."

Malik nodded, placed his torch on the floor, then jumped forward, pushing with all his might on the stones his Imam toiled against.

And it moved. Slightly, but then, as they continued to push, it continued to recede, and eventually a gap, large enough for a man, appeared between the wall and what was apparently a secret door.

Imam Ali shoved Malik through the gap, handing him a torch. "Now, push the door closed, then follow the tunnel to its end. It will open facing south." He handed Malik several bags. "Food. Water." He touched Malik's arm. "Allah be with you."

Malik nodded, stepping back into the darkness. He pulled the torch through, and the narrow tunnel was revealed.

"Now push!" he heard the Imam order.

Malik leaned his back against the wall, and pushed with all his might, the ancient doorway slowly closing, then with a final click, he heard the mechanism activate, sealing it in place.

The Imam's voice was muffled but clear enough. "Go!"

Malik didn't need to be told twice. He turned, eyeing the tunnel ahead of him, and stepped forward into what, he did not know.

Northern Wall, Vatican City
Present Day

Ermes Sabatino looked up as one of the men yelled for an excavator to stop.

"What now?"

It was like this job was cursed. This had been going on for almost three months. They were trying to replace an ancient storm drain and sewer line that ran on the Vatican grounds with a more modern one. But since day one there had been problems. Because it tapped into the Rome lines, permits were needed. These were constantly delayed or lost. There were extra inspections, environmental assessments, and any other myriad of delays thrown in his face. This should have been a three month job, but they were already at the three month mark, and excavation had only begun two weeks ago, but equipment kept malfunctioning, and some was sabotaged.

It was as if someone was trying to stop the job.

But why? *It's only a goddamned sewer!* He stopped and looked at where he was, then made the sign of the cross.

He heard the mighty machine turn off. *Okay, this might be bad.* Had they hit a gas line? He looked through the window of his trailer, and there was no indication of panic. If anything, he'd call it excitement.

He grabbed his hard hat and shoved it on his head as he stepped from the air conditioned cool and out into the midday heat. Trotting over to the crowd gathering, he pushed his way though, and when he reached the site, he gasped. The teeth of the excavator had broken through the ground, revealing a chamber underneath.

He felt the ground shift under him.

"Everybody get back!" he yelled. "This ground may not be stable."

He began to step back himself when he felt the ground give way, and he plunged into the depths below. He heard several others cry out as they fell along with him.

His arms flailed, looking for anything to grab onto, but found nothing but empty space. Then he hit. Hard. His head snapped back, but the helmet did its job, absorbing the blow. He looked about but couldn't see anything, just darkness around him, and a light above, blocked by dust.

"Are you okay?" yelled a voice from above.

He wasn't sure. He sat up. Nothing felt broken. "I'm okay!" He looked about but couldn't make out anyone else. "Who else is here? Are you okay?"

"It's Luca. I think I broke my leg."

"Filippo. I'm okay."

A flashlight snapped on. It was Filippo.

"How many are missing?" he called up.

"Three of you fell in!"

"Okay, we have one injured man down here. Call for an ambulance and fire department. We're going to need some special equipment to get us out of here."

"I'm on it!"

Sabatino looked around.

"And send some flashlights down here."

He heard the sounds of several plastic flashlights smashing nearby.

"In a bucket on a rope, you idiots!"

"Sorry, boss!"

"Let me see that," he said to Filippo, putting his hand out for the flashlight. Filippo handed it over, and Sabatino played the beam around the area. It was ancient, filled with dust and cobwebs. Several large stone boxes occupied the room. He stepped over to one, searching for the word, trying to remember what it was called.

Then he shivered.

Sarcophagus!

THE TEMPLAR'S RELIC

Outside Acre, Dominion of Saladin
1191 A.D.

Malik squinted at the sun. *Late afternoon.* The exit, or entrance, depending on which way you were travelling, was not well marked, which was clearly by design. Buried behind a myriad of rocks, exiting had involved shoving aside what turned out to be a fairly heavy hollowed out rock. When Malik had emerged from the hole and replaced the rock, he was amazed at the simplicity of it all. The stone looked like any other. Though hollowed, it was substantial enough that a single man would still struggle to move it.

He swept his foot over the sand, hiding any indication that the stone had moved, then cautiously stepped out from the rocks, surveying the area. He was alone. Squatting in the shade from one of the large rocks, he examined the provisions. *Two weeks?* It occurred to him perhaps the old man didn't eat much, or had forgotten to give him a bag.

But his first priority was to put some distance between himself and the city. To the north he could see the dust from the infidels, and smoke from fires burning in the city. The siege had been brutal. He had heard whisper of several surrender attempts, but none had been accepted. Saladin had managed to hold off the hordes by attacking the infidels from the outside every time the walls were breached.

But not this time.

He wondered why. What had changed for Saladin to not come to the city's aid once more? Could the Christians have defeated him? Were his forces too weakened to stage an attack?

He plodded through the hard rock and hot sand.

It was frustrating. Malik knew he was just a boy, not schooled in the ways of the world yet, but to him the fall of Acre, his home since birth, was blasphemous. The stunning mosque he had worshiped in since he was a boy, and lived in after the death of his parents from some sort of pestilence, was a holy place, a place infidels should never tread.

But it had fallen, and they had tread there.

It had been almost ten years that he had lived there, and those years had left very little memory of his real parents. And for that he sometimes wept, his guilt-ridden mind unable to cope.

But one day he would earn his place in Paradise, in Jannah, and see them again.

He smiled at the thought.

The neighing of a horse tore him from his reverie.

Malik dropped to a knee and looked around, finding no one. Lying down, he slithered up the embankment he was on like an asp. Cresting the top, he peered down below. His heart hammered in his chest. Four horses. He looked closely. Three men were sitting inside a fair-sized tent, enough to comfortably fit them. In front of the tent, tea brewed on a small fire as the men relaxed, obviously avoiding travel during the heat of the midday sun.

These weren't Christian soldiers. And with a spare horse, if they were men of God they would surely lend him the horse, perhaps even escort him all the way to Jaffa. Malik looked up at the heavens. *Allah be praised for bringing them to me!*

He was about to rise to his feet and announce his presence to his saviors, when he heard a noise to his left. *What was that?* It almost sounded like a child. A child sobbing. He slithered back down the embankment, then ran further to the left, toward where he guessed the sound had come. Again he crawled to the top, and, peering over the side, almost gasped.

Below, hidden behind a large stone that sat behind the tent, were four children, varying in age from what he would guess to be barely ten, up to his own age of fourteen. They were all shackled together.

Slave traders!

Suddenly a long shadow cast itself over him, the raging sun blocked. He turned over and saw the silhouette of a man reaching down to grab him. *The fourth rider!* Malik reacted quickly, and the only way he could at this moment. He raised his right knee, then extended his foot—hard and fast. The desired target hit, the man gasped in pain, grasping his now scrambled eggs, and fell backward. Malik leapt to his feet, and in a split second made a monumental decision. He could flee, and perhaps save himself, but more likely be captured by the four men on horseback, or he could fight, perhaps preventing his own discovery, and perhaps, even accomplishing something noble in the name of Allah.

He picked up a rock, and raising it over his head with both hands, dropped to his knees beside the man who was writhing in agony, his eyes closed. Malik dropped the stone hard. It immediately drew blood from the man's forehead. Before the man could react, Malik hit him again. And again. Several more blows and it was clear the man was no longer a threat. In fact, Malik wasn't even sure if he was alive.

He tossed the stone aside and dropped back on his haunches, holding his blood soaked hands in front of him. *Forgive me, Allah!* He had never struck a man before, and he had certainly never killed a man. Tears filled his eyes as he looked down at the man, unmoving, even his chest failing to rise and fall with the life giving breaths it should.

He must be dead.

Malik wiped his hands in the sand, ridding them as best he could of the blood staining them. He rose, looking about for the man's companions, but found himself alone. As he stepped away he stopped. Around the man's chest was a leather cord, and attached to that was a ring with keys. Keys that just might fit the shackles imprisoning the children he had found. He yanked it off the man's neck, the cord snapping with little effort.

The keys slipped from his fingers, and as if in slow motion, slid down the loose end of the cord, falling through the air, Malik's mouth gaping in horror as they clattered against a rock. The sound seemed to roar across the landscape as Malik's heart pounded, his ears filling with the rush of blood, removing all stillness from the setting.

He dropped to the ground.

Listening for the others, he tried to steady his breathing, the din in his ears hindering his ability to listen for the telltale sounds of feet on sand. He closed his eyes, and said a short prayer, asking Allah for strength and guidance.

The roaring quieted. He opened his eyes and looked.

No one.

And no sounds.

He carefully picked up the keys, this time gripping them tightly, and crawled toward where he had seen the children. He found them, still alone, still shackled.

"Pssst!"

The small hiss, meant to attract their attention, sounded like the horns of the Christians. One of them looked up, a boy about his age. Malik put his finger to his lips, urging him to remain quiet. The boy nodded, then tapped the others on the shoulders, his own finger to his lips, then pointed to Malik. One was about to say something when the older boy put his hand over the young one's mouth, shaking his head. The little one nodded.

Malik crawled down the embankment and quickly reached the cover of the rock. Without saying a word, he showed the keys to the older boy, whose face lit up with a smile and wide eyes. He grabbed the keys, and flipped through them quickly, selecting one he had obviously seen used before. He slid it into the keyhole on the shackles gripping his ankle, and turned. They fell to the ground.

This got the other kids excited.

"Me next!"

The older one slapped his hand over the young one's mouth, and they all froze, listening for the slavers. The murmur of their voices was all that could be heard, and it didn't seem to have changed.

The oldest one unlocked the remaining children, then they all quickly ran with their back to the rock, putting as much distance as they could as quickly as they could between them and the slavers. As they left the captors behind, the scrambled combination of ducking and running turned into an all-out run, with Malik and the oldest alternating between dragging and carrying the others, who were quickly exhausted.

Malik spotted a group of rocks, and pointed. The older boy nodded, and they adjusted their direction toward the stones and the precious cover they would provide. Within minutes they were safely tucked in behind the stones, Malik and the eldest peering out for any sign of pursuit, the other three lying on their backs, gasping for air, one crying softly.

Satisfied there were no pursuers, Malik sat down, his back to a rock, and calmed his hammering heart. The eldest held out his hand, saying something that had Malik's heart drumming again. He spoke in the tongue of the invaders.

He was an infidel!

Corpo della Gendarmeria Office
Palazzo del Governatorato, Vatican City
Present Day

"Out of the question!"

"What do you mean? How can you say that? It's protocol, we've always done it this way!"

Inspector General Mario Giasson, head of the Corpo della Gendarmeria dello Stato della Città del Vaticano, or the Corps of Gendarmerie of Vatican City State, stared at Father Jonathan Brandis. *Where has he been this past year?*

"I'm sorry, Father, but with two serious security breaches"—he held up a finger—"at least two serious security breaches, in the past year, there is no way I can let a team of outside archaeologists swarm all over the city."

Father Brandis dropped into a chair, clearly frustrated. "But Monsieur, this is an archaeological find. Surely you don't propose we destroy it and continue on with the construction."

Giasson ran his hand over his shaved head, willing the tension into his fingers, and away from the pounding headache he now had. This was quite possibly the worst scenario they could be facing. They were using the sewage upgrade as an excuse to seal off the entrance to the Vault that had been discovered several months ago, and it was clear someone was trying to stop it, or at least delay it.

And now this.

This threatened to not only stop the entire project indefinitely, but bring in outsiders, who might stumble upon the Vault, which was absolutely not acceptable.

Unfortunately Father Brandis was right. There was no avoiding it. The discovery had to be investigated, there was no choice. This was history, and it needed to be preserved.

But they also needed to seal the security breach, and it couldn't be done from the inside, as that would expose the Vault. It had to be done from the other end.

He turned to Ermes Sabatino who had sat patiently through the exchange. "Can you reroute?"

Sabatino nodded. "Of course. The good news is that the Roma side of things won't need to change, so no new permits. We can reroute the new pipes around the discovery, depending on how big it is."

"What about sealing the old pipe?"

Sabatino shrugged. "No change there. We can still tear up the half we were going to do regardless. Cap the Vatican side, fill in the rest with stone as requested. Why you don't just use dirt is beyond me, but hey, it's your project."

Dirt is too easy to dig through. Concrete can be bored through. Stone, when removed, collapses.

But of course Giasson couldn't tell him the real reason. In fact, if he could do the job himself, he'd be out there right now. There were only a handful of people who knew about this ancient, secret passageway, and he could trust them. He chuckled to himself. *Maybe I'll call Hugh, James and Laura and have them come out and help me.*

He snapped his fingers.

"I've got just the two archaeologists who'd be perfect for the job!"

Father Brandis leaned forward. "Who?"

"World renowned."

"Who?"

"Well respected, one's even been in numerous magazines."

"Who?" Brandis was getting frustrated.

"And, we can trust them implicitly."

"Who!"

Giasson smiled.

"Professors James Acton and Laura Palmer."

Outside Acre, Dominion of Saladin
1191 AD

Malik drew his knife, and held it out in front.

The boy's eyes bulged and he held up his hands, waving them at Malik. He pointed at his chest. "John."

Malik assumed it was a name. He slowly lowered the knife. Obviously this boy had been kidnapped by the slavers. And if he was a boy, he wasn't a soldier. *He's just a kid like me*. And he knew if they were to get out of this alive, they would have to work together.

Malik pointed at his own chest. "Malik."

"Mahh-lick."

Malik nodded, then pointed at the boy. "Jan?"

"Jaawn."

"Jaawn."

John nodded, then pointed at the boys Malik had rescued. He clasped his hands together and bowed. "Thank you."

Malik had no idea what the words meant, but the sentiment was clear. He just smiled and nodded, then reached into one of the bags over his shoulder, pulling out a skin of water, and some food. The boys eagerly drank and ate, it clear they hadn't done so in quite some time.

After a few minutes of rest, Malik rose and surveyed their surroundings again. There was dust on the horizon, possibly from horses, but the sun was almost set. He was sure the slavers wouldn't try to pursue them in the dark. It would be dangerous, and they'd have no trail to follow.

But it was clear they couldn't stay here. Malik surveyed their surroundings, and spotted a depression nearby. He tapped John on the shoulder and pointed. John nodded, and gathered the three young boys.

"Keep quiet, and follow us," said Malik.

The boys nodded. *So they're not infidels.*

He stepped out from behind the rocks and began to run toward the depression, his hands gripping two of the boys, John and the third boy taking up the rear. Within minutes they were in the depression, and out of sight of any possible pursuers. The sun was a mere sliver now, the stones casting long shadows, the sand kicked up by the hooves of horses now settled. It appeared their pursuers had given up.

For now.

Now was the time they would have to put more distance between them and the slavers, and pray the winds covered their tracks.

"Let's go," Malik whispered, then pressed on. They walked for hours until finally the young ones could go no more. Then they each took turns carrying one, then two, until at last both John and Malik collapsed in exhaustion. Malik had no idea how far they had travelled. But what was clear to him was that his mission, his mission for Allah, was not being accomplished. He pressed his hand against his precious charge tucked under his robes.

He lay, staring at the stars, praying for guidance, when fatigue finally overcame him. But his dreams were restless, tormented, filled with nightmares of pursuit, of the siege, of the collapse of the outer wall, the infidel hordes pouring through.

He awoke with a start, John leaning over him, shaking him.

"What, what is it?" asked Malik as he pushed himself up with his elbows.

John said something in the infidel tongue, then pointed. The snort of a horse caused Malik to spin toward the sound. His heart leapt into his throat. Three infidel knights on horseback stared down at them.

Acton Residence
Stowe, Vermont
Present Day

I can't believe I'm about to do this!

Professor James Acton swung his parents' SUV into their driveway and came to a stop under the carport. With a quick check of his teeth in the mirror, then his hair, and a deep breath, he closed his eyes, and said a silent prayer. Turning off the engine, he climbed out and looked about the neighborhood he had grown up in. The neighborhood, when as a kid, he had dreamed of this day. What would it be like? What would they be like? Who would it be? He smiled and shook his head as he opened the door.

"I'm home!"

He heard footsteps as the love of his life, Professor Laura Palmer, came out of the kitchen. "Hello, Dear," said Laura, her face and an apron she was sporting covered in flour. "Your mother is just showing me how to make tea biscuits."

Acton chuckled. "I think the flour goes in the bowl, Babe."

His mother poked her head out, clucking at him. "Leave the poor girl alone."

Acton felt his chest tighten and tears filled his eyes. "But I don't want to." His voice was dead serious.

Laura smiled, then gasped, her hand darting to cover her mouth as Acton dropped to one knee.

"Ellsworth!" screamed his mother. "Shut off the game and get in here!"

Acton stretched his hand out and pulled Laura closer. "Two years ago I thought I was happy. I had a great job, great friends, travelled the world, and was intellectually satisfied. But when I met you, I realized I had a hole in my life, a gap that had gone unfilled for so long, an emotional hole that I didn't know I had. These past two years with you have been the best of my life." He grinned. "Despite almost getting killed on several occasions."

"Oh, James," whispered Laura, tears streaming down her face. He quickly glanced at his parents as his father walked into the room. His mother was biting her finger, tears streaking her cheeks.

"I guess what I'm trying to say, is that I love you, and that I always want to be with you, so"—he choked up—"I'm sorry, I rehearsed this a thousand times, but I've gone blank." He reached into his pocket, pulled out a small velvet case, and flipped it open, revealing a diamond solitaire engagement ring. "Laura Angela Palmer, will you marry me?"

Laura extended the fingers on her left hand and nodded. "Yes!" she whispered.

Acton slipped the ring on her finger, his mother jumped up and down, his father turned to hide a tear that had escaped, and Acton rose, taking Laura in his arms. He kissed her gently, then whispered in her ear, "Thank you."

She hugged him harder. "No, thank you. You've made me the happiest woman in the world."

Acton glanced at his mother who had stopped jumping, but now was clapping her hands together. "I'm not sure about that, have you seen my mother?"

Laura let go and looked at Dorothy who immediately stepped forward and grabbed Laura in her arms. "Congratulations, my dear."

"Thank you, Mrs. Acton."

Dorothy pushed her back, holding her shoulders. "Call me 'Mom'. I'd really love it if you would." More tears burst from both women, who hugged each other again.

Acton looked at his dad and shrugged his shoulders. "Women."

Ellsworth tilted his head slightly and, palms facing upward, said, "Whatcha gonna do?" He extended his hand and Acton grasped it. He felt his father squeeze it then pull him, giving a rare hug. "I'm proud of you, son."

Acton felt his chest tighten and didn't trust himself to say anything. He took a deep breath then stepped back.

"Now let's see that rock!" said his mother, and Laura obliged by extending her hand.

"It's not much, I'm sorry, but I'm only a professor."

Laura smiled, never taking her eyes off the diamond. "It's perfect, James, absolutely brilliant." She looked at him then buried her head in his chest, hugging him hard. He returned the hug, and they just stood there.

"Let's give them some space," whispered his dad.

Acton opened his eyes slightly to see his dad physically pull his mother away from the room, the smile on her face as large as any he recalled seeing.

"I love you," he whispered in Laura's ear.

She looked up at him and smiled. "I love you too."

The phone rang, but Acton pushed it out of his mind. This was their moment, and he didn't want anyone to ruin in. The last time they had visited his parents, he had wanted to propose, but the timing had been definitely bad. It had been three months, and nobody had tried to kill them lately, so he felt now was the time. With the way their life had been these past couple of years, death could come knocking at any minute.

"It's for you, Jim!"

It was his mother. He gave Laura a squeeze and pushed away, smiling. "Well, at least it's not a military chopper this time!"

She laughed and took his hand, following him into the kitchen. Acton grabbed the phone. "Jim here."

"Professor Acton, it is Mario Giasson, how are you today?"

"Hi, Mario, I'm fine. In fact, I just proposed to Laura."

"And did she accept?"

"What, you thought she wouldn't?"

Giasson laughed. "My friend, when I proposed to my wife, I wasn't certain if I would ever see her again."

Acton chuckled. "She said 'yes'."

"Then congratulations, my friend." He paused. "Perhaps the timing is bad, but I would like to offer you and your fiancée a job."

"Huh?"

The room turned to look at Acton.

"We have made a discovery here. Quite interesting. And with the security breaches, I don't trust bringing in outsiders that I'm not personally familiar with."

"Are you sure you want us? Every time we go to the Vatican, all hell breaks loose."

Giasson cleared his throat, and Acton made a mental note to watch his language, even the mild expletives.

"There is no danger; this is an archaeological find, discovered while construction was underway. We need some experts to examine what we've found."

"And what is it you've found?"

"Something I think you both will find very thrilling."

Outside Acre, Dominion of Saladin
1191 AD

They had travelled for days. Perhaps even weeks. Malik wasn't sure anymore. The knights had taken them with them, but seemed to be going in circles, for what purpose, he didn't know. And apparently neither did John. These infidels apparently spoke a tongue different than John. Which was something Malik found interesting. He had always assumed that the infidels all spoke one language, like his people did. At least however these knights seemed to be treating them okay, simply urging them to follow their horses, but providing them with food and water when Malik's supply ran out.

But what was their purpose? Were they going to deliver them to someone else when they came upon a town? And what about *his* mission? Malik had to get to Jaffa, but couldn't just head out on his own. These were the infidels, and would most likely kill him should he try to leave. Besides, he felt some sort of obligation to the boys he had rescued.

Malik wasn't sure what day it was when they came across another group of infidels on horseback, but this group of at least a dozen riders, had several score of what appeared to be prisoners with them, all roped together at the ankles.

John immediately tried to communicate again, and this time appeared to have great success, conversing with one of the knights. At one point John collapsed against the horse, hugging the knight's leg, the man patting the boy on the head. John looked at Malik and smiled wide, it clear they had been saved.

They travelled with the now large group, Malik, John and the other three free of the ropes binding the others. Malik dared not talk to those who were bound, terrified that if the infidels knew he was Muslim, he too, and the other boys, would be taken prisoner.

He had to figure a way out. He had to complete his mission, and he knew it would only be a matter of time before his secret would be discovered. All it would take would be for one of the little ones to say something in his native tongue.

Then they'd all be doomed.

And he couldn't have the safety of one of Mohammed's greatest treasures resting on the mouths of babes. He needed to escape.

One of the infidels yelled, pointing ahead.

Malik looked, and his chest tightened in dismay.

On the horizon were thousands of souls, prisoners and infidel soldiers, all amassed at the foot of the Al 'Ayadiyeh hill, a hill he knew well since childhood.

It appeared there would be no escape.

Allah forgive me.

Ciampino Airport
Rome, Italy
Present Day

Both Acton and Laura looked at the limousine with Vatican markings. The last time this had happened, it hadn't turned out good. Acton led the way down the stairs from Laura's leased Gulfstream V. The ridiculous amount of money she had inherited from her brother when he died allowed them to live a life of luxury if they chose to, but they didn't. They lived a normal life, except for the fact they travelled when they wanted to, in the style they wanted to. And they sponsored their own digs when funding from other sources wasn't available.

So a G-V to Europe wasn't out of the ordinary, especially if time were of the essence. And the last time they had landed in Rome, a limousine much like the one that stood before them now had resulted in a harrowing experience.

The door opened.

And Giasson stepped out.

"Professors, it is okay, come, come," he said, waving his hand for them to join him.

Acton breathed a sigh of relief and smiled, glancing back at Laura who also looked relieved. They descended the stairs, and one of the ground crew at the charter terminal unloaded their bags. The chauffeur loaded them in the trunk as the traditional cheek kisses were exchanged.

"It is so good to see you again, Professors. After last time, I decided it best I should pick you up myself."

Laura climbed into the back of the limo and Acton followed her.

"It's appreciated, Mario," said Laura, settling in. "I haven't sat in the back of a car since without feeling some trepidation."

Giasson climbed in and the chauffeur shut the door. "Nothing to worry about on this drive, I assure you."

Acton looked at Giasson. *He looks tired.*

"So, why have you brought us here?"

Giasson leaned forward. "We're in the process of sealing the secret entrance to the Vault."

"Not the one in the—"

"No," interrupted Giasson. "That one must remain. I mean the one that was used to abduct you."

"Ahh, okay. That makes sense."

Giasson massaged his temples. "We've been trying to get this going for months; since the very day after those events were concluded. But we've run into delay after delay. *Inexplicable* delay after delay."

"What do you mean?" asked Laura.

"Because the passage actually is just a link to the sewage system that's been there, shared with the city of Rome for over a century, we need permits from the Italian federal and Rome municipal governments to proceed with the work. We're calling it a modernization of that portion, claiming a cave in."

"Cave in? How'd you get them to believe that?"

"I planted a small explosive charge on the ceiling and detonated it."

Acton smiled. "So there *was* a cave in."

"Absolutely," said Giasson with a grin. "Which of course demanded a repair. His Holiness naturally was in on the plan, and ordered Vatican City to take the opportunity to upgrade that part of the sewage line rather than just repair the old line. And that's when the problems started."

"Such as?"

"Delays in getting permits. An unusual number of environmental assessments, building code inspectors, engineering studies—it never ended. Also, almost every form we ever submitted was lost. Replies were lost. We ended up having to hand deliver our paperwork. In all my years I've never seen such a thing."

"Sounds like somebody was trying to keep you from plugging their leak."

Giasson nodded.

"It didn't end there. Once we had everything in place, we had a hard time getting contractors. People wouldn't bid on the job, or they'd drop out. Once we finally got a firm, after offering a large bonus sum, equipment began to be sabotaged or stolen." Giasson shook his head. "It is terrifying that they have this much power."

"Surely you haven't called us in because of this," said Laura. "You found something?"

Giasson nodded. "Once we finally started excavating, we stumbled upon something."

Laura leaned forward. "What?"

"Some sort of crypt."

Acton and Laura exchanged excited glances. Acton motioned with his fingers. "Details!"

"I don't have any. Some of the construction workers fell in the hole, and discovered several sarcophagi. They were pulled out and the area stabilized so it would be safe for a team to go in. But with all the problems we've been having, I wasn't about to let more outsiders inside the city to investigate. Which is when I thought of you."

"Why?"

"Because I trust you. And so does His Holiness."

Acton sat back in the leather seat, eyeing Giasson. "There's something you aren't telling us."

Giasson frowned. "You are very astute, my friend." He snapped open a briefcase, removing a file folder. He flipped it open, revealing a sheaf of papers. "These have been found on the job site, inside paperwork. Everywhere." Flipping through them, it was evident they all were the same. Each contained the symbol of the Triarii, with a red cross through them.

"So the Keepers of the One Truth are involved."

"Undoubtedly."

Acton took Laura's hand.

"Which means none of us are safe."

Al'Ayadiyeh, Outside Acre, Dominion of Saladin
1191 AD

Tears streaked Malik's cheeks. He couldn't help it. He was terrified. Screams echoed off the hill at their backs as the infidel Frankish soldiers charged with sword and lance, a massacre unlike anything he could have imagined, beginning. He held onto the other children, trying to shield their eyes from the horrors he couldn't help but take in.

His eyes, unblinking, red, blurred as the thousands hemmed in by the horses and tents of the invaders, pushed themselves back toward the hill, and away from the advancing army. Women and children pled to Allah, the men prayed as they tried to shield their wives and loved ones from the onslaught.

But it was hopeless. The hill was too steep, there was no way to climb it. And the armies surrounded them on the other three sides, slashing and stabbing their way forward, decapitating and goring hundreds at a time, the hoofs of their beasts crushing any survivors.

And through it all he saw John, standing beside the knights that had rescued them, the knights who had ultimately turned them over to the garrison now committing the slaughter, all on one whispered word of a small boy whose head was now buried in Malik's thigh.

John had pled to them, but they had refused to let us go, instead lashing us to the group of prisoners they had already collected, leaving only John free. He had fought valiantly against the knights, but when one drew his sword to cut him down, Malik had yelled for John to stop. The words weren't understood, but everyone knew what was meant, and John, resigned to the fate of his companions, dropped to the desert floor and wept.

"Malik!"

Malik turned toward the voice calling him. It was Imam Ali, fighting his way toward him. Malik began to push through the crowd, toward his Imam, but it was almost no use, the crowd surge carrying both of them toward the base of the hill. But in time, each made a little progress, and eventually they clasped each other's hands.

"Malik, my boy, why? Why are you here?"

Malik felt the shame fill his chest and stomach. "I am sorry, Imam, but I came across these boys"—he pointed at the three with his chin, his arms still around them—"being held prisoner by slavers. I felt compelled to rescue them."

The Imam nodded, reaching out and feeling the scroll tucked in its case under Malik's robes.

Malik's voice broke. "I'm so sorry I failed you!"

Imam Ali smiled at his pupil. "You did Allah's will, by saving these boys." He patted each on the head as they all struggled to maintain their balance, the crowd jostling them in their desperation.

The infidel soldiers were less than fifty paces away.

Malik looked down at the three sobbing boys, then at his Imam. "But to what end? At least with the slavers they would have lived! All I have done is kill them!"

"It is Allah's will. They have earned their place in Paradise."

And with that he turned to face the infidels and yelled, at the top of his voice, "Stop, and listen to my words. Give yourself to Allah, and face your enemies with courage in your eyes, and peace in your heart, for today we enter Paradise, to celebrate our sacrifice with our loved ones for eternity, at Allah's and the blessed Prophet's side." He held up his hands. "Do not run, but turn and face your enemy. Show them your bravery, show them your faith, a faith these infidels can never have, can never understand, for they will never know the love of Allah and the Prophet, peace be upon him."

Malik thought Imam Ali's words wasted, but the screaming began to subside, as did the jostling, and those nearest him stopped, and turned, then others, and soon the mass of screaming flesh, desperate to attempt the impossible climb, stopped.

And so did the infidels.

The few hundred prisoners that remained all stood, most still weeping, but quieter now, their faces, rather than their backs, toward the murderers, murderers who would now need to look their victims in the eyes as they did the Devil's work.

A shout from one of their leaders urged the onslaught forward, and the screams of those nearest them cried out against the sobs and prayers, but the survivors held their ground. Malik gripped the boys tight, shielding their eyes as best he could. He felt Imam Ali's hand on his shoulder as he recited a prayer from the Koran. They were paces away now. He looked at his Imam, regret on his face, then shock, as the sword of a knight arced through the air, cleaving the holy man's head cleanly from his shoulders.

Malik turned to face his own murderer, a knight hidden behind a helmet concealing enough of his features that he would be impossible to identify, but Malik took comfort in knowing that Allah knew all, and this soldier, this infidel, this murderer, would pay the ultimate price in the afterlife. For what he did here today, was not the work of the Christian god, but a labor in service of evil, an evil that left the blood of thousands to stain the desert for time without end, and a thousand infidel souls to burn in damnation for eternity.

Malik never felt the blade that sent his soul to Paradise, and thankfully, was spared the sight of the massacre of three innocents, who knew not why they died.

Northern Wall, Vatican City
Present Day

Acton looked about. The Keepers of the One Truth. They were sworn to protect the secrets of the Vault, which for over a millennia had hidden away the blasphemous, the heretical, the unexplained. And as events a few months ago had proven, they would stop at nothing to do so. His eyes came to rest on one man who seemed to be staring a little too intently. The man continued to stare at Acton, before turning and talking to someone beside him.

I'm getting paranoid.

But that was the problem. They could be anyone, anywhere. They had two thousand years to get their fingers into whatever pie they needed to protect their secrets. And they'd proven that they were willing to stop at nothing to do it.

Including murder.

He took one last look before climbing down the ladder, and into the newly discovered crypt. Laura immediately followed. Though it was daylight outside, it was still dark in the crypt. One large portable light had been lowered in, its bulbs flooding the room with light, casting long shadows past anything of interest. Acton had told them to wait before putting any additional lighting in, as he didn't want to risk damage to any of the find by untrained workers.

It was damp, musky, the heavy, stagnant air not having exchanged with the fresh air from above. It was breathable, barely. But Acton had been in worse. Far worse.

"Look."

Acton looked to where Laura's flashlight was pointing.

"There used to be an entranceway here, but it's been sealed."

Acton nodded, running his hands over the masonry. "It looks old. At least five hundred years. We'll carbon date the mortar. That should give us a good estimate as to when this was done."

Acton continued to survey the perimeter, ignoring the sarcophagi. He was itching to examine them, but like when he was a kid, he was eating the vegetables first, saving the meat for last.

Unless there was gravy.

His stomach rumbled.

"Was that you?"

He shrugged his shoulders. "A man's gotta eat."

Laura shook her head. "You're the one who insisted on skipping lunch and getting started."

Acton chuckled. "Hey, I'm allowed to make a mistake now and then."

He caught Laura shining her flashlight on her engagement ring. It sparkled against the wall. He cleared his throat. "Hey, we've got work to do here."

She looked at him, a smile on her face. "Busted?"

"Busted." He pointed at the sealed entrance. "This seems to be the only way in or out. For whatever reason, this room was intentionally sealed off, which is kind of odd."

"Agreed," said Laura from the other side of the chamber. "I could see it being forgotten about over the centuries and eventually cut off from new construction by accident, but this is one room, with just the doorway sealed up." She paused. "I wonder what's on the other side of the door."

Acton tapped the stone with a small hammer. "We'll find out when we open this up, I guess. This could just be the tip of the iceberg." He turned on his heel and shone his flashlight at the four sarcophagi occupying the center of the room. "So, what have we here?" he said, more to himself than anyone else. Laura too switched her attention.

They were each about six to seven feet long, three feet wide, and the sarcophagi themselves were about three feet high, but sat atop platforms each several feet high. The four tombs were orientated with the head of each in the center of the room, with the bottom-most of the sarcophagi having its feet pointing toward the stoned up entrance. Two stone steps wrapped around the entire outer area of the four sarcophagi, then the third to fifth steps broke off from the base steps into four distinct groups, ending surrounding their respective sarcophagus.

"A lot of work went into this."

Acton nodded. "Whoever they were at one time commanded a lot of respect to have this"—Acton waved his arm at the scene before them—"done for them. I wonder what changed to have them walled up and forgotten."

Laura climbed the steps nearest her and gasped. "James, look!"

Acton climbed the steps surrounding the sarcophagus nearest him, and he felt his heart hammer in his chest in excitement. He had expected the sculpted form of the knight that lay before him, the detail of the armor and the standard chiseled face of a warrior with long hair unsurprising. But what he hadn't expected was the shield.

He pulled a large, soft-haired brush from his tool kit he had bundled in his satchel, and gently began to clear the centuries of dust and recent debris from the shield as Laura circled around to join him. Done, he stood back and they both shone their flashlights at what he had revealed.

"Is that what I think it is?"

Acton nodded. "That's a Templar Knight's shield." He shone his light quickly at the other three stone carvings topping the sarcophagi. "They're all Templar Knights."

Laura placed her hand gently on the forehead of the carving. "At least now we know why you were forgotten."

Al'Ayadiyeh, Outside Acre, Dominion of Saladin
1191 AD

John covered his mouth and nose with his sleeve, batting away the flies with his free hand. His tear-filled eyes sought his friend, his friend who he had met only days before, and who he had never shared a conversation. But there was a bond there, a bond he knew he would feel for the rest of his life.

He had watched Malik die, powerless to stop it, the horror of the massacre imprinted on his memory for eternity. How King Richard could order such a thing was incomprehensible. *What could possess a man to such evil?*

A horse whinnied and a voice called out. "You there, we are leaving. Saladin's men are returning!"

John waved the knight off. In the horror of yesterday he hadn't realized that a small band of Saladin's men, after witnessing the start of the massacre, had attacked, in a heroic, albeit useless, attempt to stop the slaughter. They had fought valiantly, but ultimately their sacrifice was for naught, evil triumphing in the end.

After seeing what his fellow Christians were capable of, he no longer believed they had the moral high ground. And as far as he was concerned, death at the hands of Saladin's men was deserved, for he was responsible for Malik's death, and the death of the three young boys who had been his companions by chance.

His father had left for the Holy Land ten years before, when John was just a boy. And when John had turned fourteen, he had left to find him, to the protests of his mother. It had taken over two years to arrive in the land told of in the Bible, and that had been relatively short only because his wealthy cousin had agreed to let him accompany his contingent. Well-funded, they had little problem securing passage when necessary, fresh horses, supplies. And when they had arrived, he had found his father quite quickly, his name, Sir Guy of Ridefort, apparently well-known and respected.

It was a triumphant reunion. His father had a banquet in his honor, attended by King Richard himself. John had shaken the butcher's hand. And after, in the few brief months they were reunited, father and son, he had continued his instruction in becoming a knight, training his cousin had begun on his two year journey. He had become quite adept at the use of the sword, at how to move freely in the heavy equipment they wore into battle, and in hand-to-hand combat as well.

Though only sixteen, he knew how to handle himself, and sufficiently impressed, he was due to be accepted into the Poor Fellow-Soldiers of Christ and of the Temple of Solomon, or, as the common man knew them, the Knights Templar.

But that was before his dad was killed, and John was captured.

It had been cowardly, ambushed in their sleep by the very Bedouin slavers Malik had freed him from. They were both asleep, under the stars, when their attackers slit the throats of the guard supposed to watch over them, most likely themselves asleep at their posts. And he had been taken prisoner, the only survivor.

Until Malik.

John gasped, recognizing the face of one of the little boys who had been his companion for weeks, amongst the throngs of dead. He bent down, moving arms and legs, revealing the face.

It was him.

Tears flowed down John's cheeks, and he followed the tiny arm, its hand grasping a larger one, and John knew who it was. He pushed the headless body of an old man aside, revealing his friend, still holding the hand of the first boy, his other arm around the other two.

John collapsed on top of Malik, sobbing. For it was his fault. If he hadn't of called out to the knights, if they had just found a village instead, they might all be alive. But instead he had trusted in his fellow Christians, and this was the result.

The pounding of horse's hooves broke the eerie silence, the sound of the rider jumping off causing John to turn. It was his father's Sergeant, Raymond.

"Sir John, thank the good Lord you are alright!" he exclaimed, running over to him. "When we found your father's encampment, and you were gone, we feared the worst."

John didn't say anything. *Sir John?* He placed a palm on Malik's chest, and felt something hard underneath.

"Sir, we must leave at once. Saladin's army is coming, and there will be no quarter for those he finds, not after this."

John moved aside Malik's robe, and found a long tube, a strap holding it around his friend's neck. He gently removed it from his friend's body. He touched Malik's forehead. "I will take care of this for you now."

"Sir, we must hurry!"

John stood and took one last look at his friend and their three tiny companions. He wiped the back of his hand across his soiled face, clearing it of the tears burning streaks of sorrow down his cheeks. He turned to his father's most trusted companion.

"Why do you call me 'Sir John'?"

Raymond placed a hand on John's shoulder. "For you are the eldest, and with your father's death, you inherit his wealth, his title, and, should you accept it, my loyalty."

John nodded, suddenly feeling a heavy weight fall on his shoulders, as the realization of his new position, his new responsibilities, sank in.

He gripped Malik's tube, then slung it over his shoulder. Raymond called for another man to bring a horse, and John, Sir John, mounted the beast, it already skittish from the pounding of thousands of hooves as Saladin's army closed in, hell bent on revenge.

Sir John dug his heels into the sides of the mighty beast, urging it forward, as the remaining Christian soldiers beat a hasty retreat to the secure walls of Acre, leaving behind thousands of nameless innocents, including the bodies of four who would forever remain burned in his memory.

Rest in peace my brothers.

Northern Wall Construction Site, Vatican City
Present Day

"If these are indeed the bodies of Templar Knights, then you're right, we now know why they were sealed in and forgotten."

Laura ran her finger along the edges of the distinctive flared cross extending from top to bottom of the shield, and across to the sides. "The shields would certainly suggest they're Templar's."

"Agreed."

Acton swept more dust away, below the shield and his heart skipped a beat.

"There's an engraving."

Laura rounded the sarcophagus to get a better look as Acton ran his finger along the text, reading it aloud. "Here rests Sir John of Ridefort, son of Guy, and Knight of the Order of the Temple, died in Rome, 16 July in the year of our Lord 1215, as he lived, a hero, saving the life of an innocent, and honoring his Lord our God, and the Holy Roman Catholic Church. May he forever rest in peace." He looked at Laura. "I guess that settles that."

She nodded, patting the boot of the stone effigy. "I'm afraid, Sir John, that we will be interrupting your rest, at least for a short time."

Acton resumed cleaning the top of the sarcophagus. With these being Templar's, it was understandable that the Church had sealed this chamber off. The Templars were once the mightiest of orders, probably even rivaling the modern day Triarii for how widespread they were. Founded in 1119 with the approval of King Baldwin II of Jerusalem by Hugues de Payens under the auspices of providing protection to European pilgrims on their way to the holy land, they were given special dispensation in 1139 by Pope Innocent II to be exempted from all local laws. They were poor, at first, hence their emblem of two men riding on the back of one horse, and their official full name of the Poor Fellow-Soldiers of Christ and of the Temple of Solomon.

But they quickly grew wealthy through money paid by the pilgrims, and bounty collected from the criminals they killed. Their power grew, and at their peak had twenty thousand members, of which almost two thousand were knights. A vast administration ran their business; their wealth grew exponentially when they began to offer the first international banking system, where a pilgrim or other traveler could deposit their wealth at a Templar office, receive a piece of paper confirming the value of what was deposited, then, travel in safety with nothing of value to have stolen. When they reached their destination, they would hand over their 'check', payable only to them, and receive the equivalent value.

Less a service charge of course.

But as with all wealth came jealousy, and bad business partners. King Philip IV of France borrowed a fortune from the Templars to wage war against England, and was unable to pay the money back. Rather than own up to this, he convinced Pope Clement V to prosecute the Templars on many charges including apostasy, idolatry, heresy, obscene rituals and homosexuality, financial corruption and fraud, and secrecy. On Friday, the 13th of October, 1307, Templars across France were arrested en masse, and charged. Eventually the arrest order was extended across Europe. Most of the leaders were burned at the stake. In the end, none confessed to any crimes except under torture, and once freed, recanted.

The Templar network had been destroyed, and what remained was folded into the Knights Hospitallers, thus ending the most powerful order of knights to have ever existed, all due to a French king who didn't want to pay his loan back.

And with the Templars shamed, the walls of this chamber were most likely sealed, these four men no longer considered worthy of the honor bestowed upon them, and conveniently forgotten by the time the Church categorically but quietly forgave all Templars in 1308 of any wrongdoing.

With the top cleared off, Acton knelt down and unrolled his leather tool kit. Selecting a long, thin probe, he carefully inserted it between the lid and the sarcophagus body. It slid in easily. He continued probing several more times, then replaced the tool and stood up.

"It's not airtight, so we're safe to remove the lid."

Laura nodded. "I'll have them start bringing down the equipment."

Acton ran his hand along the lid of the sarcophagus containing Sir John. *You died as you lived, a hero, saving the life of an innocent.* He wondered what the story was, what could have killed this man, in Rome of all places, when he had survived so many battles of the Third Crusade.

Rome

1215 AD

Sir John of Ridefort felt much older than his forty years, what with much of those years spent in battle and the harsh climate of the Holy Land. But his years of fighting were over. He was heading home, to a home he barely remembered, and to a family that may no longer be alive. There had been no communication in almost five years, which had led to this journey.

He looked over at Raymond, his faithful servant these almost twenty-five years. His weathered face, almost a thick leather, the creases so deep they camouflaged the battle scars littering his visage. Raymond had been his father's confidante, and had quickly earned the trust and admiration of the son. They had fought at each other's side through countless battles, and when Sir John had suggested Raymond retire and return home, Raymond had refused. "My place is at your side."

Loyalty such as this was rare, even more so when it was mutual. There was a friendship here forged in battle, in prayer, in peace. They knew each other's secrets, desires, wants, and sins. They were brothers in arms, they were friends until death, and they were Templars.

"Look."

Sir John followed Raymond's gaze. Saint Peter's Basilica, built by Emperor Constantine the First, in 326 AD. It was impressive, it was inspiring. To think that Saint Peter himself was buried under its foundation. Sir John wondered what the first Bishop of Rome would have thought of the crusades. Would he have hailed them as the work of God, or decried them as the bloodlust of man disguised with the trappings of Christ's church.

Sir John felt the words fill his heart with joy, the ancient Latin he was now able to understand thanks to years of instruction from the faithful Raymond. "And I say also unto thee, That thou art Peter, and upon this rock I will build my church; and the gates of hell shall not prevail against it."

Raymond looked at him, a smile creasing the tanned face. "Your Latin remains excellent, I see."

Sir John chuckled. "With you drumming it into my head for twenty years, it better be."

"Well, someone had to teach you some culture. The heathen child I met at Acre was in desperate need of teaching beyond the sword."

Sir John nodded. "What was it you always said? 'Wisdom wields more power than the sword'?"

"Correct. But do you believe it?"

Sir John thought back on the years of battle, and the years of administration involved after a victory. Conquering a city meant running that city, and the Templars had many holdings throughout Christendom. In the past decade, most of his time had been spent pushing parchment rather than a blade, and that had suited his weary bones just fine. He placed his hand on his friend's shoulder.

"Absolutely, but"—he held up a finger—"*not* for years."

"With age comes wisdom."

"Then you are the wisest man I know."

Raymond frowned. "And apparently little respect."

They both roared with laughter, and urged their steeds on.

Suddenly a shout rang out, then more. Raymond and Sir John spun in their saddles to see what the commotion was, and Sir John gasped. A cart had broken loose and was rolling down the cobble stone road they now occupied. Quickly he scanned the road, and his heart leapt. There was a group of children playing, ignorant of the threat that now bore down on them. He jumped from his horse and ran toward them, shouting for them to move. They looked up at him, but not at the danger he pointed at.

The roar of the wood wheels on the ancient stone echoed through the street, and finally the children realized the danger, most of them running out of the way, leaving one tiny girl crying on the road, frozen in terror. Sir John's legs pumped, protesting against the effort they were now unaccustomed to, as he grew ever closer to the wailing child. He glanced over his shoulder and saw the cart, laden with heavy bags of flour, almost atop them both.

There wasn't time.

He dove, grabbing the girl, and shielded her with his body. The impact was jarring, more powerful, and more painful, than anything he had ever experienced. He pulled the screaming girl closer as the rear wheel smashed into his already broken frame. It surged over him, continuing on its destructive path, ended with a crash into the side of a building at a bend in the road.

Sir John couldn't move. Pain racked his body, the little girl's screams actually providing him some comfort.

She was alive.

A woman ran over, crying, and pried the tiny girl from Sir John's arms, thanking him profusely. He couldn't speak. He gasped for air, but he knew it was no use. His lungs had collapsed. He looked up and saw the little girl hugging her mother, apparently unharmed, and he smiled.

Raymond was at his side in moments.

"Sir John, are you okay?"

But Sir John could tell his friend already knew the answer. He was not. He could feel himself weakening, and he knew he only had moments to live. He reached up and grabbed Raymond by the back of the neck, pulling him closer.

"Save the scroll."

And with that, a hero of the Third Crusade to free the Holy Lands, the survivor of innumerable battles against Islamic hordes and pilgrim-harassing bandits, and one of the most respected of the Templar Knights, died as he had lived, rebalancing the scale of life, his silent prayer for the future of the small child he had just saved. For as Malik had died from saving a young Sir John, Sir John now died to save the life of this little child, and he prayed she would earn the reward she had just been granted.

Northern Wall Construction Site, Vatican City
Present Day

"Heave!"

Acton and several of the construction crew pulled the ropes now running under the lid of the sarcophagus, the lid having been pried up earlier with crowbars to position the ropes. The lid didn't budge, but the slack was removed from the rope, the teeth of the pulley system preventing the rope from slipping back.

"Heave!" ordered Laura again.

The men pulled again, and this time the lid moved.

"Once more, heave!"

They pulled, grunting at the weight and the humidity. The lid lifted. Acton handed off his rope to another worker, and stepped toward the lid. He and Laura swung it clockwise, perpendicular to the body of the sarcophagus.

Acton heard Laura gasp and he took a quick look, feeling his heart begin to hammer in his chest. He quickly returned his attention to the ropes. Reaching up, he grabbed a small rope tied to the teeth.

"Okay, when I pull this, lower the top as gently as you can. Ready?"

The Italian crew nodded after one translated.

Acton reached up and yanked the line, the teeth snapping free. Grunts surrounded them as the men slowly let the line out the couple of inches they had raised it.

The lid came to rest atop the sarcophagus, the stone meeting stone echoing through the small room. Acton tested it for stability, then gave a thumbs up to the crew.

"Great work, guys. Now take a break. We'll move this out of the way after we've completed our first examination."

The men let go of their ropes and began to climb the ladder out of the chamber as Acton joined Laura at the sarcophagus.

"Look, James. It's incredible."

Acton shone his flashlight inside, revealing the skeleton of Sir John, encased in his nearly perfectly preserved armor and dress of the day, his heraldic and Templar symbols proudly displayed, his sword, pointing downward to his feet, held tight against his chest by gloved hands. It was like countless other finds, however this was Acton's first Templar, and definitely first knight discovered on Vatican soil.

No valuables, no treasures, were evident, Templar Knights taking a vow of poverty upon joining the order. This disappointed Acton only slightly. Treasures were common, especially of that era. What interested him more as an archaeologist and anthropologist was how this man lived, and how he died. What secrets would be revealed by the x-rays that would be taken of his body, what small trinkets might he have on his person to remind him of loved ones back home, of his comrades in arms.

Acton froze, shifting his light back to where it had just been. "What's this?"

He leaned forward, as did Laura, both shining their lights down the left side of the body. A tube, not two feet long, made of some sort of hardened animal hide, lay on the bottom of the sarcophagus, almost out of sight. Acton reached in and carefully removed the item as Laura provided extra light.

"What do you think it is?"

Acton examined it closely, careful not to rotate it, aware that whatever was inside hadn't been disturbed in almost eight hundred years, and was likely very fragile. He looked at the seal at the top. Wax.

He looked at Laura. "This needs to be opened under the right conditions."

She pointed at the wax. "If that seal didn't fail, whatever is inside might actually still be intact."

Acton nodded, his heart hammering in his chest.

What secrets could this tube hold, important enough for a Templar, sworn to poverty, to have buried with him?

Sapienza University, Rome, Italy
Two weeks later

Acton felt Laura's hand grip his, as they both waited on the other side of the glass. The scroll had been transported to the Sapienza University's state of the art restoration lab, x-rayed and sampled in a vacuum, and it was quickly determined that there was a single rolled piece of parchment of some type inside, and there was some type of writing on it. The seal was broken in a vacuum chamber, and the parchment sampled. It was vellum made from cow hide, very durable, yet from the scans, appeared to only be a scrap, perhaps a left over piece from some previous written work.

And it was old.

Far older than the knight, whose bones were carbon dated to within twenty five years of his death as inscribed on the sarcophagus. The scroll had been dated much older, to around 600 AD, plus or minus 65 years. What could be written on it, Acton didn't dare imagine. The parchment had been created around 600 AD. The writing could be from any time after that, and was impossible to date. But even so, regardless of what was written on it, or when it was written, it was a piece of history about to be revealed.

The sample taken had first been used to determine the condition of the parchment, then was destroyed to carbon date it. And the condition was good. Rehydration techniques had been applied, and the scroll was ready to be revealed for the first time. On the monitors close-up images of the cutting were displayed, Acton alternating between the video, and the real thing.

He couldn't remember the last time he had been so excited.

"This better not be Al Capone's safe."

Laura chuckled, looking around. "Nope, Geraldo isn't here, I think we're good."

Acton gave her hand a squeeze. "Look!"

The technician had the tube in his left hand, and a pair of tweezers in the right, his hands and arms covered inside the sealed, climate controlled chamber to prevent contamination.

He reached in with the tweezers and Acton held his breath.

A gentle tug, with the open end of the tube tipped slightly.

The technician was rewarded with a tiny scrap of the paper.

He held it up to the camera.

Acton let his breath out.

Not promising.

The technician's voice could be heard.

"Should I continue?"

Acton gave him a thumbs up and activated the intercom panel next to the window.

"Once more."

The man nodded, and again, a small scrap.

Acton pressed the intercom button. "Try gently rolling the tube, squeezing slightly. It may just be stuck in one spot."

The tech nodded and set aside the tweezers, laying the tube flat. Placing both hands on top, he gently rolled the tube, it warping slightly as he applied pressure. Repeating this several times, he retrieved the tweezers and again pulled.

And the scroll slid out smoothly.

Laura jumped, giving Acton a hug.

He pressed the button on the intercom. "Get every camera you've got on that now. I don't want the scroll held open any longer than we need.

Monitors flickered as cameras were redirected, everything now focused directly on the scroll, including some that would record beyond what the human eye could see.

The technician spread out his fingers, and gently unrolled the parchment. Acton wasn't focusing on what might be written, but was instead watching one monitor with an extreme close-up, making certain that the ancient parchment didn't begin to break apart.

It didn't.

Laura gasped.

"It's Arabic!"

"We're clear!" called another tech, who was controlling the cameras. The tech with his hands in the chamber gently let the scroll slowly roll itself up, then removed his hands.

The text appeared on all the monitors, very clear, the contrast still good after all these years. Acton saw several copies roll off a printer, and one of the techs brought them each out a copy.

"What do you make of it, Professors?"

Acton looked to Laura. "Arabic is your thing. What does it say?"

She quickly scanned it, and gulped. "If this is what I think it is, this is an incredible find." She looked at Acton with fear in her eyes. "And an incredibly dangerous find."

"How so?"

"It's from the Koran, but it's different."

"What do you mean?"

"It's one of the more famous lines from the ninth Surah. It's been used to justify killing non-Muslims for a millennia, but this is different."

Acton's chest tightened. "How," he said, his voice low as several of the technicians gathered around to see what had been found.

"It says, 'And when the sacred months have passed, then kill the polytheists, but only the polytheists, wherever you find them and capture them and besiege them and sit in wait for them at every place of ambush. But if they should repent, establish prayer, and give zakah, let them go on their way. Indeed, Allah is Forgiving and Merciful.'" She paused. "Then it says, at the bottom, 'As recited to me by the Prophet Mohammad, peace be upon him'."

Acton whistled. "So this is an original verse, before the Koran was formally compiled."

Laura nodded. "It would appear so. I don't think anyone would dare make the claim in those days."

"Agreed."

"You said it's different. How?" asked the tech who had worked on the scroll.

"The original doesn't have the words, 'but only the polytheists'."

"What's a 'polytheist'?" asked a young undergrad that Acton had been introduced to earlier.

"Antonio, was it?"

The young man nodded. "Antonio Esposito."

"Well, Antonio, it's someone who believes in more than one god, like the ancient Greeks or Romans. Essentially what we commonly call a pagan," replied Acton.

"Ah, pagan, I see."

Laura pointed at the printout. "This verse over time has been reinterpreted to essentially lump all non-Islamic people in with the polytheists, because of a verse later in the same surah, that states, 'The Jews say, "Ezra is the son of Allah"; and the Christians say, "The Messiah is the son of Allah." That is their statement from their mouths; they imitate the saying of those who disbelieved before them. May Allah destroy them; how are they deluded?'"

"In that verse it says 'May Allah destroy them'," said Acton. "So in other words, leave it to me, I'll take care of them. But in this verse"—he pointed at the printout—"it's instructing the reader to attack the polytheists."

"And *only* the polytheists. The version of the Koran that exists today, and has existed essentially unchanged since the first compilation, doesn't have those four critical words. If they were there, then there could be no misinterpretation of this verse."

Acton rubbed his chin, lowering his voice. "You realize that there are millions of fanatics who would kill to make sure this never sees the light of day?"

Laura nodded. "That's exactly what I was thinking."

Acton turned to the scientists in the room. "Nobody, and I mean *nobody*, tell *anybody* about what you've seen here today. We need to keep this quiet, and arrange to get it into the proper hands. If this gets out, this university will become a prime target."

Acton looked through the glass at the scroll, and felt goose bumps spread across his skin.

We need to get this out of Europe. Fast.

La Taverna dei Fori Imperiali Restaurant
Rome, Italy

Antonio Esposito was itching to tell somebody his secret, but he knew he couldn't. But then, who was this American professor to tell him what to do? *The arrogance of the man!* This wasn't Professor Acton's secret to keep. This was an Italian secret, and it was up to Italians whether or not it should be kept. Hell, it was up to Italians to decide whether or not it was even a secret.

He downed his glass of wine and poured another.

Where is she?

He grabbed a roll and tore off a piece, swirling it on a small plate of oil and balsamic vinegar.

"Tony!"

He looked up and smiled. There she was. Gorgeous. Angelic. Sexy. There was something about wearing clothes that hid almost everything that just sent the imagination wild. He had only met her three weeks ago, and this was only their third real 'date', the rest lunches or coffee breaks at the university.

And he was afraid perhaps she didn't want to be anything more than friends. They hadn't even kissed yet. But that hard to get game of hers made her even more intoxicating.

His heart hammered in his chest as he rose. She rushed up to the table, removing a light jacket from her shoulders, and placed it on the back of a chair. Antonio leaned in to give her a hug, but he was greeted with a hand on his shoulder, gently holding him back, and air kisses on either side of his cheek.

She sat down, a large smile on her face. "So, how was your day?"

"Good. Yours?"

"Good? I heard you worked on some ancient artifact today and it's all secret. Can you tell me?"

He shook his head. "Definitely not." He leaned in and smiled, touching her frowning cheek with his finger. Her head darted back. He hated when she did that. It was as if he were repulsive. But her smile returned, and it melted his hardening heart immediately. "But I'll give you a hypothetical situation."

Now she leaned in. Their heads were only inches apart, both leaning across the tiny table.

"Tell me your story."

He looked at her hands, clasped in front of her. *God how much I want to hold her hand right now.* He sighed. Inside.

"Let's just suppose that there was an ancient scroll, a scrap of parchment, found on the body of a Templar Knight from the thirteenth century."

"Uh huh."

"And let's just suppose that that parchment was carbon dated to within sixty-five years of six hundred AD."

"You mean Common Era?"

He frowned. *Only people who don't believe in Jesus say Common Era.*

He waved his wrist. "Whatever. Now, let's suppose we were able to rehydrate this parchment, and unroll it. What might we find on it?"

She shrugged her shoulders. "I have no idea." She reached forward and gripped his hands with hers. He looked down and she immediately let go, blushing. "Sorry."

His jaw dropped. *Sorry? How could* she *be sorry.* He reached over and squeezed her hands, but let go almost immediately, rather than suffer the pain of having her withdraw. "Never say you're sorry for holding my hand."

She blushed again, looking away. "So what was on the scroll," she whispered.

"The *hypothetical* scroll, you mean."

She looked back at him with a smile. "Of course."

"Well, this *hypothetical* scroll had writing on it. Arabic writing."

Her eyes jumped. "Really? What did it say?"

"Well, one of the Professors said it was a verse from the Koran, but—"

He stopped, remembering the conversation around the implications.

Maybe this is *a secret that should be kept.*

"What? What did it say?" She grabbed his hands, and this time didn't let go. "Please, tell."

He didn't look at her hands this time, lest it scare her off again. He just looked into her eyes, her beautiful, dark eyes.

"It was a passage about killing the pagans, but it was different than what is in the Koran today."

She sat upright, her back straight, her shoulders square, her hands nowhere near his. "Then it must be fake." Her voice was cold. Stern. Uncompromising.

"No, it isn't. It said at the bottom something like, 'As told to me by the Prophet Mohammad, peace be with him' or something like that."

There was no trace of excitement on her face anymore. "You said it was different. How?"

"Apparently it had a few extra words than what is now in the Koran. Something about killing the pagans, but only the pagans. It wasn't pagans though, it was some other word, I can't remember."

"Polytheists," she whispered.

"Yeah, that's it!" He frowned. "How'd you know that?"

"Because I'm Muslim you idiot!"

Something scooped out his stomach and cinched his chest. He felt bile begin to fill his mouth as his heart broke.

"I-I didn't know."

She glared at him. "How could you not know? Look at how I dress. My name is Fatima! How could you not know?"

"I-I guess it didn't matter to me what religion you were. I just liked you." His voice cracked and his chin dropped. "I thought you were pretty."

Her tone softened slightly, her eyes glistening.

Then she stood up.

"I have to go."

She grabbed her jacket and left, Antonio staring at the void that had been her, wondering what had just happened.

If only I had kept the damned secret.

Wahhab Residence, Rome, Italy

"Home so early, Dear?"

"Yeah, Mom." Fatima hung her jacket and pulled off her shoes.

"Your friend from the university wasn't there?"

"No, she was, but—" Fatima stopped. "Is Dad home?"

"Of course he is. He's in his study."

"Thanks."

Fatima quietly walked down the tile hallway, and knocked gently on the door.

"Enter."

It was barely a whisper. *He's praying. Maybe I should come back?* She decided it was too late anyway, and opened the door.

"Hello, Father."

Her father was kneeling on a cushion, his hands open to Allah, his lips moving silently.

She waited patiently.

After several more minutes, he rose, and turned to face his daughter, opening his arms with a smile. She stepped forward and hugged him, as he kissed her on the top of her head.

"Fatima, my child, what is it you want?"

She wasn't sure how to start. In fact, she was second guessing whether or not she should say anything. *Does it really matter?* She wasn't a fundamentalist, she was barely a practicing Muslim. *Oh no! I'll have to tell him I was with a boy!*

And poor Antonio. She shouldn't have left him like that. She shouldn't have treated him the way she did. He did nothing wrong. He had exciting news, and he wanted to share it with her.

But how could he be so stupid to not know I'm a Muslim?

But what did that matter? She liked him, but she was taking things at her speed. Far slower than the average Italian girl, there was no doubting that, but he seemed to be okay with that, respecting her boundaries.

He's such a sweetheart.

"Fatima?"

Fatima shook her head. "Sorry, Father. I really shouldn't have disturbed you."

He took her by the arm and directed her into a chair. He sat down beside her. "Tell me what's troubling you."

It was his voice. It was so soothing. Whenever he spoke, she just spilled her guts. It got her in trouble countless times when she was a child.

"I was out with a friend."

"Yes. Your girlfriend from the university, Frieda, wasn't it?"

She shook her head. "No, it was"—she lowered her voice in shame—"a boy."

Her father said nothing.

Which was worse.

She looked at him, pleading. "He's a very nice boy, very respectful, you'd like him father. He's just a friend. His name is Antonio Esposito. He's an undergrad. But that's not what I wanted to talk to you about."

"Then what?"

"Well, he told me about something that happened today."

"Yes?"

She quickly told him Antonio's "hypothetical" story as best she could, and could tell her offense of going out with a boy unaccompanied was slowly being forgotten. When she was finished, her father stood, and began to pace, the fingers of his right hand pulling on his long, graying beard.

At last he stopped and turned to face her. "Are you sure of this?"

She nodded.

"Do you think he's correct? I mean, you don't think he is mistaken?"

"I don't see how."

He resumed his pacing, his stroking.

And stopped.

"Leave me. I need to make some phone calls."

She nodded and headed for the door. When her hand clasped the knob, she heard him say, "And tomorrow, we will discuss your dating habits."

She flushed.

"Yes, Father."

She quickly left the room, carefully closing the door behind her.

Sometimes I wish he wasn't an Imam.

Viale della Moschea Mosque,
Rome, Italy

Rahim's eyes had long glazed over, his mind wandering to the football match from last week. He smiled as he remembered Totti's last minute goal for the win. It was everything he could do to not scream GOAL!

He prostrated himself, going through the motions of prayer, automatically saying the words he had said every day for as far back as he could remember, but the words unheard as Totti's victory run played in his mind.

He had been a pretty good striker when he was younger, but with 9/11 fresh on everyone's mind, a Muslim stood no chance of moving up the ranks, especially with an obvious name like Rahim Islam.

I hate them all. Europeans. Whites. Americans. Christians. Jews. Catholics. Especially those so-called Muslims who preach peace with the infidels.

GOAL!

His thoughts quickly returned to football, this weekend's upcoming game pushing the hatred from his heart. He'd have to listen to it on his radio, since he'd be working anyway, cleaning the toilets of privileged white infidels.

What was that?

The Imam said something that tweaked, and he began to listen.

"...Roman Catholic Church hasn't even told us of its existence! We must demand they return what is ours, stolen from us during their unholy crusades, where their infidel armies tried, and *failed*, to conquer us. Today we must take back what is ours. We must march on that bastion of

Catholicism, and demand they hand over that which does not belong to them!"

Rahim was puzzled as to what *that* was, but he could hear the murmurs of assent around him grow into a roar, and he felt it in his chest as his heart welled up in fervor.

"Allahu Akbar!" he screamed at the top of his lungs.

There was a chorus of angry yells, joining him in his praise to Allah, as the hundreds gathered jumped to their feet, rushing to the door to retrieve their shoes, and begin the march.

He found himself swept along with the crowd, scampering as he tried to slip his shoes on his feet, and once successful, pumping his fist in the air with the crowd, yelling 'Allahu Akbar' with each physical affirmation of his faith.

This wasn't a stroll, this was a quick march, and their numbers grew as Imams across the city released their faithful with instructions to march. The mosques scattered about the city may have been few in number, but there were dozens of known prayer rooms, and possibly scores of unknown, sending their own handful. Cellphones were on the ears of hundreds, then thousands, as they called their friends and families who weren't able to attend Friday morning prayers, and urged them to join the march.

And when Rahim reached the gates to Saint Peters Square, there were already thousands there, with thousands more behind him, fists pumping the air. A cordon of Roma Polizia tried to keep them from the gates, but there was no use. Rahim saw a policeman push one of the marchers back. They tripped and hit the ground, hard.

Rahim felt his chest tighten, and the roar of blood filled his ears. He charged, charged at the officer who had pushed a Muslim to the ground, charged at the infidel who would dare lay a hand on one of the Prophet's followers.

He slammed into the officer, taking him down, then rained blows on him as hard and fast as he could. He felt hands grab at him, pulling him away from the bloodied man. He kicked out, landing a final blow to the head of the infidel, then heard a roar from the crowd, and he was suddenly let go, falling unceremoniously to the ground. He looked and saw the crowd charge. He jumped to his feet, gave the cop one last kick, then shoved his way toward the gates, then through.

He raced across the cobblestone square, his heart pounding in excitement, fear, and fervor.

The Vatican is ours!

Papal Office
Apostolic Palace, Vatican City

"What is it they're chanting?"

Giasson joined His Holiness at the bulletproof glass of one of the Papal Office's many windows. He looked at the mass of protesters that had surged into Saint Peter's Square. They appeared to have stopped at the cordon of classically dressed Swiss Guard, their garish uniforms possibly deterring the crowd from violence. Whatever was holding them back, probably wouldn't last long.

"We think they're saying 'Give us what is ours', in English, but most of them don't speak English, so they're just imitating the sound."

The elderly Pontiff nodded, stepping away from the window. "So sad. Here is something wonderful that has been discovered, yet they are so filled with hate, they don't see it."

"I wouldn't be surprised if most of them didn't really know why they're here. The crowds didn't show up until after their morning prayers at the local mosques. They were probably told to come here by their Imams."

The Pontiff dropped into his chair, shaking his head. "This is the problem with that religion. There is nobody at the head of it, nobody controlling their actions. There is no one I can talk to directly to try and defuse the situation."

"What about the Grand Mufti?"

"I've tried, and he has sympathized, but says until the scroll is handed over, he cannot help me."

"And who did he suggest it be handed over to?"

The Pontiff chuckled. "That is exactly what I asked him, and you know what he said?"

"What?"

"'Allah will guide you.'"

Giasson's eyebrows shot up. "What gall!"

"It's unfortunately what I've come to expect. Too often one will say something inappropriate, then the others will deny he speaks for them, but because there is no head of their church, there isn't much we can do. But"—he raised a finger—"I did think of someone who might be able to help us, and who we have dealt with in the past. As well, he's in one of the rare parts of the Muslim world that is actually relatively peaceful."

"Who?"

A small explosion shook the room and flames licked the side of the building, black smoke and soot staining the window they had just been in front of.

"What was that?"

Giasson flipped open his phone and hit the speed dial. "Report."

"They've started throwing Molotov Cocktails, sir."

"Clear them out."

"How? We don't have the personnel for that kind of operation."

"Contact Roma Polizia, request assistance. Close the gates, lock down the city. Once the riot police arrive, let them in and they'll deal with them. Have fire and ambulance service standing by."

He flipped the phone closed and it immediately rang. He answered.

"Giasson."

"Mario, it's me, Jim."

"Professor, what's your situation?"

"Not good. We've got hundreds at least rioting outside the university. Police have just arrived and are starting to push back. I just saw on the TV that they've begun rioting inside Saint Peter's Square. Are you and His Holiness okay?"

"Yes, as a matter of fact, I'm with him now."

The Pontiff raised his eyebrows.

"Professor Acton," said Giasson, covering the phone.

The old man frowned. "Are he and Professor Palmer okay?"

"For the moment, but the university is surrounded by protesters."

"I think it best if they and the scroll return here."

Giasson looked out the window. "It doesn't look much better here, but I think you're right." He uncovered the phone. "Professor, I am sending a helicopter for you. It should be there in fifteen minutes. Try to get to a clear area where it can land."

"Okay, will do. Thanks, Mario."

Giasson flipped the phone shut then turned to Father Morris. "Please arrange a helicopter to pick up the professors." Morris nodded and stepped from the office. Giasson returned to the window, scanning the crowd. "There's tens of thousands out there. I think we're going to need to prepare for the worst."

"What do you mean?"

"A crowd that size can easily overwhelm us, unless we're willing to use deadly force."

"Out of the question."

"For the moment, I agree, but if it is a choice between preserving this church, this institution and all its treasures, we may have no choice. We've seen what Muslims have done in the past. Look what the Taliban did to the statues of Buddha that had stood for fourteen hundred years. The West stood by and did nothing, and now an irreplaceable piece of history is gone. And just recently in Timbuktu." Giasson leaned on the Pontiff's desk. "Your Holiness, if they get in here, they will destroy millennia of art, the frescoes of Michelangelo, the works of the most famous artists the world has ever known. They don't care. Not only are they a mob, hell-bent on destruction, they are Muslims, who believe most of what we stand for is blasphemous."

"I have to believe that there is some sanity in that crowd. Someone who is not here in a frenzy of bloodlust."

"There very well could be. And that's who I fear the most."

And with 1.6 million Muslims in Italy alone, he knew the chances were too good that his fears could come true.

Jaffri Residence
Borough of Tor Bella Monaca, Rome, Italy

"How can we turn this situation to our advantage?"

Hassan Jaffri looked at the five others gathered in his basement apartment, a hole in a low class neighborhood. A perfect hiding place. No one wanted to know you, you didn't want to know anyone else. People minded their own business, and, as with most low income areas of Europe, there was nothing strange about devout Muslims living there, going about their business.

And he was devout.

Born in Afghanistan, his parents had fled the Russians and wound up in Italy. But he had returned, as soon as he could, and had spent the past three years training in Pakistan in weapons, bombs, tactics. He was ready to fight the infidel, and was just waiting to be activated. He and the men in this humble room were what the West, the infidels, liked to call a "sleeper cell".

But today, played out across one of the few infidel comforts he permitted himself, a television, was an opportunity that would wake this scorpion amongst their midst.

It was time to take action themselves, rather than wait for their masters hiding in Pakistan.

Rahim Ali leaned forward. He was the youngest, and most eager of the group, and also the most impulsive. Hassan constantly had to keep him on a tight leash, his mouth far too often flapping in public. "We have weapons, explosives. Why not just go in, kill every infidel in sight, and blow up the basilica?"

Hassan nodded. "Yes, we could do that, and I think we should do something similar. Ridding the world of that blasphemous example of idolatry would certainly please Allah, but I'm thinking bigger."

"What is it, Hassan?"

Hassan smiled at Mahmoud Ziti, his trusted second. At least thirty years older, Ziti was well respected, but had refused the mantle of command, leaving it to someone young enough to fulfill Allah's will. Instead, he was the bomb maker, with several missing digits to prove it.

"They have something of ours. In fact, we know they have many things that belong to us."

"You mean relics?"

Hassan jumped to his feet. "Exactly! They have looted our mosques, looted the homes of our leaders, and kept these priceless treasures within the walls of their city, within their blasphemous 'Secret Archives'." His fist pounded an old wardrobe that had seen much better days. This elicited a pounding from upstairs, the old lady who was his landlord never pleased when she could hear a peep from her tenants. He lowered his voice, looking back at the group. "It is time we took something of theirs."

There were nods from the group. Rahim spoke first. "Just what did you have in mind?"

Hassan smiled, returning to his seat, lowering his voice even further. "Something they would never expect, and something that would cause them to hand over everything we ask for, without hesitation."

They'd hand over the Pope himself if we asked it.

Sapienza University, Rome, Italy

Acton gripped the hermetically sealed case containing the parchment in his hand, the other holding Laura's. They stood in a doorway, shielded from view from the hordes on the streets, who for the moment seemed much more peaceful than those at the Vatican. They both had watched in horror on television as the crowd surged through the gates, and feared the worst.

But fortunately the crowd had stopped, and the news channels were attributing it to one man, an Imam, who had brought a megaphone, and had beseeched the crowd to calm itself, then had begun the chant now echoing from the crowd here as well.

"Give us what is ours."

The chorus of hundreds from the street sent chills racing down Acton's spine, as he recalled his recent experience in Saudi Arabia.

"We have to get out of here, now."

Laura pointed over a nearby rooftop. "Look!"

Acton followed where she was pointing and felt the tightness in his chest ease slightly.

A helicopter.

Usually they sent his heart racing, but in this case, it was slightly calming. As the chopper approached, the Vatican markings became visible, and he took Laura by the hand, stepping out onto the lawn. As its intentions became clear, the few students who were still venturing outside scattered, leaving the lawn empty save Acton and Laura, who sprinted for the chopper as it landed.

Two Swiss Guards, dressed in their blue regular duty uniforms to probably draw less attention, jumped out, urging the professors forward. A scream rang out to Acton's left. He looked over his shoulder and saw the front gate collapse, the crowd rushing over it, two police officers trapped underneath the wrought iron.

It was hopeless. The few dozen officers present tried to stop the crowd, finally giving up, instead focusing on trying to lift the gate, despite the hundreds clamoring over it.

Someone tugged at his arm, and he looked. It was Laura, fear in her eyes. He resumed his sprint to the chopper, and pushed Laura to safety, then climbed in himself as the two guards jumped back inside.

"Go! Go! Go!" one yelled as the crowd raced toward them. Acton could hear the engines power up, and then the skids slowly lift off the ground.

The entire craft shook.

The pilot cursed, banking to the left slightly. "Someone's hanging on the skid!"

The craft shook again. "Another one!" he yelled, looking out the opposite side.

"Just get us some altitude!" yelled one of the guards.

"What about those people?"

"They'll kill us if we don't get out of here!"

More power was applied, and again the chopper shook, but it began to rise, and soon was too high for anyone else to climb on.

"We can't keep going, not with those people!" cried Laura. "They'll die if they fall!"

One of the guards, who Acton now recognized as Gerard Boileau, one of Giasson's most trusted men, slid open the door. Wind howled through the cabin. "Get us over the crowd, twenty feet!"

The pilot nodded, banking back toward the crowd, lowering the craft. Boileau pulled his baton. "Jump, or I'll make you jump!" he yelled as Acton positioned himself at the door to see what was happening.

The man shook his head, and was about to yell something when Boileau's boot stomped on the man's hands. He yelped and dropped to the ground below, the crowd catching him, or more accurately, acting as human padding. Boileau slammed the door shut, momentarily quieting the cabin, then moved to the other side. He opened the door.

And was grabbed by someone on the skid, and pulled out of the chopper. Acton leapt forward, grabbing for Boileau. His hands ran down Boileau's legs, then finally managed to grip the man's boot. Acton felt himself slipping toward the door as the weight of Boileau pulled him out.

Laura screamed.

He felt hands grab his belt, and his forward momentum jerked to a halt. Someone hit him in the back, and his shoulder blade cried in agony. Gripping Boileau by one boot, he swung his free elbow back, blindly, and felt it connect with something that gave. He repeated his motion, and was rewarded with the sound of someone crying out in pain, then the view of them falling to the ground.

"Pull!" he yelled.

He felt his belt tighten against his waist as who he assumed was the other guard yanked him back inside. With his free arm, he reached down and grabbed Boileau's belt, never letting go the death grip he had on the man's boot, tucked under his armpit. He saw another pair of hands reach out and grab Boileau by the belt as well, a pair of hands he knew well, and together he and Laura pulled Boileau as the guard hauled Acton the final few feet.

As Boileau's waist cleared the lip of the cabin, Acton saw him reach back and pull his baton from a loop on his belt, then swing hard at an unseen target. The target cried out, a rapidly quieting scream indicating he had dropped to the crowd below.

With one final tug, they were all safely inside, and Laura slammed the door shut.

"Let's get the hell out of here!" she yelled.

Acton rolled onto his back, catching his breath, as Boileau did the same.

Boileau slapped him on the chest. "Thanks."

Acton didn't bother gasping a, 'You're welcome.' He was pretty sure it would just come out as a grunt, but he gave the other guard a smack on the leg and a nod.

They rode in silence the rest of the way, Acton wondering what chaos awaited them at their destination.

Saint Peter's Basilica, Vatican City

"Faster! Faster!" Giasson heard the elderly priest yell, as Saint Peter's Basilica was stripped of its treasures. All around him the most precious of objects that could be moved were carried or hauled away, deeper into the complex, and ultimately toward the Secret Archives, that vast storage area that preserved history not only from the elements, but from those that would destroy or steal it. It was secure. Any treasures that made it inside, would be saved.

But that was the problem.

Most of the basilica's treasures couldn't be moved. The building itself was a treasure. The frescos, the altars, the architecture. Even the doors held significance.

And underneath were the tombs, in the grottoes, and under that, the necropolis, where even the bones of Saint Peter himself rested. The outer entrance to the grottoes and necropolis had been sealed off by a massive metal security door, that only an incredible blast could open, and the inner entrances were sealed now as well with metal security doors built into the floors a decade ago at his predecessor's insistence. He had feared Islamic reprisals after the response to 9/11, and his fears now appeared prescient.

The tombs were secure.

Giasson allowed himself a moment to gaze at the ceiling of the dome topping the largest church in Christendom. It was breathtaking, the architecture and the artwork by masters like Michelangelo and Bernini, the statues of the saints by sculptors as reverent as Marchionni and Duquesnoy. Statues too heavy to move in time. He felt a lump in his throat, a tightness in his chest. *Could we few in this room, now, be the last to see these treasures intact?*

Things could be repaired, but they were never the same. Even if you couldn't see the difference, you knew they weren't as the sculptor had delivered them. They weren't the original brushstrokes of the painter. They weren't the original carvings of the mason. It was a restoration, but worse.

His phone vibrated.

Flipping it open, he sighed. "Giasson."

"Sir, the helicopter with Professors Acton and Palmer is inbound. ETA two minutes."

"Okay, have them met at the heliport, and brought to my office immediately."

"Yes, sir!"

Giasson flipped the phone shut and took one final look around.

If they get in, they'll destroy this place. Out of ignorance, and hate.

Over Vatican City

Acton pictured the fall of Saigon. Dozens of helicopters, landing and taking off, filled the airspace around the Vatican. News choppers, as well as police and military, competed for airspace at their designated altitudes. As they flew over Saint Peter's Square, and over the basilica, toward the heliport at the opposite end of the tiny country, Acton could hear the roar of the massive crowd below, its undulating sea of human flesh, fused together in a sea of hate, filled the massive square, and poured out into the streets surrounding the city.

It was terrifying.

The flicker of police lights indicated blocked off streets, cutting off reinforcements from joining the occupiers, but it was too late as far as Acton could tell. There was no way they were going to be able to take back the square, not without either force, or a protracted siege, forcing them out with thirst and hunger over days.

But during that time they could wreak havoc. Acton's heart ached at the treasures that could be lost to humanity forever, simply due to the ignorance and hatred of others.

All because someone had let word slip of an artifact that belonged to a 'rival' religion, and that Acton was positive would have been handed over to Islamic scholars at the earliest possible moment, now that what it was had been confirmed.

"Hang on! As soon as we touch down, get out, get down, get clear!" yelled the pilot.

Everyone in the back gave a thumbs up. Acton leaned against the window, and watched as a helicopter lifted off the pad, making way for their rapid descent. Acton reached up and grabbed a handhold, smiling at Laura, who at the moment had her eyes closed, white knuckle-gripping a support with both hands.

The skids hit and the helicopter bounced slightly. The door was pulled open by Boileau, and Acton jumped out, turning around to help Laura down. They bent over and ran toward a man who was waving at them to join him. Acton heard the engines power back up and he glanced over his shoulder. The two guards were right on their heels, and various aged Vatican residents were loading on the chopper.

The man who had been waving Acton recognized as Alfredo Ianuzzi, one of Giasson's men. He opened the door of a car and they climbed in. Ianuzzi jumped in the driver's seat, and started the car as he slammed his door shut, the din from the helicopters suddenly cut off.

"What's going on?" asked Acton.

Ianuzzi slammed the car in gear and it jumped forward. "We're evacuating the elderly. All of the exits are blocked by protesters."

"What's the situation in the square?" asked Laura.

"Not good. Latest estimates have about thirty thousand, with tens of thousands more outside trying to get in."

"Any casualties yet?"

"Injuries, yes, fatalities, not yet. But things are about to get a lot worse. There are reports that Catholics are starting to mass for a counter protest."

"That could get ugly."

The man nodded as he came to a halt near the rear of the Palazzo del Governatorato, or Palace of the Governatorate, the main administrative building of the tiny city. The three of them climbed out of the car, and Acton followed Ianuzzi, holding Laura by the hand. The air was filled with the chanting of the crowds on the other side of the massive complex.

Ianuzzi held a door open for them, and once inside, the noise from the crowds was replaced with the shouts of people inside, as organized chaos greeted them.

"What's happening?"

Ianuzzi urged them forward. "We're trying to get the most precious and significant artifacts into the Archives, so they can be protected should we lose the city."

"Is it really that bad?" asked Laura.

"I guess you haven't seen the news?"

Acton shook his head as they jogged toward their destination which he guessed to be the security offices. "No, we've been pretty much cut off the past couple of hours."

"Well, Muslims are protesting around the world. The usual craziness you'd expect in Pakistan and the Middle East, but they're also protesting in the West."

"If it turns violent here, I shudder to think what might happen around the world."

Acton nodded at Laura. "Agreed. This needs to be stopped, and fast. Otherwise we could end up with a hell of a lot of dead people."

Ianuzzi held the door open to the security office. "I don't see how we're going to clear those people out."

Giasson looked up from his glass enclosed office and waved them in.

"Thanks for the escort, Alfredo."

Ianuzzi nodded and rushed out of the security office.

Laura and Acton entered Giasson's office and he rose to greet them with his standard double-cheek kiss and a handshake. "I'm glad you two are safe." He nodded at the metal case Acton carried. "Is that it?"

Acton patted the case. "Yes."

Giasson ran his palm over his shaved scalp. "We need to get that out of here. Fast."

"Agreed. I suggest we get it into the hands of an Imam, in a Muslim country, today if possible."

"We're trying, but no one wants to touch it."

"What?"

"No one we talk to wants to be seen cooperating with Christians—not when their flock is so fired up."

"That's ridiculous!" exploded Laura. "They're the ones demanding we return it, but when we offer, they refuse? What kind of daft thinking is that?"

Giasson frowned. "You're preaching to the choir, Professor. I think in some cases they are afraid to get involved, in other cases, they relish the chaos that has been created."

"If not holy men, then what about governments?"

"Our diplomats are working on that, however we don't have much of a presence in Muslim countries, therefore we're forced to work through proxies, usually my home country, Switzerland. And as we all know with diplomacy, it takes time."

"Time we don't have," said Laura.

Suddenly the entire room shook, as if jolted by some mighty force hitting the building, and a moment later, a terrifying rumbling sound rolled through the security area.

Everyone was on their feet, with Giasson sprinting out of his office.

"Report!"

Nobody said anything, then a single phone rang. It was picked up by the guard at the entrance. The entire room turned to face her. She spoke quietly, then looked at Giasson, the phone covered by her chest. "Sir, an explosion has been reported on the southern wall of the basilica!"

Gasps filled the room.

Giasson pointed at one of his men.

"Unlock the armory, issue all personnel with side arms, all forward guards with automatic weapons. This is about to turn violent." The man jumped from his desk when Giasson added, "And bring myself and the professors side arms and body armor as well. We'll be in His Holiness' office." He motioned for Acton and Laura to follow him as he strode quickly from the office. He looked at them, his expression grave. "His Holiness must be convinced to get out of here before it's too late."

Northern Side of Saint Peter's Basilica, Vatican City

Hassan smiled as he saw some of the guards rush toward the explosion. It was merely a diversion, to lure them away from where he wanted to go, and draw most of the eyes in the opposite direction. He walked backward, his fist pumping the air, looking toward the explosion, but moving against the crowd, hopefully unnoticed, along with three of his cell.

And there it was. Completely exposed. No one had thought to defend it for some reason, the focus more on the façade of the basilica, the guards safely behind the massive wrought iron gates.

But something was different.

His fist froze in the air, then slowly dropped as he realized *what* was different. A massive, metal security door had been dropped in place, a security measure he had never noticed in the dozens of times he had roamed through this prime example of Christian idolatry and decadence.

The rest of his cell stopped as well, exchanging puzzled expressions.

He pushed forward. They had to at least try, otherwise it meant the backup plan, and it was generally agreed that it had a much lower chance of success.

The rest followed, and they hovered on the edge of the crowd so as to not draw attention. Hassan nodded at Mahmoud Ziti, their bomb maker. "What do you think?"

Ziti eyed the door. "It depends on how thick it is." He paused, as if unwilling to say what he was about to say.

"Out with it."

Ziti frowned. "If I were the infidels, I would make it thick enough to withstand any blast that we could throw at it. It isn't the door that is expensive, it is the mechanism. Whether the door is one inch or two inches thick, doesn't matter from a design or expense point of view enough for them to have done a cheap, thin door. That door"—he jabbed at it with his index finger, less a knuckle lost during his bomb making training—"is definitely at least two inches thick." He shook his head. "We're not getting through there."

"Are you sure?"

"We won't even dent it." He pointed with his chin at the guards behind the façade's gates. "That's why they aren't guarding it. They're not in the least bit concerned about it."

Hassan frowned. Ziti was right. Which meant the backup plan. A plan he didn't even like. It would take far more time, and was much more dangerous. Danger didn't bother him, but danger meant more chance of failure.

They had to do this right.

The first time.

Ziti looked at him. "Backup plan?"

Hassan nodded.

"Backup plan."

Papal Office, Apostolic Palace, Vatican City

"Your Holiness, we must get you out of here now!"

Acton recognized Father Morris' voice as they stepped into the antechamber outside the Pope's office, the hand carved inner doors uncharacteristically opened as people rushed about with purpose. Acton stepped aside as a large portrait was carried out.

Giasson pushed through, and Acton with Laura followed him into the Pope's office.

The old Pontiff looked up and smiled at his guests. "Professors. I am pleased to see you are unharmed."

"Barely."

Giasson interrupted. "Your Holiness, we must get you out of here. Now."

The Pontiff turned to Father Morris. "What's our status?"

"All guests, invalids and elderly have been evacuated, along with the Sisters. All that remains is you, Your Holiness."

The old man dismissed the plea with a wave.

"And our charge?"

"All documents, scrolls and books of historical importance are secure in the Secret Archives."

"And the art?"

"The Basilica has been emptied of everything that it can be, and so have much of the adjacent buildings. The problem is that some of it is just too large, too heavy to move, or is part of the buildings themselves."

"The frescoes," whispered the old man, staring at nothing, his eyes glazing over. He looked out the window, shaking his head. "Such hate. Were we really once like this, hundreds of years ago?"

Giasson stepped forward, his voice low. "Your Holiness, that is a debate for another time. For now, we must get you to safety. The Church cannot suffer a second death, under violent circumstances."

"I am ready to die."

"But for what?"

The old man raised his eyebrows.

"For what, sir? To be a martyr, fighting a mob of insane fanatics, upset because we found an old piece of paper, a piece of paper their own leadership demands we hand over, but won't accept? If you die at their hands, it will ignite a war around the world. Catholics will demand retaliation, and when they don't get it from their governments, they will take it out on Muslims on the street.

"There was almost no backlash after nine-eleven against Muslims. Only isolated incidents. But this is holy ground, and they"—he waved his hand at the crowd without looking—"intend to destroy it, for no other purpose than it doesn't agree with their Koran. These are the same people who want to destroy the pyramids because they honor false Gods." Giasson lowered his voice. "Your Holiness, what right do we have to allow Saint Peter's church, to let the rock upon which we stand be destroyed by a mob. *You* are the Church, its symbol. We must get you out of here, to lead the negotiations and get that thing"—his finger whipped around to point at the case Acton still held—"into their hands. Only you can do it, Your Holiness. Save the Church by ridding us of that, and leave me to try and save the buildings."

The elderly man stood silent for a moment as Giasson, Acton and Laura, along with Father Morris waited for a response. The bustle of activity continued as the workers removed the last of the relics in the room.

At last the old man sighed.

"Very well."

Giasson flipped his phone open and speed dialed a number. "Get His Holiness' chopper ready. We leave in ten minutes."

Suddenly the room rocked with another explosion.

Façade of Saint Peter's Basilica, Vatican City

The chanting of the crowd turned to panic as they rushed away from the explosion. Those that remained were the walking wounded, the dead, or Hassan. From his vantage point near the statue of Saint Paul, he could see that Ziti's explosives had done their job. A five second fuse, and a perfect toss, had turned the bomb into a grenade, and it had taken one of the gates off the façade, killing or wounding some of the guards standing behind the wrought iron, and half a dozen of the crowd too close to the blast.

He smiled.

Now for Phase Two.

He pulled his gun and took aim.

And with a silent prayer to Allah, he squeezed the trigger seven times, leaving a deliberate pause in between each, so as to extend the event, and leave no doubt in his targets' minds as to where the shots came from. And as bodies in the crowd dropped, his position near the façade, and the location of the bodies, made it clear where the shots had originated.

The crowd's panic grew, surging toward the front gates of Saint Peter's square, when five souls stepped from the crowd, walking back toward the basilica, pounding their chests, and repeatedly yelling in unison, "Allahu Akbar!"

Hassan smiled, immediately recognizing his men. But would it work?

One lone man left the crowd and rushed to join the five, his fist and voice adding to the tiny chorus.

Then another.

And another.

Then they turned in twos and threes, and within minutes, the entire tide had turned, with the crowd now chanting as one, their voices crystal clear, their words ones they had known since they were first taught to speak.

"Allahu Akbar!"

God *is* Great! Hassan's chest hurt with the sound of it, the pride, the joy, the love, the rapture. The celebration of tens of thousands of Muslims, united as one, roaring their love of God, proclaiming it without shame to those who would subjugate them, to those who would rather see them wiped off the face of the earth rather than accept them.

He shot two more rounds into the crowd.

But this time they didn't flee. His men raised their fists in the air and charged the façade and its scarred entrance. From his perch behind Saint Paul's statue, he could see the guards inside begin to back away. One raised his weapon, and Hassan's heart stopped in anticipation.

But the weapon was slapped down by one of the man's comrades.

Unfortunate.

He turned to the roar approaching, and couldn't help but grin as thousands of his fellow believers closed in on the portico. The backup plan was going perfectly, and within minutes, a plan thought crazy, a plan thought too ambitious only hours ago, would show the world the supremacy of Islam, the supremacy of a faith whose strength was in its believers, its adherents more powerful than any army, than any infidel weapon.

Today, the Vatican would become an Islamic state.

Papal Office
Apostolic Palace, Vatican City

The distinctive sound of gunfire drew the entire room to a halt, then there was a rush for the windows. Acton reached it first and pointed. "Somebody's firing on the crowd!"

"Impossible!" exclaimed Giasson.

But there was no mistaking it. There were at least half a dozen bodies lying in the square, abandoned by the roaring crowd that once stood as one, chanting in unison, it now fleeing the square in a panic.

Giasson flipped open his phone and dialed. "Report!"

He listened for a moment as the entire room turned their attention to him.

"Can you hold?"

He frowned.

"Look!"

It was Laura that caused the focus to change back to the view outside. Acton watched as several men stopped running and turned, their fists pounding their chests, yelling something. Then more of the crowd turned, and within moments, thousands upon thousands had stopped running, and had joined the others.

Then they charged.

"If you can't hold, fall back to the palace!" Giasson looked at His Holiness, then shook his head. "No, do not fire unless fired upon."

He listened again.

"I agree."

He hung up and looked out at the crowd as it poured toward the portico.

"They don't stand a chance," whispered Laura.

Giasson turned to His Holiness.

"The blast took out one of the gates. There's no way they can hold the basilica without opening fire."

"Out of the question."

"I know, I know"—Giasson clearly sounded frustrated—"which is why I ordered them to fall back. We can barricade inside the palace, but unless we're willing to meet them with force, we will lose this city."

"But who's firing now?" asked Father Morris.

"We don't know. I've been assured it isn't us."

Acton frowned. "Which means someone is manipulating this situation."

Giasson nodded. "It appears so."

The elderly pontiff dropped into his chair and massaged his temples. "What can we do?"

Giasson approached the desk and leaned forward, his hands splayed across the ancient antique. "Your Holiness, we must fight back. We are being invaded."

"Thou shalt not kill!" said Father Morris.

Giasson shook his head, turning toward the priest. "No, you and I both know it is 'Thou shalt not murder'. There's a big difference. The Bible says it is justified to kill in self-defense. This is clearly one of those times." He turned back to the Pontiff. "Your Holiness, we must fight back!"

The old man sighed and nodded.

"Again, I ask how?"

Giasson stood up straight, returning to the window. Acton looked out. The crowd was at the façade, the entrance to the basilica, but from this angle, it was impossible to see what was happening.

Giasson's phone rang again. He answered, listened, then said, "Very well."

"The basilica has fallen. Our men are falling back to the palace, but this building is too large to hold."

"What do you propose?" asked Father Morris.

"On any given day we have approximately three thousand people here. Once it became clear things were getting out of control, the administration ordered all non-essential personnel home. This means almost all the lay staff, over two thousand, are gone. But eight hundred people live here. We've evacuated the elderly and the sick, plus in this morning's briefing I believe it indicated approximately one hundred were on assignment or vacation outside of the city. That leaves perhaps seven hundred residents and staff."

"How do we get seven hundred people out?" asked Laura.

Giasson shook his head. "For one thing, almost two hundred of that are security personnel including Swiss Guard. They stay to hold the city."

"And the other five hundred?"

This time it was the Pontiff who asked.

"We take them out the south entrance."

The old man's eyebrows narrowed. "But there is no south entrance."

Giasson smiled. "Yes, there is, and if we're lucky, that crowd"—he jabbed his finger at the window—"is thinking the same thing as you."

Statue of Saint Paul, Vatican City

Ali was the first to emerge from the crowd and join Hassan at the statue of Saint Paul. Then Ziti and the others. The crowd that could surged through the blasted gate, the rest pushing against the still solid remaining gates. It was clear many were being crushed, but Hassan didn't care. They would die martyrs here this day, dying for a cause greater than any one life. Dying to assure the supremacy of Islam, of the words delivered to the Prophet Mohammad by the archangel Gabriel, and the inferiority of the decadent Western way.

Today was the beginning of the new Caliphate, and with it, the foretold apocalypse.

Hassan, as a Twelver, or what the uninformed West would call a Shi'a or Shiite Muslim, believed in the twelve Imams, those who followed the Prophet Mohammed over the centuries, divinely ordained, to keep and spread the faith. The Twelfth Imam, Muhammad ibn al-Hassan, currently hidden from mankind by God since he disappeared in 872 AD, would return someday with Isa, or as the West called him, Jesus. When man had lost its way, when God willed it, they would return to bring justice and peace to earth by imposing true Islam upon all.

And as a Twelver, just like most in his original homeland of Iran, bringing on the apocalypse was encouraged, for once it was upon us, the Mahdi would return, and bring peace to an entirely Islamic world.

The five gathered around him, their heads close so they could hear over the roar of the crowd. Hassan looked from man to man. "Today, my brothers, we take the first step in bringing Muhammad al-Mahdi back, and assuring the supremacy of the words of the Prophet, peace be upon him!"

"Allahu Akbar!" they all cried in unison.

Hassan held up his weapon.

"Ready?"

They all nodded, drawing their own weapons.

"Allahu Akbar!" yelled Hassan as he charged toward the opening in the façade. He shoved into the crowd, a mass of human flesh, unorganized, but fervent in its desire to gain access to Christianity's largest church, either to settle their bloodlust, or simply to escape the pressure from the thousands pushing behind them. The crowd pressed against him, and he could tell he risked being lost in the chaos.

He extended his hand holding the gun far enough ahead so those immediately in front of him could see it, and they parted slightly, just enough for him to squeeze through for him to display the weapon to the next group in his way. Within minutes he was at the gates, and once through, it was relatively open. The bodies of several guards who died in the explosion lay on the ground against the wall, their bodies stripped of any weapons they might have had. As he turned a corner he nearly gasped, the massiveness of the basilica breathtaking.

And he felt a rage fill his heart.

The idolatry around him, the icons worshipped by the infidels, disgusted him. And the mob now inside appeared equally incensed, some hacking at whatever they could lay their hands on, with whatever they could find. Keys, pens, their bare hands. Whatever they used, they were determined to wipe this example of blasphemy off the face of the earth.

But that wasn't his concern.

He marched through the nave at the center of the massive church, then turned to his right as he approached the Papal Altar, entering the Chapel of the Sacrament, a mostly enclosed area, where no one had yet ventured.

Surveying the floor, he found the spot he was looking for just as Ziti rushed up to join him.

Hassan pointed at the floor.

"Set the charge here."

Outside the Papal Offices
Apostolic Palace, Vatican City

Giasson led the entourage down the hallway, several heavily armed guards flanking him and taking up the rear. Acton and Laura were close behind, both armed, then the Pontiff and his closest staff of five. Two guards held the doors open to the private elevator that only ten people had a key to, Giasson one of them. The Papal staff boarded, along with Giasson and one guard; all that would fit.

Giasson looked at Acton.

"Follow the guards; they will take you down the stairs. Be quick, we won't be waiting."

Acton nodded and followed the rest of the armed party at a trot, Laura by his side, the case still gripped in his left hand. They reached the end of the hall and a winding staircase. Acton grabbed the rail and raced down the steps as fast as he could, three guards leading the way, Laura on his heels. The roar of the crowd got louder, and Acton heard the smashing of glass and shouting.

He drew his weapon tucked into his belt.

As they approached the main floor, gunfire erupted, and the screams of someone clearly in pain echoed up the stairs. They came to a sudden halt as a burst of gunfire tore the floor open in front of them. More shouting just around the corner and Acton picked out the distinct voice of Giasson shouting orders in Italian.

The guard on point motioned for them to head to the right. Acton emerged from the stairs and looked to his left. Two of the protesters, or invaders as he now thought of them, lay dead on the floor, one with a gun still gripped in his hand. At the far end of the hall another small group were climbing through a shattered window. Acton gripped the case tight in his hand, made sure Laura was at his side, then raced after one of the guards, toward Giasson's voice.

They emerged in a large room to find Giasson and the Papal entourage walking as fast as the elderly Pontiff's legs could carry him, down a long series of hallways that appeared to connect several buildings. Giasson's phone beeped. He flipped it open. "Giasson." He listened for a moment. "Merde. Can you bring it here?" Another pause. "Then do it."

Giasson continued to march down the hallway. "We've lost the heliport. They've begun tossing incendiary devices over the walls to stop the evacuation."

"How will we get his Holiness out?"

"The same way the rest are evacuating," said the old man calmly.

Giasson dismissed the statement with a flick of his wrist. "Out of the question. The helicopter will be here within two minutes, and you *are* going to be on it, if I have to carry you myself," said Giasson. He looked over his shoulder. "With all due respect, Your Holiness."

They eventually reached the end of the interconnecting hallways, and at last to a set of doors to the outside. Two guards held them open, and Giasson stepped through as a single shot roared through the enclosed space. Father Morris dropped with a cry. Acton whipped around, flicking the safety off his weapon, and spotted several rioters, one armed, rushing toward them. Another shot rang out, the glass from a window behind him shattering. Acton squeezed the trigger, and the man dropped.

Half a dozen rioters charged forward, screaming at the top of their lungs, one dropping to pry the weapon from Acton's handiwork. Acton felt Laura's hand on his shoulder as he backed away, guiding him toward the exit. The perspective suddenly changed, the sun shining down on them instead of the artificial lighting from inside, and he was momentarily blinded. A window burst into a thousand pieces to his left. He fired a single shot into the crowd rushing the door, and one dropped, but not the one with the gun as another shot tore through the mayhem.

As Acton cleared the doors, two Swiss Guards, both with automatic weapons, took knees on either side of the doors, and opened fire, ripping up the floor in front of the men charging their position. Acton saw them stop momentarily, then rush forward again, the few from earlier now numbering in the dozens.

"We can't hold this position without it getting extremely bloody!" yelled one of the men.

The whoosh of helicopter blades overhead momentarily drowned out Giasson's response. Acton watched as Giasson waved his arm for the chopper to descend quicker. The massive vehicle dropped almost like a stone, bouncing on the ground in what was definitely not a textbook landing for a civilian chopper, making Acton think this might have been an ex-military pilot.

Giasson and two of his men helped the Pope and his staff aboard as the two Swiss Guards at the entrance opened fire. Acton urged Laura toward the chopper, but the pilot waved them off and began to ascend.

"Wait!" yelled Acton, holding up the case containing the scroll, but it was too late. The chopper was beyond the point of no return. Giasson spun toward Acton, his jaw dropping as he saw the case, still held high.

Acton slowly lowered his arm as Giasson ran up to him. He pointed at the case. "Guard that with your life."

Acton nodded. *No kidding.* He knew if there was to be some sort of eventual resolution to this, it would be with the handing over of this scroll to Islamic authorities, whoever that may be. And in the panic of the evacuation, a golden opportunity to get it out had been lost. He hoped

Giasson's evacuation plan worked, otherwise they, and the scroll, may never see the light of day again.

Both Acton and Giasson watched as the chopper sped off into the distance with enough altitude to ensure its safety. They all spun toward the doors as more gunfire erupted from the guards.

"Let's fall back to the evacuation point, now!" yelled Giasson, grabbing Laura by the arm and running full tilt away from the Apostolic Palace, Acton and the guards following.

Six down. Five hundred to go?

Mass Drive, Fort Bragg, North Carolina

The doorbell rang. Command Master Sergeant Burt "Big Dog" Dawson, BD to his men, looked at his watch.

"Can someone get that? I'm knee deep in marinade out here!" called Stucco from the kitchen.

"Dude, if you're knee deep, you're doing it all wrong," replied Niner as he rose from the couch, heading to the door. Dawson popped another pretzel in his mouth followed by a chug of Bud. The game was coming on soon, and Stucco had offered up his living room for the single guys to come and watch.

Dawson glanced around at the full house, every chair occupied, and now the floor filling up. Neither Stucco nor his wife had expected everyone to accept.

He should have known better.

Dawson, leader of the Delta Force's Bravo Team, the United States' most highly trained group of operatives, surveyed his men with pride. These were the modern day heroes, men who would lay down their lives for their comrades and their country, and the world would never know. These men wouldn't be starring in Hollywood movies, their names splashed across the nation's newspapers. These men fought the unknown battles, the missions too covert for the public to know about. They eliminated the threats the average American would be terrified to know existed.

They let the nation sleep at night, secure in the knowledge that men like these were there to protect them.

Niner poked his head in the room. "Hey, BD, it's for you."

Dawson's eyebrows shot up, and he rose from the couch. Pointing at the empty piece of prime real estate, he said to the group at large. "That better be here when I get back. I didn't get here on time to sit on the floor."

"You snooze you lose!" yelled Spock as he dove over the table, spinning in the air to land on his back. But Atlas had already leapt from the ottoman he was sitting on and toward the empty seat. He stuck out a massive paw and grabbed Spock's shoulder, stopping him dead in the air.

They both dropped; Atlas on the couch, Spock slamming down on the table he had been trying to clear. The ruckus brought Stucco from the kitchen, his hands held high like a surgeon, dripping in marinade.

"What the hell are you animals up to?"

Spock looked up from the broken table, an eyebrow cocked, as if asking, "What are you talking about?"

Stucco pointed a finger at him. "You're paying for that." He leaned in and lowered his voice. "Clean it up before Sheila sees it, otherwise she'll never let me have you guys over again."

Dawson shook his head, a huge smile on his face as he went to the door. He opened it and took a step back, genuinely shocked at who was standing there.

"Colonel Clancy, sir, to what do I owe the honor this fine afternoon."

"Sorry to disturb you, Sergeant, but I need to talk to you." Clancy, the officer in charge of Delta Command, and a man Dawson implicitly trusted, stood on the step in civilian attire, something Dawson couldn't remember the last time he had seen.

"No trouble, sir, would you like to come in?"

Clancy shook his head. "No." He nodded toward Dawson's poppy red 1964½ Mustang. "You still good to drive?"

Dawson smiled. "Sure, I'm only half way into my first."

"Good. Then let's go for a drive."

They strode across the street together and climbed in the car. "Top up or down?"

"Leave it down, it's a beautiful day, and this is just two friends out driving."

Now Dawson knew something was definitely up. He respected Clancy, he liked Clancy, but never would he have described them as friends. And neither would Clancy. He was a colonel, Dawson a sergeant. Clancy was upstairs, Dawson definitely downstairs.

The engine roared to life as Dawson turned the key. With a glance over his shoulder, he pulled away from the curb. Nothing was said for a few minutes until they were out on the open road.

"I suppose you're wondering why I'm meeting you like this."

"The thought had crossed my mind."

"Something big is going down, and I need your team in place, right away, just in case."

"No problem. What's up?"

"You've seen the news?"

"I assume you mean the Vatican thing? Heard it on the radio this morning but nothing in hours. What's it all about?"

"Well, some archaeologist friends of ours discovered an ancient piece of parchment that changes the fundamental meaning of one of the Jihadists' favorite Koran verses."

"Archaeologist friends." Dawson shook his head. "You don't mean—"

Clancy nodded. "Yup, Professors Acton and Palmer."

Dawson couldn't help but laugh. "How the hell do those two keep doing it?"

Clancy shrugged. "I don't know, but our intel tells us they're at the top of the hit list. This riot appears to not just be a riot. There's a controlled element to it, and we're not sure what they're up to yet. All we do know, is not only does that element need to be stopped, but we have an American citizen who needs our help."

Dawson frowned. He had fought beside Acton, and considered him a man of honor, a man he could trust. And a man he had no interest in seeing dead. "Is this sanctioned? I mean, going in for one man?"

"This is off the books for now. Pretty much every country is prepositioning special ops teams, including us, so expect it to be by the time you arrive."

"What's the current situation?"

"The protestors, if you can call them that, have taken over Saint Peter's Basilica, and it looks like the city will be lost."

"Jesus," muttered Dawson. Though not a Catholic, he understood the significance. He also understood how it couldn't be allowed to stand.

"What do you need us to do?"

Via del Governatorato, Vatican City

Giasson flipped open his phone and speed dialed his contact at the Roma Polizia whom he knew would be trying to coordinate things on the outside. He and the professors, along with the guards and dozens of civilians they had picked up along the way were moving as fast as they could down Via del Governatorato, away from the Apostolic Palace and toward the Governatorate Palace that housed his security headquarters.

But that wasn't their destination.

The phone was answered. "Deputy Commissioner Ezio Vitale here."

"This is Giasson. We've got a plan, and we need your help."

"Name it."

"I need a path cleared on the south exit, as many men as you can spare, with as many buses as you can get."

"Mario, there is no south exit."

"Think about it. I don't want to say it on an open line, just in case."

There was a pause, then an excited, "Oh!" followed by a more subdued, "oh."

"What?"

"That's going to take hundreds of men. How many are coming out?"

"If everyone follows the evacuation order, and is able to get to the assembly area in time, five hundred."

"Five hundred! That'll be at least a dozen buses. How the hell do you expect me to do that without attracting attention?"

Giasson was sympathetic, but didn't have time to care. "Can you do it?"

"I'll do what I can. When?"

"Fifteen minutes."

"Fifteen minutes!" Several curses then a prayer for forgiveness burst forth. "Call me in ten minutes."

The phone went dead.

Giasson continued with the group, then pointed at one of his men as they approached the Governatorate Palace. "Tell all non-essential personnel to follow us!"

The man nodded and sprinted toward the front entrance.

Gunfire tore through the air over their heads and Giasson looked back. The mob that had broken through the Apostolic Palace were now spread out through the grounds, several chasing the growing group. He couldn't risk being followed.

He stopped and squeezed off several rounds at the approaching group, several of whom appeared armed. Two of his men took knees beside him. "Hold this line." He turned toward the Governatorate Palace and waved at several of the armed personnel swarming out with the civilians. Within seconds they were joined by a dozen men. "Spread out, hold this line. We can't have them seeing what we're doing. Keep directing civilians to the rally point."

"Yes, sir!" echoed the men.

Giasson looked around. "And for God's sake, try not to hit any of our own people."

"Shoot to kill, sir?"

It was a young guardsmen who reminded Giasson of himself when he had first joined the guards. *Green.*

"Yes, son. Consider this an invasion. You're protecting your country."

The young man's jaw squared. "Yes, sir."

One of the guardsmen fired, and his target dropped, only to have his weapon picked up by another.

"Hold this line, then take cover in the Palace."

Giasson turned and raced after the now large group of civilians making its way, far too slowly for his liking, down Piazza del Governatorato and past the Governatorate Palace that housed his headquarters.

Not much farther.

He saw Acton and Laura ahead, urging the people forward, and Giasson saw the silver case gripped in Acton's hand, cursing the lost opportunity. There was no one to blame but himself. Acton tried to get it to the helicopter, but the pilot had lifted off too early. Based on the pilot's orders, he had done the right thing. He had just been given the wrong orders. His orders should have been to evacuate His Holiness *and* the scroll, but they weren't.

And that was his fault.

But there was no time to waste blaming himself. He took heart that there appeared to be hundreds of staff converging at the rally point, coming in from all directions, and a quick glance over his shoulder confirmed they had no pursuers.

For now.

How long that would last, he didn't know.

Chapel of the Sacrament, Saint Peter's Basilica, Vatican City

"How big a blast can we expect?"

Ziti looked at Hassan. "Big."

Hassan frowned. Ziti never gave details voluntarily. One had to pry it out of him like a stubborn camel.

"Do we need to leave the room, or leave the building?"

Ziti shrugged. "The room should be enough."

Should.

Hassan could feel his blood begin to boil as his chest tightened. His finger stroked the trigger guard of his still unholstered weapon.

"Will it go deep enough?"

Ziti shook his head. "I doubt it."

Hassan's finger slipped onto the trigger. "What do you mean?"

Ziti looked up, his eyes ablaze, and said, teeth clenched, leaving a deliberate pause between each word, "Let me finish with the ex-plo-sives, *then* I'll answer your questions."

Hassan spun on his heel and walked away, a couple of his team snickering. He stepped into the main hall of the basilica, it now filled with thousands, most standing around in the middle, not knowing what to do, others filling the pews, chatting amongst themselves excitedly at what they had accomplished, and others still hacking at anything they could lay their hands on. The only thing saving the structure was that most things were too high to reach, and nobody had thought to bring anything with them.

He frowned.

Perhaps if I were to point out the torn apart wrought iron gate they climbed over to get in here—

"It's ready."

Hassan turned to see Ziti standing at his shoulder.

"Good. May I ask my questions *now*?"

Ziti grinned, nodding. "Of course."

"Why do you doubt it will go deep enough?"

"It's not a shaped charge. We were supposed to blow a door open, not try to do excavation work. This will make a big bang, hopefully a big crater in the floor, but it won't go deep. It should get through the marble though; then we dig."

Hassan pursed his lips. "But we could be facing twenty feet of concrete."

Ziti shook his head. "Concrete wasn't invented when this was built. Eighteenth century before we'd have to worry about that. This place is so old, I'm guessing a mix of good old sand and crushed rock. Packed into place by the weight of this"—he held up his hands indicating the building—"for five hundred years."

Hassan stopped him with a raised finger.

"You're ready?"

Ziti nodded.

"Then let's do it."

Ziti yelled for the men to leave the room, and everyone took cover around the corner, the thick walls providing them, Hassan hoped, with sufficient protection. Ziti looked at him and Hassan gave a thumbs up. Ziti flipped open a red switch on the tiny detonator, then pressed a button.

The blast was deafening.

Rock and debris blasted from the entrance to the side room and into the basilica, some of it hitting the unsuspecting crowd. Cries of pain and screams of terror echoed through the hallowed halls as a cloud of disintegrated marble rolled across the floor. As the dust settled, Hassan turned the corner, waving one hand in front of his face, the other holding his shirt over his mouth. He peered through the dust, but could see nothing.

He stepped forward then felt a hand on his shoulder, pulling him back. He spun to see who it was, and found Ziti standing there, shaking his head. "We don't know what happened to the floor. You could fall."

Hassan nodded, stepping back, his desire to maim Ziti from earlier slightly diminished. As the dust slowly dropped, revealing the ceiling, then walls, the crowd behind them began to realize what had happened, and began to congregate on Hassan and his team's position.

And they were angry.

Some began to shout, some shaking their fists at them.

Hassan looked and could see the blood lust in their eyes. He felt Ziti's breath on his ear. "You better say something, or we're going to have to open fire on our own people again."

Hassan took a deep breath, thankful the dust had cleared. Stepping forward, he made certain his gun was displayed, but not pointed at the crowd. He held up his hands, quieting the immediate crowd.

"My fellow followers of the Prophet, peace be upon him, today we have struck a mighty blow against the infidel." His arms swung, indicating the basilica, his head raised high to the heavens. "We have taken his church! *We* now hold the largest church in their decadent world, *we* now possess their blasphemous idols"—he pointed at the Papal Altar at the far end of the basilica, adorned in gold—"and Allah willing, before this day is through, *we* will control this entire city. And with it, the Mahdi shall return!"

A roar filled the basilica as the thousands inside began to scream 'Allahu Akbar', the religious fervor in their eyes a look that most Westerners mistook for insanity, having long lost the ability to feel the joy and power true belief could bring.

He raised his hands, and the crowd eventually calmed.

"Now, some of you may wonder what we are doing over here"—he jerked his thumb over his shoulder toward the room—"but rest assured, it is the will of Allah, and once we have completed our work, we will have the infidel bowing at our feet!"

Again the crowd roared. Hassan gave a slight bow of respect, then turned toward the scene of the explosion. As he entered, dust was still settling, but enough had dissipated to make him smile.

In the center of the room sat a large crater.

Corpo della Gendarmeria Office
Palazzo del Governatorato, Vatican City

"That's our man."

Boileau pointed at the screen showing footage from one of the cameras still operating in the basilica. Most of the security office that remained had gathered to watch the video. Boileau turned to one of the men. "Get his face and send it to the Roma Polizia. See if they can find out who he is. And try to get the faces of those"—he pointed out several others standing near the man—"people, and see if they know who they are as well. They appear to be accomplices to me."

The man nodded and returned to his desk. Boileau looked back at the video, wishing they had a camera in the Chapel of the Sacrament where the explosion had happened.

What are they doing in there?

He turned to Marco Ulissi, a man he had worked with for years. "Status of the evacuation?"

"M. Giasson just passed the building two minutes ago with a small contingent. We are holding a line just outside to make sure no invaders get past and see what we are doing. But if they come in numbers…" His voice trailed off and Boileau nodded in understanding.

"And us?"

"We've brought all provisions into this area. We have water, food, batteries, artificial lighting. Everything we need to sustain two hundred people for two days. The problem is going to be bathroom facilities and water. We can run out of everything except water and still survive. We have two bathrooms for two hundred people, so we'll definitely need to keep people cycling through whether they want to or not. But if we lose water pressure, it's going to get nasty in here, fast."

Boileau turned his nose up at the thought.

"Perimeter?"

"Secure. All doors are locked, chained and blocked. Windows are locked and those within reach that aren't barred have been blocked as best we can with furniture, and those rooms locked down. Each hallway where those rooms lead has at least two guards, armed." He sighed. "Bottom line, if they want in, they're getting in. There will be one hell of a lot of bloodshed."

Boileau hissed, "watch your language!" and Ulissi dropped his head.

"Sorry. I'm just—" He stopped.

Boileau patted Ulissi on the shoulder. "We're all scared." He removed his hand and pointed at the screen. "Better tell M. Giasson to hurry."

On the screen the man who seemed to be running things was pointing at the outer doors of the basilica, and men were rushing toward them.

Mass Drive, Fort Bragg, North Carolina

Dawson stood on the small porch of the on-base family housing unit that held Stucco and his family. He sighed, his shoulders slumped, but only slightly. This was the part he hated. Breaking up the fun stuff. It seemed all too often family events were interrupted or cancelled. At least today it was just the guys, and the single ones at that.

But there was also a mission.

And a mission always got his heart pounding in excitement. And he knew the men would be disappointed at missing the game and having a few brewskies, but they too would be excited by the prospect of kicking some ass and doing some good.

He rapped twice on the door then opened it. Rounding the corner, all eyes were on the television except for Stucco's wife.

"Oh, hi, BD, everything okay?" she asked.

He smiled and nodded at her as the room turned to face him. As if on cue the broadcast cut off, and a news logo appeared.

"We interrupt this broadcast to bring you a special report."

A chorus of groans filled the room, with Niner's voice cutting through the mix, "Are you kidding me? What kind of mental midget interrupts sports with news? That's like—"

"Shh!" interrupted Atlas. "I want to hear this."

An image of the Vatican appeared and a talking head Dawson didn't recognize began to speak. There was no smile, no friendly, disarming expression. It seemed obvious to Dawson that whatever news was about to be delivered, was grim, and there was no sugarcoating it. It reminded him of 9/11. There were no smiles then. Not from Aaron Brown delivering the news for CNN on his first day on the job. He remembered watching that coverage, and the horror of it all.

And he felt the same sensation crawl down his spine now.

"Ladies and gentleman, the Vatican has been lost."

Dawson stepped forward and held his hand out to Spock who had the remote. Spock looked up at him and Dawson could tell he knew what was about to happen. He didn't frown. He didn't look disappointed. He just accepted it.

Spock handed the remote over and Dawson muted the television. The room turned to him, the distinct sound of beer bottles being placed on tables as those gathered stood to face him, all knowing their fun was over without it said.

"We've been called up. Thirty minutes at the unit. I'll give Red a shout, the rest of you contact your designates."

With Stucco's wife in the room, Dawson couldn't say where they were going, but everyone knew, even she. They filed out, gave her an obligatory handshake and smile, and moments later only Dawson, Stucco and his wife remained. Dawson turned to her.

"I'm sorry for this, ma'am. We appreciate the effort you've put into making us feel at home, but unfortunately duty calls."

She smiled and nodded, tears in her eyes, tears Dawson knew were not for a ruined afternoon, but knowing her husband was willingly heading into danger yet again. The wives knew what their husbands did for a living. And they accepted it. It was what their men loved to do. The secret wasn't the job, it was the mission. No, they couldn't tell their friends and family what their husbands did, they were just regular grunts.

And that was perhaps one of the worst parts of this. The families and friends who had to be lied to on a regular basis, the wives who couldn't talk to their closest confidants when they were worried. It resulted in a close knit unit in itself amongst the spouses. Only they could talk to each other about their troubles, about their worries and fears.

Dawson said his goodbyes, and left the humble home, silently praying that all of his men returned to their loved ones after this mission.

Marawi City, Mindanao, Philippines

Corporal Florencio Padayao of the Philippine Army watched the television screen with several of his comrades, rage building within. A staunch Roman Catholic, as were most of the Filipinos, he couldn't believe what he was seeing. Not only were those filthy Muslims daring to defile the holiest place in the world, but they were now trying to destroy it.

Footage of the Pope's narrow escape, caught on camera by a news crew in an overhead helicopter, engulfed his heart in fury. He slammed his fist on the table they were sitting at, the tin plates holding the meager lunches of his platoon bouncing, the rattle causing heads to turn, including some of those coming out of a nearby mosque.

His fists clenched and he pushed himself up from the table.

"Where are you going?" asked his closest friend, Eduardo, pulling on his sleeve.

"I'm going to teach those fuckers a lesson," muttered Florencio. He ripped his arm away from Eduardo's tightening grip.

"What do you mean?"

Florencio ignored him, picking up his Steyr AUG Assault Rifle and flicking the safety to full auto. He watched as those filthy pigs streamed out of their mosque, the loud speakers strapped to the top of the minaret annoying him six times a day. He hated this posting. They all did. But they had to try and keep the peace because these assholes kept trying to cause trouble.

Our country would be better off if every last one of them were dead.

A low growl slowly built in his chest, erupting in a roar of rage that brought the entire town square to a halt. He raised his weapon and pointed it at the crowd.

"Let's see your Allah save you now!" he screamed, squeezing the trigger. Bullet after bullet belched from the barrel of his well-used weapon, the first few rounds tearing up the ground in front of the crowd of worshippers before his aim was true.

Then the mayhem began.

Screams split the calm of the square as the first, mostly adorned in traditional white, dropped, freshly torn holes in their flesh spewing forth blood that stained their owners and pooled on the densely packed dirt of the street.

His weapon clicked, and he ejected the clip, slapping a new one in and readying the weapon. He took aim at the Imam who had glad-handed them on many occasions, thanking them for helping keep the peace, and assuring them over and over that their religion was one of peace, and that they all just wanted to get along.

Bullshit!

He squeezed, and the man dropped. He continued, more controlled bursts this time, chewing through his thirty rounds, then again ejected the clip, and reloaded. Dozens were on the ground. Some moving, writhing in pain, some still. Wails of sorrow and terror filled the once peaceful town square, but nothing would calm Florencio's hatred. He raised his weapon again, taking aim at a mother and her bastard son, a future terrorist that Florencio's own son might have to fight someday.

Something tore into his side, causing him to spin around. Agony swept through his body as he dropped to the ground. His weapon flew from his hand and rattled to the ground. Reaching down to the source of the blinding pain, he felt a dampness rapidly expanding. He held up his hand

and it was covered in blood. The sun shone down in his eyes, and he began to lose focus, his hand returning to where he'd been shot, trying desperately to keep the blood inside, the pressure he managed to apply doing little.

The sun blotted out, and he saw Eduardo standing over him, his weapon in hand. He took a knee and leaned over Florencio, putting his hand on his shoulder.

"What have you done?" he asked. The horror was clear. And so was his pain. Tears filled both their eyes as Florencio looked at his friend of so many years. He felt the strength quickly draining from him as he reached up and grabbed Eduardo by the sleeve, pulling him closer.

"I evened the score."

Rally Point, Vatican City

Acton followed the crowd toward the rally point, Laura at his side. Gun fire occasionally broke the subdued, terrified silence of the crowd. The chanting from Saint Peter's Square continued, and Acton found his heart pounding almost in rhythm to it, the sound of thousands, of tens of thousands, chanting the same thing over and over almost hypnotic.

Another burst of gunfire, this sounding closer, caused a lady next to him to yelp in fear. Acton's head snapped in her direction and she bit her finger, trying to silence herself, tear stained cheeks flushed with the effort of whatever run she had been forced to endure. He gave her a reassuring smile that he wasn't even sure he himself would believe, then looked over his shoulder. He saw Giasson's bald head bouncing several dozen people behind, and slowed Laura up slightly to let the man catch up.

"Just another hundred meters!" Acton heard Giasson say as he came into sight with a man's arm over his shoulder, helping him as the man skipped along on one foot.

Giasson looked up as Acton approached.

"Sprained ankle," he said as Acton took the man's other arm and draped it across his shoulder. Together they nearly carried him the final few hundred feet where they handed the man off to others in the crowd. Giasson, Acton and Laura joined a group of guards as Giasson flipped open his phone.

"Ready?" was all he asked, then he nodded and flipped the phone closed. Giasson crossed the tracks then jumped up on the platform and held his arms up to quiet the crowd whose whispers were threatening to turn into shouts.

"I will say this once in English, since most of you understand English. Translate for your neighbor if they don't as there is no time for additional languages.

"For obvious reasons, everybody must stay as quiet as possible during this entire exercise. If anybody talks, shouts, cries out, screams, we could all be discovered. This is our last chance at escape."

Gunfire erupted from the direction they had just come, several sustained bursts interrupting Giasson's instructions. When they stopped, the entire crowd turned back to Giasson, giving Acton the impression of a tennis match.

"Now, in less than five minutes we will be opening the gates"—he pointed at a set of large doors embedded in the mighty southern wall—"and you will all file out in an *orderly* fashion, and onto buses that will be waiting for us. Follow the instructions of the Polizia outside, get on the bus they tell you to, get on and take a seat, and *keep quiet!* If we all cooperate, we'll be out of here safely, inside of fifteen minutes."

Giasson jerked a thumb over his shoulder and Acton looked, his eyebrows shooting up at what he hadn't noticed sitting there.

A train.

He knew the Vatican had a train station. It had been started by Pope Pius XI in 1929, was completed in 1933, and had the shortest track of any country in the world, only 900 feet, and only one station, which they were standing at.

But beyond that gate, it tied into the Italian railroad system, and once there, they could plow through any crowd. And if Acton remembered his geography—

His thoughts were interrupted by heavy gunfire, and Giasson reaching for his phone. He flipped it open and listened for a moment, then nodded. "Hold as long as you can, then fall back toward us if possible, if not, get into the Governatorate Palace." He hung up the phone and clapped his hands together once.

"We have no time so listen up! Those closest to the platform will get on the train, now, in an *orderly* fashion! The rest of you, line up at the gate in four lines."

The crowd didn't move.

"Now!" he yelled, and the crowd began to move, those closest the platform clamoring for position. "Calmly!" yelled Giasson. "And quietly!"

Acton, Laura, Giasson and several of the guards began to help people across the tracks as the crowd surged forward. Giasson grabbed several men and delegated them to help the others, and within minutes the platform was filled with people now boarding the small, two car train.

"That's getting full pretty quickly!" said Laura to Giasson.

He glanced over his shoulder and nodded, standing up. He raised his hands, waving them at the crowd. "The train is full. Everyone else get in the lines."

There were some cries and a few angry shouts, but Giasson turned on the crowd, pointing his finger at no one in particular. "Calm yourselves! Do you want to be responsible for getting us all killed?"

Silence swept the crowd, those who had been making noise stopping, shamed by the comment thought directed at them alone. Those who had been trying to get on the platform stopped, and shuffled toward what Acton was surprised to see were four distinct, fairly orderly, lines, just as Giasson had instructed. They urged the rest on the train, and those who couldn't fit, jumped off the platform and joined one of the lines.

Giasson motioned to Acton and Laura. "Get in line."

"What about you?" asked Acton.

"I need to open the gates." He pointed at the lines. "Don't worry about me. Get in line and get out while you can!"

More gunfire. This time very close.

"Now!" He pointed at the case. "And get that thing to His Holiness!"

Acton shook Giasson's hand, then he and Laura crossed the tracks and joined the back of one of the lines. Giasson entered the station, his phone held to his ear.

And that's when something dawned on Acton and his jaw dropped.

"What is it?" asked Laura, her hand grabbing his arm.

"Something just occurred to me."

"What?"

"Who's going to close the gates when everyone is out?"

Vatican Railroad Viaduct, Rome, Italy

Sovrintendente Marcelo Primo looked at his watch as his heart pounded in his chest.

This is crazy!

Crowds were already gathering below the viaduct the small Vatican rail line travelled before joining the main line, and he could see dozens if not hundreds of cellphones held to ears as the call went out for reinforcements. They knew something was going on. It was obvious. There were over a dozen city buses lined up on the walkway alongside the tracks, their drivers, all volunteers, having backed them in for several kilometers, there no room to turn them around. Hundreds of police manned hastily erected barricades in an attempt to prevent people from climbing up to the viaduct.

His phone rang and he tapped the display to accept the call.

"Primo."

"Opening the gates now!"

"Confirmed. We're ready. But make it quick, I don't know how much longer I can hold the crowd back!"

"We'll go as fast as we can."

The call ended, and the mighty gates of the south wall began to open, the massive metal doors parting at the center. He heard the train engine begin to move, it a small miracle they had been able to get it here in time, the engineer, his head hanging out the window, anxious to get in and out as quickly as possible. Police were positioned at several points along the massive engine's length, armed with instructions to shoot anyone who might impede its progress. This train alone would save several hundred if they could just get it into the tunnel several kilometers away.

As the gates opened the crowd roared in anger as their suspicions were confirmed, and they began to push against the metal barricades erected only minutes before, leaving little time to properly secure them together.

They won't hold.

The brakeman on the back of the engine, a volunteer from the train company, waved slowly to the engineer, and the train continued to inch toward the gates, now half way open, providing his first glance inside. He could see hundreds of people from his vantage point, less than thirty feet away. About a dozen of his men were at the gate, telling them to wait for the gates to open completely so they could exit at the same time the engine passed on the tracks.

A dozen bus engines roared to life around him as the city bus drivers started their vehicles, the doors opening. Lines of police stood along the way, ready to direct each line of refugees to the appropriate bus. And they were refugees. These were citizens and guests of a country, under attack, fleeing for their lives.

Primo sighed. If it went smoothly, they might just get everyone out before things fell apart. But things never went smoothly. Not with a mob this size determined to prevent it from happening.

Glass shattered behind him. He spun and saw the back window of one of the city buses in pieces, the long line of parked buses a prime target for anyone with the presence of mind to pry loose a cobblestone.

He looked back at the gates and saw the lines begin to rush forward as the gates finished opening. The engine was already picking up a little speed as the brakeman urged the engineer forward. His men and women, using only their hands and their voices, directed the four lines toward their designated groups of three buses, and for a moment, Primo thought this might just work.

Someone screamed.

His head pivoted toward the sound and he saw a body on the ground, a cobblestone beside it. Several people helped the person up, and continued toward the buses as blood streamed down the victim's face.

They'll get medical attention at the other end.

The four lines were almost clear of the gates, and the first bus already began to pull away, as the other buses continued to load. A cobblestone hit near his feet, bouncing directly at him. He ducked and it went over his shoulder, hitting the man behind him in the stomach.

"Are you okay?"

The man nodded, doubled over. "I will be."

"Get on one of our buses."

"I'll be okay."

"Now!"

The man nodded and stumbled toward one of the three buses reserved for their evacuation.

Bravery will get someone killed today.

He looked down at the rioters. They had to number in the thousands now, and the barricades weren't going to hold. The sound from the locomotive changed, and he prayed that meant they were hooking up to the cars inside.

Another bus pulled away.

He watched the last of the first line board, and the bus pull away, freeing up the first two from the second line. Three more buses were clear.

That's five.

He looked back at the gate, walking toward the rails, and peered inside. It was eerie. The setting sun cast long shadows across the immaculate lawns inside, the green space of the Vatican a marked contrast to the dense urban environment of a three thousand year old Rome.

But there was no one in sight.

Just the engineer, leaning out his window.

Then he saw a hand wave, and the engineer turned, pushing something, hard. He heard the distinct screeching of metal on metal, and saw the massive wheels spin, then grip, and the train lurched forward, slowly gaining speed.

He heard several more buses roar away behind him, but his eyes were on the train. Something moved behind it; several men, running. He peered into the dusk and saw others chasing the first few.

Oh shit!

He looked at the crowds then the buses. The last bus of evacuees pulled away as a Molotov cocktail was thrown. Primo watched in horror as it arced through the air, then hit the front of the bus, exploding in a fireball. The bus slammed to a halt as those inside screamed in terror.

That's when the line broke.

The bus jolted to a halt as screams and smoke began to fill the interior. Those who were in seats jumped to their feet, as everyone desperately tried to flee the now burning bus. Acton held his hand up to shield himself from the heat, he and Laura the last on, therefore closest to the front.

Except for the bus driver.

He sat frozen, paralyzed with fear, then suddenly began to desperately undo his lap belt, without success, his adrenaline, panic fueled attempts failing. Acton pushed Laura back and pulled his pocket knife, stepping over to the driver and kneeling at his side.

"Stop!" he yelled as the driver's hands continued to get in the way. The man snapped out of his panic for a moment and stared at Acton. Acton reached forward and rather than bother with the clasp, cut the belt in one stroke, then pulled the driver out of his seat, and away from the fire engulfing the front windshield and surrounding rubber.

"How do we open the doors?" asked Acton, yelling into the driver's ear, the screams of the passengers drowning out most sounds.

The man pointed at the smoking control panel he had been behind moments before.

"The lever, pull the lever all the way!"

Acton reached over and touched the lever, gasping at the heat, withdrawing his hand immediately. He looked around for something and felt a tap on his shoulder. He turned to find Laura with her hand extended, offering her scarf. He smiled and took it, quickly spinning it around his hand. He reached over again and this time grabbed the lever and twisted it all the way.

The front door hissed open, as did the rear. He grabbed Laura and pulled her out the front doors, and to what was supposed to be safety. But as they ran from the bus, they were met with the sight of dozens of rioters battling with the police; dozens more pouring up a set of stairs. To his right he could see the train just now coming through the gates, at what seemed like a crawl.

Several police rushed over and directed the passengers of the now burning bus to another one idling nearby. Acton took Laura by the hand and they began toward it when the distinctive pops of gunfire drew his attention to the gates, and what was happening inside. He turned to Laura.

"Get on the bus; I'll just be a minute."

"Where are you going?"

"I just need to make sure Mario's okay."

He gave her a quick kiss on the cheek and turned, running toward the gates. As he cleared the mighty wall and reentered the tiny city state, the platform suddenly snapped into focus. Three guards had taken a knee and were firing on a group that numbered in the dozens, with some of them armed, returning fire. One of the guards fell. Then another. The third jumped to his feet to fall back but was hit from behind.

Acton spotted Giasson step out and squeeze off several rounds at the crowd that now rushed forward, unopposed.

He doesn't stand a chance.

And that's when Acton made a decision. He sprinted forward, drawing his weapon, and took up position behind a small bush. Taking aim, he squeezed off three rounds at those carrying the weapons and leading the pack.

Two fell.

And the crowd slowed, uncertain where the shots had come from. Giasson stepped out from the control room again, and fired several more shots, and Acton advanced to a large tree. He fired another shot, taking out one of the invaders as they stooped to pick up the weapon of a fallen comrade.

Someone must have seen the muzzle flash, because an arm pointed in his direction, and some of the crowd turned toward him. Bullets ripped up the ground around him as he pressed his back into the tree trunk that he was suddenly finding far too narrow for his liking.

Muzzle flashes and the report of several shots snapped through the air from the bush he had just been behind. He peered through the darkness and his heart sank.

It was Laura.

What the hell is she doing here?

But he knew.

Saving my ass.

Acton spun and emptied his clip into the crowd as he raced toward the edge of the platform, freeing up the tree for Laura, as the bush would provide no protection. He glanced behind and saw her advance to the additional cover as she fired two more shots.

Acton looked at the crowd. There were at least a dozen bodies strewn across the approach to the platform, and the crowd was now stopped.

Two blasts from the train's horn split the night and Acton heard the powerful motors that controlled the gate kick in again. He glanced back and saw the gates begin to close, but almost as if playing on a screen at a drive-in theatre, the chaos on the other side, lit by the street lights glaring down on the police and rioters, highlighting the battle they were losing.

If those gates don't close soon, we could have hundreds more coming down on us in seconds.

He saw a group break off and head toward the gates.

"Laura, cover the gate!" he yelled.

She spun around and raised her weapon, firing two shots at the ground in front of the group. They dropped, then scrambled away, their bravado momentarily quelled as this group hadn't yet been met with gunfire.

Acton returned his attention to the other group, already hardened insurgents compared to those outside, then at the control room which Giasson still stubbornly occupied.

"Mario, let's get out of here!"

He poked his head outside.

"Not until the gate is closed and I can destroy the controls!"

Shit! Acton knew Giasson was right. If they left the control station intact, the south gates would be opened within minutes, and there would be thousands more do deal with.

Laura fired another two shots.

Acton looked back and saw the gates were nearly closed, only several agonizing feet remaining. He returned his attention to the group attempting to take the platform. It appeared they had rediscovered their balls, and were again approaching. Giasson's hand appeared out the door of the control room and several shots rang out, the muzzle flashes now distinct in the near pitch black.

Acton fired several rounds himself, and the crowd backed off as the sound of the two massive doors slamming together rolled across the lawn.

"Now!" he yelled as he fired two more rounds. Another two from behind him rang out, and a moment later Laura was at his side.

"You okay?" she asked.

He nodded. "Yeah, you?"

"Absolutely fabulous, Darling."

He chuckled. "And what happened to you getting on the bus?"

"As if I was going to let my fiancé go off alone into a gunfight!"

He frowned, but he knew she couldn't see it.

"Cover me!" he heard Giasson yell, and they both jumped up, firing into the crowd that now surged forward at the words. As they both emptied their clips, Acton watched Giasson race across the platform and dive toward their position as the unmistakable sound of a weapon set to fully automatic tore up the concrete.

Giasson cried out in pain.

Acton reloaded then aimed at the muzzle flash that was directed at their position, firing rapidly. The opposing fire ceased, and he turned to Giasson who was lying on the ground, gripping his shoulder.

"Is he okay?" asked Laura as she covered their position.

"I'll live," said Giasson. "Help me up."

Acton reached down and pulled Giasson to his feet.

"How do we get out of here?"

"Follow me."

At a crouch they rounded the southern side of the train station, and out of sight of the small mob pursuing them. Then, at a sprint, they quickly covered the south side and turned north.

"We just need to get back to the Governatorate Palace," gasped Giasson, still gripping his arm. At a jog they ran through the parking lot of the train station. Acton fished Laura's scarf from his pocket.

"Wait a sec."

They came to a halt and Acton hooked the scarf under Giasson's arm, positioning it above the wound, then tied it off tightly.

Giasson gasped then nodded to Acton. "Thanks."

"Okay, lead the way. The sooner we're out of the open, the better."

Giasson didn't wait to reply, simply running again, with Laura behind him and Acton covering the rear, the metal case containing the scroll still gripped tightly in his hand, a constant reminder as to what had caused this entire situation. That so much death could come out of something as wondrous as an archaeological find was unimaginable. Dozens were probably dead, and if he wasn't mistaken, dozens if not hundreds more would be killed before this was over.

There was no way the West could let this continue, not while precious pieces of history were destroyed by ignorance and hate. But to take back the Vatican would be a herculean effort. There were tens of thousands of protesters, dozens of those armed. And when someone is firing from within a mob, as he and his companions discovered tonight, it was almost impossible not to shoot those around them.

The blood spilt over the coming days may wash away with ease, but the memory would take a long time to erase. And would it just result in more hatred between Islam and everything else? He hated himself for singling out one religion as the problem, but he couldn't help but reach that conclusion. Edison Cole and New Slate's plan to trigger a holy war with a nuclear weapon would have worked, only because Islamists would have played directly into his hands, and repeatedly throughout the past decades it was Islamists attacking Christians, Buddhists, Hindus, each other. When almost every terrorist attack on the planet is perpetrated by the followers of one religion, and the vast majority of the adherents to that religion remain silent, perhaps that silence speaks volumes about the problems within their set of beliefs.

Had Christianity once been evil? Absolutely. The Spanish Inquisition was a prime example of how religious doctrine, run unchecked, could perform heinous acts upon the population. But that was over five hundred years ago. Christianity had progressed, modernized, and learned to live in a world of democracy, freedom, technology. But as much as he hated to admit it, Islam was still stuck in the twelfth century. Once producing leaders in scholarly pursuits, it had stagnated, and never progressed, turning in on itself in a cycle of hate and violence that eventually would lead to either its own destruction, or that of everyone else.

It was inevitable that with modern technology the uneducated masses would become educated, would become informed, and just like the Soviets that once thought their lives were better than those in the West, they too would learn the truth, and hopefully discover that hatred wasn't the way to a better life. If enough would turn their backs on the old ways, could they reform their religion like Christians had? Could they put the past behind them, and join a modern, free, peaceful world?

Acton couldn't see it happening in his lifetime. Nor his children's.

The thought of children snapped him out of his internal debate, one he felt guilty about, but sometimes confronting the truth in front of you, no matter how politically incorrect, was necessary in order to move forward and deal with the problem, rather than tiptoe around it apologetically.

But children?

He looked at Laura and smiled.

Children.

He glanced over his shoulder and frowned.

"We've got company!" he hissed as they rounded to the north side of the building.

"Just up there, a few hundred meters," gasped Giasson.

They were slowing down as Giasson weakened. Acton handed the case to Laura then caught up to Giasson and threw the man's good arm over his shoulder to take some of his weight.

"Thank you," the man grunted.

"We've gotta hurry!" urged Laura as she now covered the rear. They covered the distance quickly, but their pursuers covered it quicker, and within seconds their shouts filled the air as the tiny group was spotted.

Acton's head spun around as he heard Laura fire twice. The small mob slowed, the shots embedding themselves into the ground at their feet, but enough to stem their courage momentarily.

Acton didn't waste any time, nearly dragging the injured Giasson as fast as he could toward the building. Shouts from their left, and then their right, caused Acton's chest to tighten and his heart drum in his chest as he realized they were about to be surrounded.

Keep going!

"Weapon," whispered Giasson.

Acton pulled Giasson's gun from its holster, not losing a step, and placed it into Giasson's good hand. He pulled his own weapon out. Laura fired twice more.

"Firing," whispered Giasson, giving Acton enough warning to turn his head toward Giasson as the weapon roared a foot away from his ear. They were now in the parking lot, nearing the stairs of the Governatorate Palace, but hundreds were now converging on them. Shots ricocheted off the asphalt nearby, then more tore open the concrete steps they were preparing to mount. Acton fired to their left, Giasson to their right, and Laura from the rear, targets no longer important.

They hit the first step.

But the doors ahead of them, would they be open? Acton didn't want to think of that now. More gunfire and Laura yelped. Acton spun around and she was gripping her leg, but still climbing the stairs.

"I'm okay, just a graze!" she said, wincing. "Keep going!"

They were half way up the stairs. More gunfire tore at the façade of the building, sending chips of concrete scattering across the stairs. Suddenly the doors burst open and at least a dozen heavily armed men appeared, rushing past them. Two more came out and grabbed Giasson and Laura, carrying them inside as a steady stream of gunfire behind them sent their pursuers scattering.

Acton crossed the threshold into the building, gasping for air as their saviors retreated back into the building, the doors closing behind them. Acton and Laura stood with Giasson as they watched the defenders blockade the doors again.

One of the men walked up to Giasson, a look of relief on his face.

"M. Giasson! We thought you were dead!"

Giasson looked at his companions.

"We almost were."

Vatican Railroad Viaduct, Rome, Italy

The gates thudded shut, the metal hitting metal reverberating across the viaduct, Primo feeling the entire structure vibrate with a tingle in his legs. The motor cut off powering the gate, and gun fire continued on the other side.

But there was nothing he could do about that now.

He needed to get these refugees and his men to safety. The buses with the evacuees were gone, including one originally intended for his men. The firebombed bus it replaced continued to burn, the heat and smoke from the wreck licking at them all, the area far too small for a thirty foot fire to go unnoticed.

And with that wreck blocking the already narrow path they had come up on, the final two buses would have to tuck in behind the train in order to get around it. This wasn't going to work. He motioned Pietro Nardozzi over, a young officer he'd worked with since the man was a rookie.

"Yes, sir?"

Primo pointed at the two idling buses, the fear on the drivers' faces clear. "Tell them to leave now, behind the train, we won't be taking them."

Nardozzi's face belied his fear at the news, but to his credit he simply nodded and ran to the first bus, then the second. The heads of his men spun as they heard the buses begin to pull away, several of them shouting at the drivers in anger as they thought they were fleeing without them.

There were dozens of protesters now, if not nearly a hundred, on the viaduct, with more coming every second. They were about equally matched in numbers, but that would change.

It was time.

"Fall back!" he yelled. "Fall back! Fall back along the viaduct!"

He ran a couple of hundred feet toward where the viaduct had no more ways for protesters to access it, and stopped, grabbing his men as they caught up.

"Form a line here," he said, drawing an artificial line with his hand. "Let our men through, keep the protesters out." The dozen or so men heeded his instructions and formed a line, and as more of their comrades reached them, the line firmed up, those with riot shields and gear still intact taking up position in the front.

Primo stood in front of the line, continuing to call the retreat, and watched with pride as those that remained, fighting hand to hand with the protesters, helped each other extricate themselves, and retreat as a group, rather than leave anyone behind. Through the city and fire light, it looked as if none of his men were left behind, but some were definitely injured.

Damn. If only we had one of those buses.

Their retreat would be slower with injured, but they would make it. He looked back and he felt his chest swell. The two buses had stopped, their tires now firmly planted on the viaduct walkway and off the tracks, their drivers standing in the doorways, beckoning to them. The pride that Primo felt at that moment, the faith in his fellow man, was overwhelming. These two brave souls had the opportunity to flee, and despite having seen one of their own firebombed, they stayed.

It reminded him of a recent conversation with a friend who had said he feared society was about to collapse, and what would happen in the aftermath. Would chaos and anarchy reign?

Primo had more faith in his fellow man than his friend had.

Remember the Colorado shootings. Despite near certain death, husbands covered wives with their bodies, boyfriends shielded girlfriends, strangers performed CPR on people they didn't even know, despite the danger. When things go wrong, the best in us comes out, and as long as there are enough of us to do the right thing, society will keep itself together long enough to recover.

And this was one of those moments. The best had come out in these men. He pointed at the buses.

"Get the injured on that first bus!" he ordered as the line of officers rushed forward to form a new line just behind the last of their retreating comrades. All were now behind the line, and the protesters were pushing against it, but the viaduct was fairly narrow, only thirty feet across, and much easier to hold than the huge area they had been covering moments before.

He looked behind him and saw the injured being loaded on the first bus, the rest of the several hundred men retreating slowly down the viaduct, their eyes trained on the angry mob that advanced with them. He heard the engine of the bus roar as it pulled away and cheers rose among the men as they knew their comrades were safe.

Primo spotted Nardozzi and motioned him over.

"Tell the driver to retreat with us, just in case anyone else gets injured."

Nardozzi nodded and turned to deliver the order when Primo grabbed him by the arm. Nardozzi turned back, his eyes wide in confusion. "And thank him for staying." Nardozzi smiled and nodded. Primo let go of his arm, then slapped him on the back. "Now go!" Nardozzi rushed off and Primo returned his attention to the front line.

"Masks!" he yelled, warning his men of what he was about to do. Everyone grabbed their gas masks and began fitting them over their faces, those at the very front holding the shields assisted by their comrades.

"Tear gas!" Two of his men rushed up, loading the canisters in their riot guns. He raised his hand in the air, then dropped his arm. "Fire!" The distinctive pop of the canisters launching indicated the criticality of the situation. Two distinct puffs of smoke appeared as he fit his own mask over his face. He put himself into the middle of the pack holding the line. "Quick retreat, fifty meters, then reform the line on my command! Tell your partners." He returned to the men with the teargas. "Retreat fifty meters, then when the line reforms, put as many canisters as you can between us and the mob." The men nodded and sprinted to their new position. Primo waved his hand in the air, indicating the bus should retreat. The driver nodded and climbed in. Primo turned back to the front line.

"Now!" he yelled, then spun on his heel and ran, counting off the strides. Reaching fifty, he stopped and with both arms extended out, he indicated where the line should reform as those in the front regrouped, the heavy shields slamming into the metal and concrete of the viaduct, recreating the nearly impenetrable wall. The protesters were rushing to fill the gap, but not many, most caught off guard. He heard the pops from behind as two canisters of teargas were fired into the gap, then another two pops. They continued firing, the area quickly filling with a thick smoke, and the coughs and cries of the protesters unmistakable.

Primo turned and pointed to the bus. "Fill it with an many as can fit, then get the hell out of here!" he yelled. Those not forming the line sprinted to the bus, loading through the front and back doors, and within minutes, the bus was full, and pulling away.

"Now run!" he yelled, turning and jogging after the bus, the front line breaking with him, as they all beat a hasty retreat, the teargas continuing to keep the rioters at bay. As they put more distance between them and the cloud of teargas, he looked back and saw several of the crowd give chase but give up after a few feet, realizing they were now mostly alone, and the distance too great to catch up and do any real damage.

Instead, like the delusional individuals they were, they decided to turn the conclusion to a successful evacuation operation of an entire city into their own victory, cheering and screaming, "Allahu Akbar" at the top of their lungs.

Primo shook his head.

Yes, God is great, and tonight, he was clearly on our side.

Rue Myrha, Paris, France

"But I have to get down that street! It's my job!"

The gendarme shook his head and pointed to a narrow road on the right. "You have to go around, that way."

Philippe looked at the road—scratch that—laneway, then back at the police officer. "Monsieur, have you looked at the size of my vehicle? It's a garbage truck! It can't fit down that 'road' as you call it."

The officer stepped back, looking at the vehicle, then at the laneway, apparently realizing his gaffe. "Then you'll have to wait for the protesters to clear out, or back up and find another way."

"Back up? Are you crazy?" He leaned out his window, looking back at the line of traffic. "And just how do you propose I do that?"

Again the cop took a look.

"I guess you'll have to wait." He pointed to the side of the road. "Please pull over there as far as you can." The officer stepped back to hold the traffic while Philippe moved his truck, muttering curses under his breath. Once he had positioned himself at the curb, he leaned back out his window, waving at the officer.

"How long is this going to take? I need to finish my route and get home. My wife's having a baby!"

The man shrugged his shoulders. "It's been going all day and they haven't moved."

Philippe slammed his fists into the dash. *What the hell am I going to do?* He looked up at the chanting protesters, sitting on the road. *Those fucking Muslims. They come to France and they think they own the place. Praying in the streets, wearing their potato sacks, spreading their hatred of our way of life.* His thoughts flashed to last night's news. There were over 4.7 million Muslims in France, with a birthrate double the traditional French. And one in every eight in Paris were Muslim. *This is fucking ridiculous!* His chest tightened and his heart began to slam against his ribcage. *I need to get out of here.*

His phone rang. He grabbed it off his hip and looked at the call display. *Giselle!* He flipped it open. "Is it time?"

"Oui!"

"But I'm stuck in traffic! These fucking Mus—"

"I don't give a goddamned about any traffic. I'm about to have this baby, and if I have to call my mother to take me to the midwife, it will prove to her once and for all that you're an unreliable pathetic excuse for a man and this time she just might convince me to divorce you."

Philippe felt his heart break a little as tears filled his eyes. He wasn't the success he had hoped to be. The little shop they had opened with such expectations had failed with the recession, and he had been damned lucky to get this job as a garbage man for a private company, servicing several hotels. In fact, it had been his mother-in-law who had managed to get him the job, pulling in several favors.

I'm not doing this for you. I'm doing it for my daughter.

His stomach churned at the humiliation of the memory.

"But baby, what am I going to do? There's a protest blocking the street!"

"Go through the bastards for all I care! If you're not here within the hour, I'm calling Mama."

And she hung up.

The phone rang again and he flipped it open.

"Baby, you know I hate it when you do that!"

"Do what?"

Merde. It was his boss.

"Yes, sir, what can I do for you?"

"L'hotel Julie just called. You missed their pickup."

"No, I haven't reached them yet, I didn't miss them."

"What?"

"I'm stuck in traffic. Those Muslims protesting."

"I don't give a shit why you're late. It's your job to know what's in your way, and go around it if necessary. Finish your route, on time, or forget coming in tomorrow. I don't care if your mother-in-law is my cousin. She's a bitch of a woman, and I can't believe I let her talk me into hiring someone in a recession."

And he hung up.

Philippe whipped the phone at the windshield. He hated being hung up on. *What am I going to do?* If he didn't finish his route, which was only one more stop at L'hotel Julie, he'd be fired. And he had a new baby coming any minute, and he couldn't afford to be unemployed. He'd take any job he could get—hell, he was driving a garbage truck—pride no longer entered the equation. He'd sweep streets for cash.

He looked through his windshield at the mob sitting across the street, hundreds of them, more likely thousands, stretched as far as he could see before the street bent out of sight. *It's those fuckers who've taken all the jobs.* His ears filled with the pounding of rage. He closed his eyes and gripped the steering wheel.

I need to get through.

I need to finish my route.

I need to get my wife to the midwife.

I need this job.

He growled, opening his eyes.

Fuck it.

He turned the key, starting the truck. He leaned over, locking the passenger side door and rolling up the window, then did the same for his side. He turned the radio up, the broadcast having turned to live coverage of what these fuckers were doing to the Vatican.

God will forgive me.

He put the truck in gear, pumped the horn several times, drawing the attention of the police manning the line of the, for the moment, peaceful protest.

He popped the clutch.

The truck lurched forward, and he saw eyes bulge, as police turned to face him, still uncertain of what he was about to do. He shifted into second, and the truck surged forward again.

And little doubt remained as to what his plan was.

The police began to scatter, the barricade they had erected quickly abandoned as they surrendered their position to the oncoming truck. Philippe pushed it into third, now gaining speed, the massive truck, with a nearly full load of garbage, plowing straight for the metal rails separating the protesters from civilization.

Fourth.

He had the speed now. There was no stopping him. He heard the shouts of the police, waving their hands at him, one even had the nerve to jump in front of the truck, waving his arms, before diving aside at the last second.

He flipped the range button to high and shifted again.

Fifth.

He hit the barricade. The front of the truck jumped a good six to twelve inches as it rolled through and over the barricade, and into the crowd of now panicking protesters. They began to jump to their feet, scurrying in every direction.

Sixth.

He didn't care.

He had to get through. He had to finish his route. He had to get his wife to the midwife. He had to keep his mother-in-law off his back. He had to keep this job.

He had to just make it through this day.

He could feel the occasional bump as he rolled over the parasites too slow to get out of the way, and those who were stupid enough to run directly away from him, instead of to the sides, plowed by his bumper.

But he didn't care.

He had to get through.

His passenger side window shattered. His head swung over to see a rock sitting on the seat, and someone reaching in, trying to unlock the door. Philippe picked up the rock and swung it at the man's head. The impact was jarring, and the cry as the man fell away disconcerting. He pushed harder on the accelerator and ducked as a rock slammed into the windshield, the safety glass shattering into a million tiny fragments, but still held together. Somebody else jumped onto the running boards, reached inside and pulled the door handle, unlocking it before Philippe could stop him. He reached over to press the button again but the door was already opening. Grabbing at the handle, he pulled back, but the door was torn open and he found himself staring into the eyes of the man who had finally succeeded, his eyes filled with rage, a look of blind insanity and hatred Philippe had only seen before on television.

It terrified him.

The man lunged at him. Philippe grabbed the rock sitting on the seat and jerked his hand up on mere instinct, nailing the man square in the jaw. He winced in pain, but didn't stop, and within seconds had his fingers around Philippe's throat. Philippe jerked away, breaking the hold, but the man's hands gripped Philippe's shirt, and began to pull him toward the passenger seat.

His foot slipped off the gas, and the truck began to slow. Someone else reached in to help the first man, and within seconds Philippe felt himself being pulled out of the cab of his truck. He reached up and grabbed the steering wheel, gripping it with all his strength as he was yanked and clawed at. A set of fingers blindly grasped at his face, and entered his mouth, pulling hard. The pain was horrendous, as if his entire head were about to be ripped off.

He bit down hard.

He heard a yelp, and the fingers were withdrawn, and only one set of hands were on him. He shook his shoulders side to side, rolling his body violently, breaking the grip, and pulled himself toward the safety of the driver's side of the cabin, when the window on that side smashed. A dozen hands reached inside, grasping for the door handle, and to his horror, he saw one find it.

The door opened.

The set of hands, freed from only moments before, grabbed him by the back of his collar and pulled, then new hands from the other side grabbed at his feet as the driver side door opened.

The truck was still moving forward, but he was no longer in control of it. He felt the wheel jerk to the left as someone else grabbed it, and broke his grip. The truck lurched in the new direction, and to his horror, he felt himself slide quickly out the passenger side and into the sunlight.

He hit the ground hard, and was immediately set upon by dozens. He couldn't make out any individuals, only nightmarish flashes of faces, eyes glaring, teeth barred, hundreds of voices screaming in anger, in pain, hundreds of hands desperate to get a grip on the source of their anguish.

He kicked out, swung his arms, tried to keep moving, so they couldn't get a grip on him, but it was no use. Someone had a hold of his left leg first, then an iron grip had his right arm. Both pulled and he felt himself pop up off the ground, suspended in the air by the two pulling at him from opposite directions. He kicked out with his free leg, but someone grabbed that. Reaching over with his last free limb, he clawed at the hand holding his arm, but someone else grabbed him and pulled directly backward. Hard.

He felt a jarring pain that nearly caused him to pass out, and the fog in his brain told him his shoulder had just been dislocated. More hands got a grip on him, all pulling in opposite directions. He felt more pain on his left shoulder as another set of hands gripped his arm, at least four now, and pulled.

He felt it tear. His eyes, blinded with tears, could see nothing anymore. The white light of pain filled them, then his eyes squeezed shut instinctively as someone grabbed his face, their fingers clawing at his eyes. He screamed, a long, agonizing scream, one at first he didn't even register as his own, one he never knew he was capable of making. And he knew it was gone. He could feel it, he could sense it, he knew it was no longer there.

They had torn off his left arm.

Fists rained down on him, kicks jolted him, but he couldn't feel it anymore. The pain was too much. He felt himself beginning to slip, then the jolt of more pain as his right leg popped out of its socket. He could feel the skin, the sinew, the ligaments, the veins, pulling, tearing, and then the distinct sensation as the limb was torn free.

But this time he didn't scream.

This time the pain was too great. This time He showed him mercy. This time He let him pass out.

This time He let him die.

Chapel of the Sacrament, Saint Peter's Basilica, Vatican City

"Well?"

Hassan looked at Ziti, who stood at the edge of the crater, shaking his head. To Hassan, it looked like the explosives had done their job. A crater ten feet across, and at least five feet deep, lay before them. And he was sure after the rubble was cleared, it would be much deeper, perhaps ten feet, and Allah knew there were hundreds of willing hands on the other side of the wall to help clear it, even if they didn't know why.

But Ziti remained silent.

Hassan felt his chest tighten. "Are you going to speak?"

Ziti frowned. "It's not deep enough."

"What do you mean?" Hassan pointed at the hole. "It must be ten feet deep!"

Ziti shrugged his shoulders, his nonchalant attitude aggravating to no end. "The necropolis is five to ten meters underground. We may have barely dented the surface."

Hassan wasn't going to be discouraged. He refused to be. They were closer than they were an hour ago, and they would be closer an hour from now. He dismissed Ziti and his negativity with a wave. He motioned Ali over. "Rahim, get a dozen men from out there"—he jabbed his finger toward the basilica—"and get them in here to start moving this rubble."

Ali nodded and rushed out. Moments later puzzled men began to enter the room. Hassan put on his best smile, his arms extended in welcome, greeting each man with a hug and a kiss on each cheek. "Welcome! Welcome!" he said to each, and when the men were assembled, he pointed at the hole in the ground, a hole he noted all were staring at. "We need your assistance today. It is Allah's will that we have been able to get this far, and with your help now, we will accomplish our task. We need to dig a hole here"—he pointed at the crater—"so we can reach our goal." He raised his hand to cut off one of the men who was about to ask, he was sure, why. "Do not ask why. Know only that it is Allah's work we do here, and once finished, we will have power over the infidel like we've never had before." He slapped his hands together. "Now! To work!"

He jumped in the hole, grabbing the first stone, and handing it up to the first man, who leaned in and took it, passing it down the line that quickly formed, leading out of the room. After handing half a dozen stones up, he motioned for the first two men to join him, then handed off the work, climbing out of the hole.

He snapped his fingers at Ali. "Get another line going. There's enough room for two crews." This time there was no difficulty getting workers, as a large group had gathered outside the door and were already taking the stones, passing them back. When Ali approached, hands were held up in the air, eager to take part. Within moments a second line had formed, two more men in the crater.

Hassan smiled.

It would be long, hard work, but they had an unlimited workforce available to them, eager to help, despite not knowing what was going on. It might take hours, it might take days.

But once through, the infidel Catholic Church would bow at his feet.

Corpo della Gendarmeria Office
Palazzo del Governatorato, Vatican City

Acton winced more than Laura, as the medic treated what indeed had turned out to be a bullet graze on her left thigh. "Just a scratch" she called it. *I think it's hurting me more than her.* He squeezed her hand as the medic wrapped the leg a little too tightly for his liking.

She pulled her hand away.

"What?" he asked, looking up at her.

"You're hurting me more than he is," she said, jutting her chin at the medic.

Acton could feel himself blush. "Sorry, I just hate seeing you in pain."

"I'm not," she said, flexing her fingers. "Now that I've got my hand back." She smiled and kissed his hand. "You worry about me too much."

"Hey, you're going to be my wife. Of course I'm going to worry about you."

The medic raised his head. "You two are getting married?"

Laura smiled and extended her hand, then gasped. "My ring!"

Everyone looked, including Acton. The hand was bare, the ring gone.

Laura's eyes filled with tears as she looked at Acton, her right hand darting to her mouth. "I'm so sorry, it must have fallen off in the confusion."

Acton took her left hand and rubbed his thumb over where the ring should be. "Don't worry about it. I'll get you another one."

"But I want the one you gave me."

He smiled up at her and kissed the bare finger. "Then we'll find it."

She smiled at him, taking his cheek in her hand. "Ever the optimist." She sighed. "Something tells me that ring is long gone."

Acton stood. "We're archaeologists. If we can't find it, no one can." He struck a superhero pose and she giggled, the smile he loved returning to her face. Acton put a hand on her shoulder, his self-humiliation having worked, and squeezed. "Let's get through the night, and worry about the ring tomorrow." She nodded. He looked at the medic who snapped his kit shut.

"Done," he announced, standing. "We'll change the dressing in about eight hours if we're not out of here by then." He pointed at her. "But try to take it easy, no more heroics unless absolutely necessary."

She smiled, the story of what had happened outside already taking on near epic proportions. "Heroics done for the night."

Giasson walked up, his shoulder bandaged and arm in a sling, the bullet having been removed earlier, the damage apparently minimal.

"What's the situation?" asked Acton.

"Not good. The city's been lost."

Laura gasped. "What about the evacuees?"

Giasson gave a slight smile. "All are safe. At least that worked out, but we lost three of my men in the process."

Acton frowned. "But saved hundreds."

Giasson nodded. "They'll be remembered." He motioned for them to follow him. "There's something going on in the basilica I need you to look at."

"What?"

Giasson shrugged, then winced, his free hand darting to his shoulder. "That was stupid," he mumbled. Acton watched the man's face turn pale and reached out to grab him just as he began to lose his balance. The medic rushed over with a wheelchair, and they both helped him into the seat.

"Sir, I told you to stay in the chair. You lost a lot of blood. You need to drink and eat as much as you can to rebuild your strength and the lost blood supply."

Giasson, already recovering, tutt-tutted at him. "You're like a mother hen. I'll be fine."

"You should be hooked up to an IV."

Giasson shook his head. "Not going to happen. I need to be mobile."

"Hold the damned thing in your lap. You need fluids!"

Giasson paused. "Fine. Stick it in my bad arm, and put the sack in the blasted sling."

This seemed to placate the medic, who quickly complied. His handiwork done, he stood. "I'll check on you in an hour, and we'll keep switching out the bags."

Giasson nodded then looked around. "Now who's going to push me to my office?"

Several men stepped forward but Acton waved them off, grabbing the handles. "I'll do it, you guys have more important things to do."

He began to push Giasson toward the security offices, Laura beside him, along with Boileau, Giasson's second-in-command.

"What was this you were mentioning about the basilica?" asked Laura.

"Something's going on in there," replied Giasson.

"Yes, we've got one functioning camera, and they appear to be digging."

Acton's eyebrows shot up. "Digging?"

Boileau nodded. "Any idea what for?"

Acton felt butterflies in his stomach as he exchanged glances with Laura. He knew exactly what they were digging for.

And it terrified him.

The Green and Gold Pub, Brick Lane, London

Kirby Weeks slammed his fist on top of the bar, causing the glasses around him to bounce. The bartender, Tom, a crusty old bastard Kirby had known for years, stepped over, cleaning a glass with a rag. He held it up to inspect it in the lights of the bar and, satisfied, flipped it upside down and slid it in the holder suspended overhead. He placed his elbows on the bar, leaning into Kirby's personal space.

Kirby sat back, his eyes now on Tom instead of the television.

"What is it now, lad? What's got ya so riled up?"

Kirby took a swig of his lager, pointing at the screen. "It's what's goin' on in Rome. Can ya believe that shite?"

"What's goin' on in Rome?" asked Tom, twisting to look at the television.

"What's goin' on in Rome?" Kirby turned to the man sitting beside him. "What's goin' on in Rome, he says. Can ya believe that?" He turned back to Tom. "What are ya, daft? Have ya not been payin' attention to the news?"

Tom shrugged his shoulders, turning back to Kirby. "Never pay much mind to it, it's ne'er good."

Kirby took another swig, wiping the foam mustache off his face with the back of his hand, his chest getting tight in anger. He turned to the man seated at the bar to his right. "He 'asn't been payin' attention to the news. The fawkin' Muslims have taken over the Vatican, and this daft bastard hasn't a fawkin' clue!"

Kirby jumped out of his seat and addressed the packed bar in general. "How many of you bastards don't have a clue what's goin' on?"

"Sit down, Kirby, you've had too much, lad!"

"No I haven't. Look"—he pointed at the television—"at what those bastards are doin'. The Pope himself had to be carried out by helicopter today. The fawkin' Muslims are tearing apart Saint Peter's, they're destroying the Vatican, and you fawkers are doin' nothin' about it."

"What would ya have us do, Kirby?"

Kirby peered through the crowd, now all staring at him, their own conversations no longer as interesting as his rant, but couldn't find his interrogator.

"What would I have ya do? Christ, man, the biggest fawkin' mosque in London is just down the road on Whitechapel. Let's go show them what the fawk we think of them."

"Go home and sleep it off!"

"No! He's right!"

Heads spun toward the new voice, near the rear of the bar. Kirby looked through the crowd and saw a man standing there, maybe thirty, with a shaved head, sporting a knock-off London Olympics jersey. "It's time we stood up to these foreigners, and showed them that they can't come to our country and push us around." He walked toward Kirby, the crowd parting. "They come to our country, and try to make *us* change, rather than change themselves. Right now, almost three million Muslims live in our country, almost one million of the eight million people in this city are Muslim! And they are growing at a rate ten times our own." The man pointed at the television screen. "And now, they destroy one of the most important symbols of Christianity while the world stands by and does nothing."

He had reached Kirby now, and put his arm around Kirby's shoulders. The man looked at Kirby, then the crowd. "This man"—he pointed at Kirby—"is the smartest of us all. He recognizes what is happening, and he recognizes that it is people like us who need to rise up and fight back. When people like us take action, then our government will notice. When we are joined by our fellow Christians around the world, their governments will take notice." He squeezed Kirby against his side, his voice steadily rising. "Together, together we can send a message, not only to our government, not only to the Muslims, but to the world. Together we can send a message that England has had enough. That England is prepared to fight, to fight to defend our country from foreign invaders, to fight to defend our beliefs against those who would destroy them."

He took Kirby by the hand, raising it in the air. "Now, who is with me, who is with this man? Who will join us and send a message?"

The crowd roared, glasses held in the air, including Kirby's.

"Then let's go and send a message!"

The man headed for the door, Kirby in tow, followed by most of the patrons who downed their drinks, slamming the empty glasses and bottles on the bar top as they filed by. Moments later Kirby found himself on the street, not quite sure what had happened, but definitely feeling the adrenaline build.

The man beside him, who he had never seen before tonight, turned to the crowd and yelled, "Britain for the British!", his fist pumping the air, repeating it, over and over, until the crowd behind him echoed his call, and then the march resumed. As they traveled down Brick Lane, past more pubs, some of the crowd would rush into each of the establishments, and the crowd would grow. Cellphones were in full use, friends were being called, posts were going up on Twitter and Facebook, and word was spreading.

Whitechapel.

They crossed the street, and turned left, not bothering to clear the road, the crowd now in the hundreds, the chant, "Britain for the British" continuing. A police car pulled up and the two officers jumped out, rushing up to the crowd.

"You can't block this road!" yelled the first at Kirby and his companion who still led the march.

"I suggest you let us pass," said the man, who didn't slow down, causing the officers to back up. "We have no quarrel with you. Join us in sending a message that what is happening in Rome is not acceptable."

"Is that what this is about?" asked the second cop. He ran back to the squad car and grabbed the radio. Kirby could hear him requesting backup as they marched past it. The other officer returned to the car, and Kirby looked back as he saw the vehicle pull across the road and over the center divider, racing toward their destination, the mosque. Up ahead he watched the car cut across, blocking the street to prevent any more of the oncoming traffic from approaching them.

His companion squeezed Kirby's shoulder.

"See, we have already won a victory. The police are on our side."

Kirby wasn't so sure of that, it looked to him more like the police were just trying to keep the situation from getting further out of hand. Horns honked across the street and Kirby looked as three white vans screeched to a halt. His companion hailed them as the doors were thrown open and what looked like several dozen young men jumped out, all with shaved heads, carrying what looked like a variety of weapons, including crowbars and cricket bats. They merged in with the crowd, their own fists pumping the air as they joined the chant.

Kirby felt a twinge of fear. This wasn't what he had had in mind. Or was it? It might have been, but it wasn't any more. He had wanted to express his outrage. He had wanted to send a message. But this was turning into something bigger.

He looked down the road toward the mosque, now only minutes away. Two more police cars had arrived, and they were hastily blocking the road, redirecting traffic. But would enough arrive before things got out of hand?

Kirby doubted it. He heard more honking as several cars pulled up, their passengers, more skinheads, jumped out, running over to join the crowd.

They were at the mosque now; the crowd stopped, filling the street to capacity on both sides, the chant continuing. A bottle was thrown. One of the windows of the mosque shattered, then another. Then to Kirby's horror, he watched as one of the new arrivals lit the wick to a Molotov Cocktail, then threw it through the now broken window.

It erupted inside.

More bottles flew, their volatile contents adding to the inferno, and within minutes of arriving, flames roared, people screamed, and Kirby pulled away, desperate to have no part in what he had started.

But the man continued to grip his shoulders.

"Stay and watch. Isn't this what you wanted?" said the man, leaning over, placing his mouth at Kirby's ear. "Isn't this the message you wanted to send?"

Kirby shook his head, vehemently. "No, I-I never wanted this."

The man squeezed Kirby tighter. "Search your soul. I think this is exactly what you wanted."

And Kirby gasped a small cry. A cry of shame. A cry of horror.

For this was exactly what he had wanted.

But it was a want that was never supposed to have come true.

He bent over and vomited a night's worth of courage onto the road.

Emergency Response Command Center, Rome, Italy

"Let me guess, you received an urgent phone call too, ordering you to Rome?"

INTERPOL Agent Hugh Reading smiled at his old partner, Detective Inspector Martin Chaney of Scotland Yard. Chaney grinned, extending his hand.

"I had a feeling I'd be seeing you here."

Reading lowered his voice. "Are you here on *other* business?"

Chaney nodded, whispering, "Proconsul himself called me."

Reading chuckled. "You're turning into the go-to man for them." His ex-partner was a member of the Triarii, an ultra-secret organization that had been protecting the crystal skulls for almost two thousand years, and had managed to spread itself across the world, injecting its influence into almost every government on the planet.

Including England's.

Including the Vatican's.

Hence their current orders.

A man walked into the large tent that had been set up several hundred meters from the front gates to Saint Peter's Square, manned by dozens of officers with laptops and other equipment coordinating riot control and the cordoning off of the city. A round of cheers went up and many of those working took the time to come over and shake his hand.

"Wonder what that's about," said Chaney, leaning in so Reading could hear over the congratulations.

Overheard, a nearby officer stepped up. "It's because Sovrintendente Marcelo Primo"—he pointed at the man—"organized and successfully executed the rescue of over five hundred refugees, and his two hundred officers, despite being attacked by protesters throwing firebombs and rocks." He extended his hand and Reading took it, happy there was no kissing. "Deputy Commissioner Ezio Vitale, Scene Commander. And you are?"

Reading took out his badge, showing the man his INTERPOL identification. "Agent Hugh Reading, INTERPOL."

Chaney pulled out his warrant card. "Detective Inspector Martin Chaney, Scotland Yard, here on special assignment."

"Ahhh, yes, the two specifically requested by His Holiness," said the man, tapping his chin as he looked back and forth between the new arrivals. "When I heard you were coming, I of course pulled your files."

"Of course," said Reading.

"Very interesting reading. Very incomplete reading, but very interesting, nonetheless."

Reading smiled. "Police reports involving diplomatic incidents often are."

DC Vitale nodded. "Agreed." He slapped his hands together. "But, now that you're here, what can I do for you?"

"Can we get a sit rep?"

The man nodded, directing them to a large whiteboard with a breakdown by the numbers, but in Italian, so Reading had no clue what he was looking at.

DC Vitale explained. "Based upon our current understanding of the regular population of the Vatican"—he pointed at the top number—"and who was visiting that day"—another number—"and who was away"—yet another—"we believe there were almost twelve hundred people inside when Saint Peter's Square was stormed."

Reading whistled as he looked at the chart. "I hope those next numbers are people who got out."

DC Vitale nodded. "Yes, we managed to evacuate a large number through other exits, and by helicopter, including his Holiness"—he paused to make the sign of the cross—"and most of the senior staff."

"What about Giasson?"

Vitale shook his head. "No, he's still inside. He heroically remained to make sure the southern gates closed during the mass evacuation, once the train cleared."

"Train?" Chaney's eyebrows shot up as he exchanged a quick glance with Reading.

"Yes, M. Giasson had the idea of evacuating through the south gates, which most people don't think of, since they are for the Vatican's rail line. We successfully evacuated over five hundred, hence"—he pointed at Primo—"the celebration."

"How many are left?"

"According to our latest report, there are almost one hundred-fifty in the Governatorate Palace where M. Giasson is now. As well, there are another hundred unaccounted for, possibly spread across the city, hiding, or, hopefully, not in the city, perhaps having been gone for lunch, or some other activity. We have put the call out for all Vatican personnel to check in and are slowly reducing the list."

"Bottom line?"

"Bottom line is we need to take back the city. They are destroying it"—he gestured toward a television set—"and things are starting to spread across the world." He paused. "Did you hear about London?"

Both men shook their heads.

"I'm not surprised, the reports are just coming in now. Apparently a mob firebombed the East London Mosque. At least one Imam is dead, now the Muslims are marching. In Paris a truck driver plowed through a crowd of peaceful protesters, killing dozens before they managed to pull him from the truck." Vitale's voice cracked. "They tore him limb from limb, on live television." He shook his head. "Most disturbing thing I've ever witnessed."

Reading was thankful he hadn't.

Vitale regained his composure. "But, this might be of interest to you. There are reports that two evacuees, a man and a woman, reentered the compound, armed, and saved Giasson, allowing the southern gates to be closed."

Reading's head fell back as he already knew what he was about to hear.

"Tell me their names."

"Professors James Acton and Laura Palmer."

Chaney laughed.

As did Reading.

He couldn't help it. *Of course they're here!* He looked at Chaney. "How the bloody hell do they keep getting mixed up in these things?"

Chaney shrugged his shoulders. "Characters in a book?"

Reading shook his head. "Nobody'd believe it." He turned back to Vitale. "Please tell me they're okay"

"The lady was shot"—he raised a hand as Reading's jaw dropped—"but it was just a graze, she's perfectly okay. Professor Acton was unharmed."

"Thank God." Reading had become close to the two after the events in London a couple of years ago, despite him initially trying to arrest both of them. He considered them his friends, his good friends, despite not being able to see them often. But even his friends that lived in London he didn't see much of, he more of a loner since his divorce many years ago. He motioned around him. "So, what's next?"

"We've sealed off the city as best we can, except for the front gates where there are still too many protesters. We've blocked all the roads leading to the Vatican so no new protesters can reach the city, and are immediately breaking up any groups that try to form. We have a contingent massing now to clear the front gates, that will hopefully be ready within the next two hours, and we will push these protesters away from the gates, and down the surrounding streets, where we can continue to funnel them away, and pull out the agitators, and hopefully eventually calm the crowd and break it up. The goal for now is to secure the entire city, preventing anyone else from getting in."

"Then?"

"That's not up to me."

"What do you mean?"

"The Vatican is a country. We have no jurisdiction to enter there. The Pope must grant us permission, and as of fifteen minutes ago, no direction has been received."

"Where is he?"

"He's at his summer residence, Castel Gandolfo, about half an hour from here."

"Can you have us taken there?"

"He isn't taking visitors. He wouldn't even see me."

"He'll see *us*," said Chaney.

Corpo della Gendarmeria Office
Palazzo del Governatorato, Vatican City

"You know something."

It was Giasson.

Acton looked at the screen, then at Laura. "What do you think?"

She nodded. "I can't see there being any other reason to dig there."

Acton agreed. He too could see no other reason.

"You're sure they're digging?"

Boileau nodded. "There was a massive explosion in there earlier, then about twenty minutes later they started forming those lines you're looking at now, clearing the rubble."

Acton shook his head. "Could that be what this is all about?"

"What?" asked Giasson, sweat beaded on his shaved scalp, clearly still weak. "Would someone tell me what the hell is going on?"

The room stopped, even Acton, who barely knew the man, knew him well enough to know he didn't swear. What the average American might not even notice anymore in casual conversation, stood out like a beacon in this man's speech.

And he stopped, the anger wiped off his face, a look of shame replacing it. He raised his hand. "I apologize. I shouldn't have used such language. I am tired, frustrated, and weak, but still, that is no excuse. It won't happen again." He paused, as if gathering his strength. "*Now*, will someone please tell me what's going on." He looked squarely at Acton.

Acton decided not to waste any more time.

"They're trying to get into the Necropolis."

The entire room came to a halt, several gasps preceding the silence that now consumed them all, for they all knew the ramifications. No one knew when the Necropolis, or Scavi, had been originally built. But it had been there before the founding of the church, and in 324 AD, Emperor Constantine I had ordered the construction of the first Saint Peter's Church, in honor of the martyred apostle, on the very spot where he was believed to be buried—the Necropolis. He ordered most of it leveled, and filled in with dirt, except for the portion believed to contain the remains of the first pope, and over the next thousand years, it was forgotten that the Necropolis even existed.

It wasn't until 1940 when Pope Pius XII ordered excavations under the current Saint Peter's Basilica, in an attempt to find the saint's grave, that the ancient structure was found. For nine years much of the site was excavated, revealing a honeycomb of chambers underneath, including one originally believed to be the final resting place of Saint Peter.

But there were no remains.

It wasn't until an archaeologist examined the opposite wall, sometimes referred to as the Graffiti Wall due to prayers, mostly etched in Latin, carved into the stone over generations by worshippers almost two thousand years ago. On the wall he found a burial niche, dating to the fourth century, and coinciding with when Constantine was supposed to have reburied Saint Peter. The loculus, the only one found in the entire structure, had been carved into the wall, and lined with marble, then remained sealed, unbroken until 1941. Inside they discovered bones wrapped in a purple cloth, highlighted with gold thread, the same colors adorning the monument to Saint Peter. They were set aside, in the Vatican Grottoes, until 1953, when the discovery was made.

Upon realizing what they may have found, the bones were examined, revealing that they belonged to a single man, matched Saint Peter's presumed physical appearance at his martyrdom, with the age at death determined to be between sixty and seventy. In addition, they found dirt on the bones indicating they had originally been in an earth-grave, which was how Saint Peter was originally buried, and the dirt was of the same type as where he was believed to be initially buried, much of the other dirt in the area of a different type.

The conclusion was that the bones had been moved and placed in this special place of honor, and forgotten for almost two thousand years, until by chance, they were rediscovered.

And if these terrorists got hold of them, there was no telling what Catholics around the world might do.

Giasson broke the silence.

"They must be stopped."

Castel Gandolfo, Papal Summer Residence
Outside Rome, Italy

True to Chaney's word, they were immediately permitted access to the Summer Residence, and escorted to His Holiness' office. In less than five minutes, they had an audience, a roomful of advisors waved out by the old man who remained silent until the room was emptied. Father Morris, in his familiar role, closed the doors behind them.

The elderly pontiff extended his hands in welcome. Reading shook the man's hand, followed by Chaney, then they both took seats in front of the man's desk.

"I am pleased you were both able to make it here so quickly."

Reading gave a half smile. "We were left with little choice."

Chaney agreed. "Little."

The man smiled broadly, opening his arms. "I hope I didn't take you away from anything too pressing."

But he didn't wait for an answer.

"As you are well aware, we have a crisis. And I needed people I could trust. As well, you may not be aware that two of your friends are once again involved—"

"Yes, we found that out just a little while ago."

The old man shook his head. "How they keep managing to get involved in these things…" His voice drifted off as he stared at the ceiling. "God must have a plan for them."

Reading frowned. "Well, let's hope it includes them staying alive."

The old man turned his palms toward Heaven. "It is in His hands." Any trace of a smile left his face. "You are aware of what is happening around the world."

"To some extent."

"As we speak Italians are rising up, marching on the Vatican now, and the police are having to hold them back, fighting a second front as it were. I've recorded a statement that will be broadcast on all stations shortly asking for calm, and to turn to prayer instead of violence, and my cardinals and bishops are doing the same around the world. We need to bring this to a stop, and quickly."

"How?"

"This all started with the discovery of the scroll."

"What scroll?"

"In the construction work to seal up the"—he tapped his chin, as if trying to find the right words—"unauthorized entrance—"

"That's one way to put it," muttered Reading.

"—we discovered a crypt. Inside were several Templar Knight sarcophagi, and in one of them was a scroll. We had the scroll examined, and it looks like it is a verse from the Koran, written in the presence of Mohammad."

"Pretty valuable. How did it get there?"

The pontiff shrugged his shoulders. "No one knows, but it appeared to be of some importance to the Knight we found it on as it was carefully preserved. But, the value aside, what is truly important about this scroll, are the words inscribed on it."

"A verse from the Koran," repeated Chaney.

"Yes, but the words don't match what is actually written in the Koran. It contains several additional words which change the meaning of one of the most violent quotations, to something much less violent."

"That's going to piss off a lot of zealots."

The Pope gestured at several television screens showing the violence playing out around the world. "You have a gift for understatement, Agent Reading. When word got out about the scroll, the Imams in Rome urged their worshippers to march on the Vatican and demand the scroll be handed over."

"And why didn't you?"

"We tried, but no one would take it!"

"What?" echoed Reading and Chaney.

"Nobody. We couldn't find a single Muslim cleric or academic to accept delivery of the scroll. And that's before this all got out of hand. Now no one will even accept my calls."

Reading paused for a moment, watching coverage of the Paris and London incidents. "Where is it now?" he finally asked, turning back to the Pontiff.

The old man, elbows on his desk, ran his fingers through his thin hair. "In the confusion of my evacuation, it was left behind."

Chaney leaned forward. "Left behind?"

"Do we know where it is?"

The man nodded. "Oh yes, we know."

And then it dawned on Reading. A forgotten crypt. An ancient scroll. Two archaeologists.

"Jim has it, doesn't he?"

The old man nodded. "You know your friend well."

"Too well sometimes." Reading let out a long, exhausted breath. "What's the next step?"

The old man's eyes filled with tears. "I find I am at an impasse. I honestly don't know what to do. I know we can send in thousands of troops with a single phone call, but the bloodshed would be horrendous."

Reading nodded, frowning. "But it might be the only way. You can't leave them there, and the longer they stay, the more damage they will do."

"I know, I know, and I have prayed to God for guidance, but he has left me to solve it alone."

Reading suddenly stood, as did a surprised Chaney. "Not alone, sir. There are hundreds if not thousands of people waiting for word from you. But you are right. An invasion could kill hundreds."

"Then what—"

Reading didn't let the man finish. "I propose we remove the excuse."

"The excuse?"

"The scroll is what they are supposedly after. I suggest we get in, get it, get out, then physically shove it into the hands of an Imam." Reading pointed at the screens. "And that last part, you do in front of every damned news organization in the world."

The old man smiled slightly and stood as well. "You have a plan for this?"

"Get in, it, out? Yes. *You* need to come up with the final part."

The old man nodded, smiling. "I will redouble our efforts." He rounded the desk and shook Reading's hand, then Chaney's. "I was mistaken when I said God had not answered my prayers. He sent you both to me, and now my hope is restored."

The doors opened as if the old man had sent a telepathic message to the Father outside, and Reading along with Chaney exited the office. As they walked toward the waiting police car in the court yard, Chaney leaned in.

"How the bloody hell do you propose we 'get in, get it, get out'?"

Reading grimaced.

"I haven't the foggiest."

Four Seasons Hotel, Cairo, Egypt

"This is Tim Kensington, reporting live from Cairo. The footage you are about to see, taken only minutes ago, is graphic. I highly recommend our more sensitive and younger viewers not watch." Tim took a breath. *Are you kidding me? This stuff is NC-17. We shouldn't even be airing it!* He motioned with his hand, out of sight of the camera, for the footage to roll. His cameraman whispered into his mike for the footage to roll in Atlanta, then nodded to Kensington.

"As you can see, what started off as a peaceful protest quickly turned ugly. Christians are a minority in Muslim dominated Egypt, and under the former dictator Musharraf coexisted mostly peacefully with their Muslim counterparts. But now, in a state dominated by an Islamist parliament, Christians are no longer safe, as evidenced by the events you are watching now.

"This march, meant to demonstrate against the frequent violence they have been subject to, had an added meaning tonight with the events occurring in Rome and around the world. Some I talked to said they gathered not to protest, but for safety, many fearing being at home alone. 'Safety in numbers' were the thoughts of many, and how false that turned out to be.

"Within minutes of marching, Muslims began to line the streets in a counter protest, and in less than thirty minutes, the thousands of Christians that had gathered for protection, and to denounce violence, were set upon by the massive crowds. The unarmed marchers, including women, children, and the elderly, were massacred with machetes, clubs, bats, all manner of weapons.

"All of this as the police watched on. It wasn't until they realized they were being videotaped by our crew, that they took action, and that action was to come after us, rather than stop the crowds. Fortunately for us, we already had an escape route, and were able to get away to send this broadcast. Carson?"

The cameraman, Jason Sharpe, gave a thumbs up as Tim breathed for a moment as he waited for the anchorman's voice over his ear bud.

"We're glad you're all okay, Tim. The footage we're viewing now is absolutely horrendous, very difficult to watch. It is actually very reminiscent of Rwanda."

Tim nodded. "Indeed, Carson, it is. Having covered that conflict as well, I felt a sense of déjà vu as I witnessed the machetes raised in the air, the mobs acting with impunity. The hatred, the madness in the eyes was truly disconcerting, and reminded me very much of the Hutu massacre of the Tutsis so many years ago."

"Are there any other signs of trouble in the streets where you are now?"

"No, Carson, we're at our hotel, shooting on our balcony. As you can see"—he motioned for the cameraman to take a shot of the road below—"things are quite calm where we are now, and this area is not known for having a large Christian population."

He noticed his cameraman jabbing his finger at the road below. Tim looked over the balcony and felt his chest tighten as his heart slammed against his ribcage. Police. A lot of them, jumping out of their vehicles and rushing into the hotel.

"Carson, we seem to have a possible situation here. I'm going to ask you to keep us on the air, live, so the world can bear witness. A contingent of police have just stormed the hotel, and may be here for us."

"Tim, what is your situation, are you secure where you are?"

"Negative, we're in a hotel room."

Pounding on the hotel room door caused a lump to form in his throat. He had been in many harrowing situations before, but what he had witnessed today, with the police doing nothing, was something unique.

"They're at our door now, Carson. We won't be opening the door, and we will stay on the air as long as we can."

"We're contacting the US embassy now," he heard the producer's voice say over his ear bud. "Just stay calm, keep your hands up, tell them you're a CNN crew and are on live. Jason, try to get a shot of their faces when they come through the door, but keep the camera low."

"Okay, Carson, we're receiving instructions from our producers now. We're going to stay on the air as long as we can."

The door burst open.

"They're in the room. The door has just been kicked open, and they're in the room!" Kensington raised his hands, his mike still in his left, as Sharpe dropped the camera low, the red light still on, his other hand raised in the air, as was their guide's.

"Tim, are you okay?"

Kensington didn't answer at first, the dozen or more policemen charging toward them, automatic weapons drawn, screaming at them in Arabic. Their guide said something in reply, and two shots rang out. He dropped.

"Tim!"

"Oh my God, they just shot our guide. The Egyptian police have just shot our guide. I think he's dead." The yelling continued as they advanced on the balcony. "We're a CNN crew, we're press! You can't do this!" yelled Kensington.

"Tim, show them the monitor, show them they are live!"

Tim pointed at the display he used to monitor what was broadcast. "We're live, we're on the air right now! The world can see what you are doing!"

More yelling, then a hail of gunfire shattered the monitor, then tore holes in Sharpe, who screamed in pain, then went silent.

The gunfire stopped, then all the weapons were pointed at Kensington.

"Carson, can you still hear me?"

"Yes, Tim, we can, but we've lost video."

"Tell my family I love them."

One of the policemen stepped forward, raising his weapon to Kensington's head.

He never heard the shot.

Hotel Alimandi Vaticano, Rome, Italy

Reading and Chaney exited the elevators of the hotel that had been arranged for them across the street from the Vatican. Chaney pointed at a door. "Two-oh-four. That's me."

Reading nodded. "Come to my room in fifteen."

"Will do," said Chaney, inserting his keycard and opening the door.

Reading continued to the next door, 206, and was about to insert his keycard when he heard voices on the other side of the door. Then laughter.

He checked the room number again, then the little envelope that had contained the card to confirm.

206.

Could the maid have left the telly on?

It was probably that, but he wasn't sure. And it was times like these that he was thankful he had taken the time to get his weapon back from the Rome Police. He slipped the keycard in, and he heard the click, impossibly loud in the hall.

The voices stopped.

Shite!

He pushed the door open, weapon extended in front of him, and loudly announced, "Police, everyone freeze!"

And they did.

Reading smiled, lowering his weapon as he advanced into the room. "What the bloody hell are you blokes doing here?"

Dawson stood up and approached Reading, his hand extended. "Good to see you again, Agent Reading."

"And you, Sergeant."

Suddenly pounding on the door caused the entire room to tense up.

"Hugh, are you okay?"

Chaney.

"Just a second!" called Reading as he stepped back to the door, opening it.

"I heard you yelling. Is everything—" He stopped when he saw the occupants of the room, his eyebrows shooting up his forehead. "What the bloody hell are you blokes doing here?"

The Asian one Reading recalled as Niner came out of the bathroom. "Hey, BD, there's some kinda weird fountain thing in there if you're looking for something to drink. You gotta bend over real low though. Must have been made for kids."

Reading and Chaney looked at each other, then burst out laughing as Chaney entered the room, closing the door behind him. Reading stepped forward. "That's a bidet, Sergeant. It's meant for cleaning your"—he paused, searching for the right words, but Niner beat him to it.

"Ass." He shook his head. "Yeah, *I* know that, *you* know that, but he"—he jabbed his finger at Jimmy—"doesn't. Within five minutes I would've had him drinking out of that damned thing, then had *years* of fun with it."

Jimmy's jaw dropped. "I can't believe you'd do that to me after all we've been through!"

Niner shrugged his shoulders. "It's what I do."

Jimmy shook his head. "Even after I kept your secret all these years."

"What secret?"

Niner sounded wary.

"Remember that time in Bangkok, where you picked up that girl?"

Niner shook his head slowly. "What the hell are you talking about?"

"Hey, I never told anybody that I saw her later standing at the urinal, taking a leak in the bar downstairs, after you had, you know…" His voice trailed off, but he made several suggestive hand motions.

Niner blanched. "That never happened!"

Jimmy waved his hands in the air, shaking his head. "Nooo, of course it never happened. It's our little secret."

Niner, horror on his face, looked around the room from face to face. "I swear, it never happened!"

Jimmy burst out laughing, then the room erupted. Niner punched Jimmy in the shoulder as he got up and gave him a hug, then sport humped his leg like a dog. Niner pushed him off, and Jimmy feigned indignation. "What, I thought that's what you liked?"

"You're not my type," said Niner, trying to regain the upper hand.

Jimmy smiled, then headed to the bathroom. "I'm thirsty. Fountain, eh?"

Atlas, who had sat quietly in the corner, broke his silence, his impossibly deep voice filling the room. "One of these days, one of you is going to go too far. I just hope I'm there to see it."

Niner bowed, and in his best Chinese accent, said, "His kung fu strong, but mine stronger." He jumped in the air and performed a spinning kick, landing on the ground as Jimmy came out with a glass of water.

"I hope that's from the tap."

"Toilet."

Dawson clapped his hands together, ending the frivolity. "We all know why we're here."

Reading looked for a chair and Atlas stood up, offering him his. "I've been sitting all damned day. Go ahead."

Reading nodded and sat down. "Actually, why *are* you here?"

Dawson smiled. "Officially, we're not. But, we have rioting on the streets around the world, and this incident, if not diffused quickly, threatens to tip the world into a religious war. We already had one zealot attempt that last year, and we barely stopped him. I'm not about to let him succeed, not after so much was lost the last time."

Reading nodded, recalling Edison Cole and his New Slate organization. And he recalled his first visit to the Vatican in connection to that, and the horror of that day.

Dawson pointed at the television screen that was playing silently on the wall. "The Egyptians just massacred thousands of Christians while the police watched, then when CNN aired footage, they stormed the hotel and shot the entire crew, live on the air."

"Bloody hell!" muttered Chaney.

"This isn't getting out of hand, this is already out of hand. And our professor friends are in the thick of it again," said Dawson.

Reading shook his head. "How they manage it, I'll never know."

"Well, my instructions are to do whatever I can to diffuse the situation. Our intel tells me that the Professors are trapped inside, in the Governatorate Palace, with almost one hundred-fifty armed security personnel, so they are secure for now, but with thousands swarming the city, they won't be able to get out without it being a bloodbath."

"As well, from what we're hearing, they don't want to leave, they want to take back the city, but the Pope won't give the go ahead."

Reading took a deep breath. "I think I may have convinced him there's a way around the bloodshed."

"What's that?"

"I may have told him I had a plan for getting the scroll out, and into his hands, so that he could hand it over publicly to an Islamic representative."

Dawson leaned forward, his elbows on his knees, his hands dangling in front. "And what exactly is your plan?"

Reading smiled. "Hadn't the foggiest until I walked into this room and found you lot."

Corpo della Gendarmeria Office
Palazzo del Governatorato, Vatican City

Acton's phone vibrated in his pocket. He pulled out his Blackberry and his eyebrows shot up when he saw the call display. He flashed it to Laura who also seemed surprised.

"Hello?"

"Jim, old buddy. How are you?"

Acton chuckled as he found a quiet corner away from the bustle that had broken out after the security staff realized what was going on. Everyone was trying their external contacts to find out how long it would be before an armed response could be mustered, and Giasson was trying to talk to His Holiness to get the authorization.

"I would think since you're calling on a night like tonight, you know exactly how I am."

Reading grunted. "Since I don't know how secure this line is, let's be brief and vague."

"Agreed."

"You have the item."

"Yes."

"We need to get it out of there."

"Agreed."

"The *man* is trying to arrange a hand-off, hopes that will diffuse everything."

"Sounds like a good idea."

"But we need the item in order to do that."

"Agreed."

"Our *friends* are here, and are willing to help."

Okay, that left a lot of possibilities. Delta? Triarii? Hassassin?

"Umm…"

"Think your favorite dog."

Acton smiled.

"Ahh!"

"Exactly. I'll call you soon with an update. How's your charge?"

Acton glanced at the battery display. "Nearly full."

"Okay, keep safe."

The phone went dead, and Acton returned it to his pocket, heading to Giasson's office just as he slammed the phone into its cradle. He looked up as Acton and Laura entered his office. Giasson gestured at the phone.

"His Holiness is on an extremely important phone call and cannot be disturbed." He grasped at his head, as if searching for hair to pull.

"I have news."

Giasson and Laura both looked at him.

"What news?" Giasson leaned back in his chair, sighing. "Please let it be good news."

"Bravo Team is here, and they're coming in to get this"—he held up the case—"so it can be handed over by the Pope to an Islamic representative."

"The important phone call?" surmised Giasson to no one in particular. He looked at Acton. "When?"

"Don't know yet, but hopefully I'll hear something soon."

"Okay, when they get here, I want you two out of here, along with that thing."

"What about you?"

"I can't move too fast, and my responsibility is the city. I need you to get that thing"—he jabbed his finger at the case—"to safety.

"You don't have to tell us twice." Acton turned to Laura. "Are you okay to run?"

She nodded. "Don't worry about me." She nodded at the body armor sitting on Giasson's desk. "Just let me know when to gear back up, and I'll be ready."

Acton leaned over and squeezed her hand. She rubbed her thumb over where the ring should be and frowned. He winked at her. "When this is all done, Mario will tear this city apart to find your ring."

Giasson, lost in thought, grunted at the sound of his name. "Huh?"

"Nothing, just committing your resources to a search and rescue later."

Giasson looked at Laura's naked finger.

"Get that case to safety, and I'll personally look for it."

"Sir!"

All heads turned to the young man who stood in the doorway.

"What is it?"

"They're trying to get in the front entrance!"

Dearborn, Michigan

"Woah! Mother fucker, can you believe this shit?"

LJ, or Lil' Jeff, pointed at the screen as the incident from just hours ago in Egypt was replayed. The entire room sat in silence, beer bottles forgotten, weed left to smolder, as everyone watched what was playing out across the world.

"This is fucked up!" yelled Vince, throwing his hand at the screen. "Fucked! Up!"

"This is so wrong, man, so wrong." LJ pointed at the screen as scenes from London were shown. "That's what we should be doin'."

"Whadaya mean?"

LJ jumped to his feet and grabbed the gun sitting beside the television, waving it in the air. "This"—he shoved the gun out—"this is what I'm talkin' about. We should go downtown to that fuckin' Islamic church, and fuck it up!"

Vince pulled his gun out from his pants and joined LJ in front of the television, the horrors of the past day now the backdrop to a new one. "He's right. I say we go down there, and show these fuckin' Muslims that they can't come to our country and take over."

The rest of the room, all twelve of them, jumped to their feet, guns waving in the air, alcohol and drug induced bravado fueling the moment. LJ led the way as they filed out of the apartment and raced down the three flights of stairs to the street below. LJ jumped in his Escalade, and Vince in his old Navigator as the crew filled up both vehicles, readying their weapons.

This is gonna be epic.

He fired up the engine, old school Tupac roaring from the premium audio system, and slapped the vehicle in gear, peeling away from the curb. As he neared the end of the block, he was waved down by his buddy Chevy.

"Whassup?"

LJ leaned out the window. "We're gonna go fuck up some Muslims. Get yer crew 'n come wit."

Chevy smiled. "Right behind yo ass!" He stepped back and waved up at a balcony packed with partiers. "Less go! Werk ta do!" The balcony emptied out as Chevy jumped in his car, an old Buick. Soon his crew were racing out the front door of the apartment, jumping in his car and others. Within minutes they were a convoy of six vehicles, and cellphones were in full gear texting for more soldiers.

This is gonna be off the hanger!

Dearborn wasn't big, and it didn't take long for the convoy to arrive. Dozens of vehicles were pulling up at the same time, the word having spread via text message, Twitter and Facebook that something was going down at the Islamic Center. LJ climbed out of his Escalade, stood in the middle of the road, facing the façade of the massive complex, the largest in the country. His crew and the others lined up on either side.

LJ's heart pounded in his chest. The adrenaline fueling him made him feel larger than life as he looked around at the crews standing at his side. He felt the intoxication of power, the overwhelming sense of importance, the surge of respect now shown to him.

He looked from side to side, and smiled as he saw dozens if not hundreds of cellphones held up, recording for history what was about to happen, what *he* was about to do.

He raised his gun, hand turned to the side, his most dangerous looking sneer displayed for the cameras.

"Yo, fuckin' Muslims! Go back to your own fuckin' country!"

Then he squeezed the trigger, firing at the wood doors of the building, and the roar of dozens of other weapons, some handguns, some machine guns, rocked the night, as hundreds of rounds were emptied into the front of the building.

LJ saw something flash out of the corner of his eye. He turned, still squeezing the trigger, and saw a police car arrive, careening to a halt about a hundred feet away. The lone cop jumped out, and his thick but trimmed beard told LJ everything he needed to know.

Muslim!

He turned and reloaded, then opened fire on the squad car.

Chapel of the Sacrament
Saint Peter's Basilica, Vatican City

Hassan looked at the crater. Things were progressing too slow for his liking. They needed to get through, and into the necropolis. Once inside, there would be nothing to stop them from acquiring the bones of Saint Peter, and then the Catholic Church would be at his mercy.

He snapped his fingers, indicating it was time for a changing of the laborers. A fresh dozen were brought in, and the clearing continued. It wouldn't be long before they would be able to begin digging. He smiled to himself. To think, just yesterday he was trying to figure out a way to further their cause by destabilizing the West even more. He often chuckled at their naiveté. After 9/11 the West turned inward, looking for the threat internally, adding layer upon layer of security, suspending portions of their constitutions, taking away the rights of their own populations, rather than dealing with the problem.

Because there was no way to deal with the problem.

The America of today, the Europe of today, was not the America or Europe of 2001. Europe was filled with hate, with distrust, with nationalist parties gaining more and more seats in their democratic elections, with crack downs on Muslims, from banning the building of Mosques in Switzerland, to banning the burqa in France, to Englishness tests in Great Britain. All of these things violated the fundamental beliefs of the Western democracies that lorded their superiority over the rest of the world.

And just like the Soviet Union bankrupted itself trying to keep up with the United States technologically, the West was almost there. Wars in Afghanistan and Iraq, plus an out of control security apparatus in most

Western nations demanding more and more funding to protect against a perceived threat, had almost bankrupted the mighty Western economies. A few more attacks, each using different methods, would soon tip them over the edge, and into the abyss of a global Great Depression the likes the world had never seen.

The Dirty Thirties were terrible, but people were never used to living well. A good life meant food on the table and a warm bed to sleep in. Now a good life meant two cars, a large house, multiple televisions, computers, cellphones, tablets, Internet, cable, restaurants and vacations. This time when the economy collapsed, they would have a hell of a time trying to get out of it.

And Islam would continue to spread. Hassan knew their birthrate was two to three times that of the West, and they would eventually win. But in the meantime, the West would be looking for a way out of their economic calamity. And a way would be offered, by the military industrial complex and the security apparatus that had sprung up around 9/11.

War.

War brought the economies of the world out of the Great Depression, and war would bring the economies of the world out of the next one. But who would be the belligerents? Would the West continue to be terrified of a powerful China, who would weather the downturn better than most? And would Russia ally themselves with the Chinese, with the same hopes as they had previously when they allied themselves with Germany? The Chinese would want the oil to sustain their economies, the Americans and Europeans would need it as well. War could easily breakout. A faked attack. A misunderstanding. It didn't matter. When people are desperate, they are willing to do desperate things. Stupid things. Irrational things.

And when someone tells a desperate population that all their problems can be blamed on the Chinese, the population will demand something be done. And in the aftermath, when the so called powerful nations of the world have destroyed themselves, Islam would spread. And with the Armageddon brought on by their war, the Mahdi would return, with Jesus, and bring paradise to Earth, bring justice and order to the masses, all under the flag of Islam.

And tonight it would begin, all with a few bones of a long dead man who meant nothing to Hassan, but everything to over one billion of the planet's richest.

Over a decade ago the armor had been chinked, and the West had responded in what they thought was a strong way. With war. But in fact, they had dismantled the very things that had made them great. And now, with the bones of Saint Peter in his hands, Hassan would begin the dismantling of the Church, and its moral compass that had at one time, guided the West, but now had been pushed aside, in the name of the new morality of political correctness and the assumption of cultural equality.

And with one final push, the nation that claimed, In God We Trust, just may lose one more beacon on the path of righteousness.

Hassan's heart filled with joy at the thought, at the thought that he had been chosen by Allah to assist bringing on the end of days.

And the return of the Mahdi.

Corpo della Gendarmeria Office
Palazzo del Governatorato, Vatican City

Giasson stared at the security footage checkered across the wall. He pointed at one. "What in God's name is that?"

Acton leaned forward.

"A tree?"

"What the devil are they doing with a tree?" asked Laura.

Giasson and Acton looked at each other, and both said, "Battering ram."

Giasson snapped his fingers. "I need eight marksmen on the roof. Four corners, two on the sides, two to cover the roof itself in case anyone tries to climb up there. Take out anyone with a weapon, and anyone that tries to ram the door." He pointed at Ianuzzi. "You're in charge up there."

Ianuzzi nodded, and walked away, beginning to bark orders, gathering a group of the heavily armed security personnel around him as he disappeared around the corner.

Acton turned to Giasson. "I'd like to go with them, get a lay of the land so I can maybe give some intel to our friends."

Giasson flicked his hand over his shoulder. "Go ahead." He pointed at one of the others. "Tell Ianuzzi I said it was okay." The man got on his radio and Acton turned to Laura.

"I won't be long."

"I'm coming with you!"

"No, you stay and rest that leg. You'll be needing it soon enough, besides, it's safer here." She frowned, and he smiled. "How about you get a pen and some paper and retrace your steps, from the last moment you remember definitely having the ring, to the moment you discovered it missing. Maybe you can get a map of the city, and trace it out. That way, when this is all over, we'll know where to look."

She smiled at him, and he could tell she knew he was just trying to occupy her mind. She squeezed his hand. "Thanks, Darling, but I'll be fine."

He kissed the top of her head, then dashed off after the roof team. As he looked behind him one last time, he saw Laura grabbing a pad off a nearby desk.

He grinned and nearly ran into one of the guards.

"Roof?"

The man pointed to a set of doors. "Stairs are there, go all the way to the top. Announce yourself coming out, though, otherwise you're liable to get shot."

Acton nodded. "Thanks for the tip."

He ran for the door, pulling it open, then took the stairs two at a time, until the fourth flight when he started to tire, and switched to one at a time. It wasn't until then that he realized how exhausted he was. He hadn't had any real downtime in almost twenty four hours, and had been on adrenaline for most of that.

And when the hell are you going to find any downtime?

He reached the door and knocked, opening it a crack. "Professor Acton here! Am I cleared to come out?"

"Go ahead, Professor, hands first!"

Acton pushed the door open slowly, extending his hands, then stepping out from behind the door. He was greeted with two guns in his face, that quickly lowered when they recognized him.

"Sorry, Professor, just being cautious."

Acton nodded. "No worries. How's it look?"

"Not good, we're surrounded by hundreds of people, the vast majority at the front."

"Any suggestions for a covert approach?"

Ianuzzi squinted. "Why?"

"We may have some, shall we say, *friends*, joining us shortly to evac the item."

Ianuzzi nodded. "Follow me, and keep low, we've already taken fire up here."

They approached the north side of the rooftop at a crouch, then crawled the last few feet. They both propped themselves up at the edge. "See the road there, going north?"

Acton nodded. It seemed to wrap around the rear of the building, and join up with the road that led to the train station.

"Well, they don't seem to have any people near it, probably because of the large trees blocking their view. A small team could probably use those trees as cover, and approach the building from the rear. They should meet token resistance, and we can have a door ready for them to come in."

Acton frowned. "Not a great plan, but I don't see we have any choice."

Gun fire interrupted the conversation as they both ducked, the masonry where they had just been torn apart by the well-aimed bullets.

A single shot rang out to the left.

"Got him."

Ianuzzi and Acton didn't move, just in case the matter of fact statement was incorrect. Ianuzzi turned to Acton, and motioned toward the door he had used to come onto the roof. "I suggest you get inside, it's safer."

Acton nodded, realizing that playing the hero at this point held little value.

"I'll be back when the team is coming in."

Ianuzzi nodded, and turned back to survey the north side again.

He felt confident the team would be able to get in, and probably fairly safely. After all, their opposition wasn't well trained.

But getting out, that was another story. They would be expecting them to come back out, and with Laura injured already from a stray, he feared what the next one might do.

He looked up at the night sky, and said a silent prayer.

Dearborn Police Department
Dearborn, Michigan

Officer Roy Atkinson sat in the lounge with another dozen officers waiting for the shift change. All eyes were glued on the television coverage of what was happening around the world.

This is fuckin' ridiculous.

He could feel his chest tighten as report after report came in of tit for tat violence, each getting bloodier and bloodier. There had just been reports from New York City of an attack on a church, in retaliation for the attack on the mosque in London.

This is America! Leave your shit in your old country, don't bring it here.

"This is fuckin' bullshit."

"Tell me about it."

Atkinson looked at his partner, Charlie Zawadzki. "Why do they have to bring their shit over here? I thought the whole point of immigrating was you left the problems behind you, and came here to make a new life!"

"It's this multiculturalism shit," said Zawadzki. "They come over here and the politically correct tell them it's okay to keep their culture, and call us racist for wanting them to become American."

"Well, isn't it?"

All eyes turned to the latest voice to join the conversation. Atkinson frowned. It was Mohammad Aman, the only Muslim in the room, as far as he knew. If there were any others, they certainly hadn't made it known to Atkinson over the years, but Aman, he insisted on praying six times a day, no matter what they were doing.

And the fucking PC brass let him get away with it.

Reasonable Accommodation.

What the fuck kind of PC BS was that? Reasonable Accommodation? How about Reasonably Accommodating us? We didn't stop working when it was time to pray on Sunday unless we were off work. Yet this guy did it six times a day. Him and his friend Hasni. Another fucker who flaunted it instead of keeping it hidden away like the private thing it should be. Atkinson went to church. Not as often as he should, but he still did. And did he flaunt it? Hell no!

"Did you just call me racist?"

"No, I asked if it wasn't racist to force other people to conform to your beliefs."

"So if I want you to become American, that's racist?"

"I am American."

"Not from where I'm sitting."

"Hey, I was born here, just like you."

"Not just like me, otherwise you'd get what I'm sayin'."

"Just because I'm a different religion doesn't mean I'm not American."

"Religion should have fuck all to do with it. You don't see the Jews or Buddhists causing problems. Just the Muslims."

"Not all Muslims. Just a small minority."

"Hey, when that small minority does something, why is that vast majority so damned silent, huh?" There were a few grunts of assent. "You see, that's the damned problem. If a priest got up in front of his flock and called for everyone to go kill all the Muslims, there'd be an uproar, and the FBI'd be called. But you guys, no way, uh uh, you just sit silently and let them preach it, or worse, cheer it on. But no phone calls. No anonymous tips.

"And that's the problem. *You* don't love your country. If you did, you'd put it first before all else. I'd die for my country; I'd die to protect it. But you, you want to change it so that you can be more comfortable here, rather than adapt your ways to fit in. If what we've been doing since seventeen-seventy-six is so wrong, then why are we the greatest country in the world, why is it people like you and your parents were so desperate to get here? Was it to reshape America into your old homeland, or to come here and escape your old homeland?"

"I can't believe the garbage that's coming out of your mouth."

Atkinson jumped up, rage beginning to get the upper hand.

"Hadrian's Wall."

He turned to his partner, who still sat there comfortably, staring at the television screen.

"What?"

"Hadrian's Wall. Hadrian was the Roman Emperor two thousand years ago who ordered a wall be built across England, separating the north from the south."

"Hey, I've heard of that," said one of the rookies as Atkinson sat down. "I saw it on Discovery."

"What about it?"

"It wasn't built to keep the hordes from invading, it was meant to keep the hordes from immigrating," said Zawadzki.

"What do you mean?"

"Think about it. It was a wall. It could be breached at any time, it was just too long to protect in force. But what it did do was keep out those who would come to the south of England, where there was civilization, where Rome had established itself, and take advantage of what had been built, rather than contribute to it."

"And what does that have to do with anything?" asked Aman.

"It has everything to do with it," said Zawadzki. He leaned forward. "Look. People make the mistake of saying we're all immigrants, since all of us, except the Indians, are descendants of people who immigrated to this country. But that's wrong."

"How is it?" asked Aman.

Atkinson loved when Zawadzki talked. He was a hell of a lot smarter than most of those in the room, including himself.

"Many of those who come to this country today are immigrants. But our ancestors were pioneers. They were settlers. They came here to build a better life, to build a country. When they left their old homelands, they knew there was no going back. They left everything and everyone behind. So when they got here, they were motivated to build a better life for themselves, and in doing so, their fellowman, by helping build roads, churches, railroads, hospitals. The very things that make this country great.

"But now, most immigrants come here and there's nothing for them to do, the hard works' been done. Now they come here and figure out how they can take advantage of those centuries of hard work. They don't leave their homelands behind, instead they use the Internet to keep in touch, their cheap long distance to talk daily to the old friends and family back home. They watch television in their own language, they read newspapers and websites in their own language, they shop in their own stores, eat their own food, go to their own places of worship, and don't integrate. Now you can actually live in America and be successful without speaking English. How ridiculous is that?"

"What does that possibly have to do with anything?" asked Aman. "My parents came here and opened a restaurant. They both work hard, employ people. I joined the police force to serve my community. I go to football games, play baseball, and try to be a good person. But because I'm Muslim, I'm not American?"

"I never said you weren't American. But let me ask you this. What language did you learn to speak first?"

Aman said nothing, his jaw dropping slightly.

"Your silence speaks volumes," commented Atkinson.

"That means nothing."

"Doesn't it?" Zawadzki frowned. "When I was a kid, I remember my granddaddy saying to me that when he and my grandmother came over from Poland, they made it a point to never speak a word of Polish in front of the children, so they would learn English first, and become Americans."

"It's a different world now," said Aman.

Zawadzki nodded. "Yes, but is it better?"

The speaker in the lounge squawked. "Ten-thirteen, ten-thirteen, officer needs assistance on Altar Road. Officer Lodi requires assistance, taking heavy fire."

"That's Hasni!" exclaimed Aman as he headed to the door. He turned to Atkinson. "What, you're not going to help him because he's Muslim?"

Atkinson stood up, as did the room.

"No, we're going to help him because we're Americans, and that's what we do."

Emergency Response Command Center
Rome, Italy

DC Vitali stood in the command tent, reviewing a map laid out on a large table showing the layout of the immediate area, positions of rioters, and positions of riot police. The plan sounded simple, but to execute it successfully would be a challenge. They needed to split the protesters into smaller and smaller groups, until each group would be easy enough to disperse. The manpower necessary was phenomenal. Thousands of police from across Italy had been brought in, arriving by the busload, each sent to their designated areas upon arrival. It was a massive operation involving almost ten thousand police, with the army on standby.

If it comes to that…

Vitali shuddered at the thought. This operation was not to take back the Vatican, where tens of thousands had barricaded themselves. This was to take back Rome, from the estimated ten thousand protesters still in front of the gates, and the clusters that had gathered at various chokepoints after Vitali's men had successfully cut off further access to the tiny city.

"Sir, the last unit is in position."

Vitali nodded, a frown creasing his face. *If this goes wrong…*

"And the Army?"

A colonel stepped forward. "Mobilized and standing by should you need us."

Vitali looked at the colonel. He appeared uneager to give that command, which was a good thing. Stereotypes had the military gung ho to go into any battle. But that wasn't always the case, especially when it was on your own soil, against your own citizens, no matter how misguided they may be.

Vitali stood and addressed the room.

"Begin the operation."

Immediately orders were sent out via dispatch to all units to prepare, and for the main force of three thousand riot police to begin their push. Vitali stepped outside the command tent and watched as row upon row of heavily armed riot police, most equipped with shields, marched past double-time, pounding their shields with their batons in unison, the effect reminiscent of ancient tribal warfare, designed to shove a blade of fear in the hearts of men.

And it was working.

Vitali felt his own chest tighten instinctively, his own heart pound a little quicker. He inserted himself in the midst of his men, determined to lead the operation from the ground, his radio gripped tightly in one hand.

"Sir!"

He turned to see his aide run up carrying a helmet. "Sir, you forgot your helmet."

He hadn't, but he took it and shoved it on the top of his head. He flipped the visor up, and continued forward. As they rounded the corner, departing the staging area surrounding the Statue of Saint Michael, and onto Via della Conciliazione, he could see the massive basilica in the distance, less than half a kilometer away. He looked up at the rows of apartments lining the street, nearly every window filled to capacity with citizens cheering and waving at the police, the entire population behind them.

He felt a surge of pride.

Not only in his nation, his city, but in his job, his purpose. The police were so often jeered, disrespected, but when you needed them, they were almost always there, and if they weren't, it wasn't by choice. Today, they were needed, and the people knew it.

And today, we're here.

The distance was closed quickly, and he began to hear the chants of the crowd they were approaching over the pounding of the batons. The sea of people in front of the gates, acting as a buffer between the police and the entrance to Saint Peter's Square, turned to face the new noise confronting them. Vitali moved forward, slightly quicker than the rest, raising his radio to his mouth.

"This is DC Vitali to unit commanders. We are about to confront the main body. Form your wedge and hold it until you reach the fence, then push back to empty the square as directed. Keep your men together, and execute this quickly. Surprise is our best weapon. Out."

He moved toward the front, leaving several hundred officers ahead of him. He knew he was too old to get into the thick of the fight, but he wanted to be close enough to see how it was progressing in case he needed to change the plan on the fly.

There was a crash, the sounds of bodies thudding against shields. The shouts of 'Allahu Akbar' began to be replaced with yells and screams, cries of shock and pain, epitaphs in Italian and Arabic shouted at the officers at the front of the wedge.

And indeed it was a wedge. Vitali smiled with pride as he saw the front of the phalanx shove through the opposition. As they pushed with their shields, walking over some of those that had fallen to the ground, the formation continued through, unceasing, their goal less than one hundred meters away.

Those they stepped over were quickly grabbed by police inside the wedge without shields and handcuffed with zip ties, then passed toward the back.

Nothing stopped the wedge.

The crowd began to push back, and the pace slowed, but the wedge edged forward, a pace at a time, inexorably shoving toward the short fence that separated Italy from Vatican City and Saint Peter's Square. He could see it now, and there would be no stopping them in reaching it. The crowd was split in two, and those in front, still between the tip of the wedge and the fence, were scrambling now, their support behind them constantly decreasing, as some tried to jump over the waist high fence and into the square their supporters still held, others tried to split off to the sides, and away from the oncoming force.

Something hit him on the side of the head and he dropped. He felt arms grab him under the shoulders and haul him to his feet.

"Are you okay, sir?"

He nodded, feeling where he was hit, thankful that he was wearing the helmet. He looked at his feet and saw a cobblestone lying on the ground.

One of his fellow officers tapped his helmet. "They don't just look sexy, they serve a purpose," he said with a smile.

Vitali chuckled, and waved them on as he gathered his composure.

He heard a slam, this one different. It was plastic on metal.

They were at the fence.

The wedge continued forward, ever expanding outward, the men forming a line with their shields between those inside Saint Peter's Square, and Italian territory, and as the thousands of police poured in behind the expanding wedge, they pushed the crowds back, hauling individual protesters into the mass of police, who would cuff and hand the prisoners toward the back, and the waiting dozens of city and chartered buses.

Vitali stopped in the center of the square, nodding to himself, pleased at how well it had gone. They had the square, those inside the Vatican were now trapped inside, and those who were outside, had been split into three groups; those hauled inside the cordon of officers, and two larger groups, split evenly, exiting the area to the narrow roads to the north and south of the walled city.

What he knew, and the crowds didn't, was that thousands of police had been prepositioned. To the north the mighty walls of Vatican City protected anyone from gaining access, and would be the easier of the mop up operations. If things went to plan, the protesters would be pushed up Largo del Collonato and past the last access point to Saint Peter's Square, the entire time a line of officers would continue to build a fence of flesh and reinforced polymer between the two cities, until they reached the wall.

And as the masses would be forced northward, they would hit the Piazza del Risorgimento, a large paved area where over one thousand of his men were amassed in a formation that would split the crowd into three much smaller groups, forcing them down three northern routes, continually pressed, and along these three routes, groups of officers would force them down side streets, dozens at a time, simply creating openings along the way, and then creating a barrier of riot shields across the street, funneling small groups into the side streets, where they could be detained. And as each group would be funneled off, the line would pull back, letting the bulk of the rioters continue forward, the process repeated as each batch was cuffed and bused.

And by the time the reduced crowd would reach the tree lined boulevard of Viate delle Milizie, their numbers would be so reduced, that the wall of men waiting them should be able to easily contain them.

But that was the north, and the report coming over his radio told him the plan was already working perfectly, the first of the crowd hitting the riot squad at the piazza and splitting into three groups.

But the south was another matter, and Vitali ran toward Via Paolo VI, the road ringing the south side of Saint Peter's Square. His men would have rushed into position up the southern portion of that road, forming a barrier between further penetration into the ground of the Vatican, and forcing the approaching mass to the south, where they would again be split into three groups, and at this point the southern wall of the ancient city would provide the protection it needed. Then if all went well, the mop up would proceed in similar fashion as to that in the north.

As he rounded the southern side of Saint Peter's Square, the massive columns that surrounded the north and south sides of the square towered overhead, the colonnade they formed providing the one wrinkle to the southern plan that the northern didn't face. Because of the layout of the streets to the north, they only had to contend with less than a third of the northern arc, but to the south, they had to deal with almost the entire arc, and the dozens of entrances and exits it provided from the square, albeit separated by the same waist high fence.

As he rounded the bend, he was relieved to see a line of his men forming the plastic barrier between the square and the road. But they were under fierce attack, with hundreds of protesters pushing at their shields. He raised his radio. "This is DC Vitali. We need reinforcements on the south side of the square, permission to use teargas and water cannons authorized, over."

He heard the voice of his second in command respond.

"On its way, over."

Vitali continued round the southern side, and saw the front line of his men attempting to force the crowd to the south. It wasn't going well. This was the only portion of his plan that relied heavily on man power forming a ninety degree wall.

As he neared the front of his men, he could see it had once again turned into a game of inches, and the crowd, rather than being chased, had begun to stand its ground. He raised his radio.

"Status on northern operation?"

"Proceeding as planned. We've cleared the square and the northern side of the columns. The rioters have split into three groups as planned, and the first groups are being separated and bused to holding areas. It appears they're losing their will to fight, over."

Vitali smiled. "Okay, as soon as you can spare the men, send them to reinforce the border of the square, and assist on the southern operation, over."

"Roger that, over and out."

Vitali looked ahead, the smile wiped off his face. The crowd was pushing back, and his men were starting to falter. If the reinforcements didn't arrive soon, this side might be lost. The roar of an engine from behind sent him spinning on his heel with a smile. The water cannons had arrived. He waved at the driver of the first vehicle and jumped on the running board as it slowed down. He pointed at the faltering line.

"Hit them with everything you've got!"

The man nodded, and pulled ahead as Vitali jumped off, directing the second vehicle to follow the first. The third truck he flagged down and jumped aboard. "I want you to push back these crowds"—he pointed at the rioters inside Saint Peter's challenging the cordon of officers forming a barrier along the border. "Push them back, try not to direct any sustained spray at the architecture!"

The man nodded and positioned the truck after Vitali jumped off. He heard the crowds yell in protest as the two streams of high pressure water from the first two trucks engaged the rioters, and within minutes, the front line had reformed, and was advancing again, the two trucks inching along with them, blasting at the crowd as it was forced into the narrow street. Within minutes of the water cannons arriving, the rioters had been pushed back, past the human wall of officers, and down the road with more formidable buildings penning them in.

Vitali looked over his shoulder and saw that the crowds inside the square had begun to withdraw as their comrades on the outside disappeared, out of sight, and the water cannon took its toll.

We might just win this thing.

Gunfire erupted, and he saw two of his men go down.

He looked up, and saw two men, standing on top of the colonnade surrounding the southern side, with automatic weapons, firing down on his men below. The men dove for cover, those with shields raising them as a barrier, reminiscent of ancient Roman soldiers shielding against arrows.

The two men above rained fire upon the water cannon, the officer manning the turret taking several hits, the spray stopping as he died. Vitali raised his radio. "We're taking heavy fire from two hostiles on the top of the southern colonnade, we need armed backup!"

Vitali jerked backward as he felt a sharp pain in his shoulder. He fell back, hitting his helmeted head on the pavement. Looking up, he saw his shooter take aim directly at him.

He said a silent prayer as the muzzle flashed against the night sky.

Hotel Alimandi Vaticano
Rome, Italy

Dawson watched through the window at the action below. He nodded in appreciation at a well-orchestrated plan coming together, its execution, from the small portion he could see from Reading's hotel room, performed perfectly. As the rioters were pushed north along the outer wall of the Vatican, they were met with what looked to him to be almost one thousand officers, split into several groups, forcing the rioters to split into three distinct streams.

Brilliant.

Three streams, each now numbering around two thousand, were far easier to deal with than a single mass of six thousand. And if whoever planned this operation did what he would have done, these smaller groups would be split even further, into manageable groups, siphoned off into batches that could be bused away.

If the entire operation went as smooth as what he just witnessed, they could have the perimeter of the city secured within minutes.

Which wasn't a good thing for them.

"Okay, we better get moving while they're still occupied."

"How do you plan to get in?"

"Oh, I think you know how."

Reading and Chaney exchanged glances.

Dawson smiled. "Consider myself *extremely* well briefed."

"You know about the secret entrance?"

Dawson nodded. "After the incident that we had to get involved in, CIA's been keeping a close watch on things here. Emergency demolition and construction at the Vatican, involving the city of Rome, is unusual. It didn't take long to figure out what was going on. The only question that remains is where it leads."

"It's something I can't tell you about, nor can you ask about."

"But you're going to show us the way, nonetheless."

Reading frowned, but nodded.

"Then that's all I need to know. The rest of the team is already inside, waiting for us."

"What?"

Dawson smiled at Reading's outburst.

"How long have they been there?"

"Since we arrived. We took advantage of the chaos to preposition most of the team and the supplies. We"—Dawson flicked his hand indicating the rest of the team—"are tourists, out for a stroll, who, when clear, will cross the street and go through the construction entrance, and into the city. From there, you will show us the way."

Chaney grinned. "You blokes have thought of everything."

Reading looked at Dawson. "What if you weren't going in? You'd have done all that work for nothing."

Dawson smiled out of half his mouth.

"Agent Reading, we were *always* going in."

Islamic Center of America
Altar Road, Dearborn, Michigan

Atkinson peeled around the corner and slammed his brakes on, barely avoiding the cruisers already on the scene. He and his partner, Zawadzki, jumped out, drawing their weapons, and rushed forward to join the approximately one dozen officers already there, taking cover behind two cruisers. A lone cruiser sat about twenty feet further on, its owner sitting on the ground, behind the rear tire, his arms at his side, his head lying on his shoulder.

"Is he alive?" asked Atkinson.

"I think he's breathing," said Aman. "I swear I see his chest moving."

Atkinson ducked as another burst of gunfire hit Hasni's cruiser.

"What are we up against?"

"About twenty gangbangers were shooting up the mosque, now they're all hiding amongst their cars. Seems to be just one guy though firing at the unit. No shots at us yet."

"Has anyone tried to approach yet?"

Aman nodded. "I did, but the guy opened up again, so I backed off."

Atkinson peered over the hood of the unit he was behind. "Do we know where the shooter is?"

"Behind the black Escalade."

Atkinson looked at the row of vehicles, mostly oversized SUVs. *Sometimes crime does pay.* One thing though was clear, the shooter didn't have a good angle, not unless he wanted to expose himself to fire from the officers at the other end of the street. The shooter was covered from that end by another SUV, parked slightly ahead of his position. This allowed him about two feet of room to pop out, shoot, and pop back in.

But not a good angle.

Atkinson looked about, then pointed. "Okay, we've got to get Hasni before he bleeds out. Let's take that cruiser, put it in neutral, and use it as cover, pushing it up the right side, until it taps the rear bumper of his unit. Put him on a stretcher, and drag him out, while pulling the cruiser back."

Aman smiled. "Good plan." He pointed at a nearby paramedic. "We need a stretcher, not a gurney."

The man nodded. "I'll get you a back-board."

Atkinson turned to Zawadzki. "Get some rope out of the trunks, tie them together, then tie it to the cruiser. Enough rope to get us those twenty feet."

Zawadzki scurried away, and Atkinson turned his attention back to the scene in front of them. Another couple of shots rang out, causing them all to duck again.

"Where's SWAT?"

Aman huffed. "On their way, ten minutes out."

"He could be dead by then."

The paramedic arrived with the backboard, dropping it on the ground as he dove on top of it, another shot ripping at the pavement.

"Jesus Christ!" he yelped.

Atkinson grabbed him and pulled him against the car, relinquishing his spot by the tire. "Anything I need to know?"

The paramedic shook his head. "I'll go with you. Without knowing his injuries, moving him the wrong way could kill him."

Atkinson shook his head. "No way, I can't be responsible for you getting shot."

The man squared his jaw. "I'm going, it's my job."

Atkinson looked at the man's name tag. "Goldstein? You've got balls." He snapped at a nearby rookie who was cowering behind another cruiser. "Get this guy a vest."

"From wh-where?"

"Give him yours, then see if there are any spares in the trunks."

"Wh-what?"

"Give him your vest, then fall back."

The kid nodded, unbuckling his vest and tossing it forward. The paramedic grabbed it but never had a chance to thank the kid, as he was already sprinting toward the rear of the mass of cruisers now assembled. Atkinson and Aman helped him into the body armor, when Zawadzki arrived with the rope and rolled under the cruiser they were going to push. He rolled back out a few moments later and nodded.

Atkinson moved to the cruiser, opening the door and reaching in, shifting it to neutral. "Okay, let's go. Keep your heads low, keep behind the tires if you can, and let's make this quick."

He pushed the car with a grunt, and it started to roll. He grabbed the steering wheel with one hand, the paramedic with another. "Keep on my ass until we get there."

The man nodded, and Atkinson steered the vehicle around the unit he had been hiding behind moments before, then aimed for the rear bumper of Hasni's unit. Zawadzki was right behind him, pushing with the rear window frame, and a line of a dozen officers now had taken up position to provide cover fire if necessary.

A shot rang out, and a flurry of shots from behind hit the SUV just past the Escalade.

They were almost there. Mere feet away.

They hit, the bumper gently tapping the rear quarter panel of Hasni's unit.

The paramedic immediately went to work, checking over the disturbingly still man.

"Is he alive?"

"Yes, barely."

"Can you move him?"

"Yes, help me get him on the backboard."

Atkinson closed the door and crawled over to Hasni.

"Grab his legs, and let's get him on the board."

Zawadzki scurried over, and together they lifted Hasni onto the board, the paramedic quickly buckling him in.

Several shots slammed into the cruiser, and again another volley of fire was returned over their heads. The paramedic grabbed one end of the backboard, Zawadzki the other, and Atkinson grabbed the steering wheel, waving for the car to be pulled back. Several officers grabbed the rope that had played out behind the cruiser, and pulled. The car began to roll, and Atkinson could feel the adrenaline starting to ebb as they neared the cover of the other cruisers.

Suddenly dozens of shots rang out, from multiple weapons, tearing up their cruiser from the other side.

That's not coming from our bangers!

"Keep pulling!" he yelled, as bullets continued to hit the cruiser. He felt the car jolt as a passenger side tire was hit. He looked back. They were almost there. Only feet away. Three officers were lying on the ground, pulling at the rope as hard as they could, as the others looked for cover from this new angle of attack, then returned fire.

The paramedic yelped, and dropped. Atkinson looked over and saw Goldstein grabbing at his ankle. *Probably a ricochet.* Atkinson grabbed him by the collar and pulled with all his might as he steered the car, at a crouch, painfully aware that he too could be hit at any moment. Zawadzki pulled the stretcher alone, the backboard scraping on the pavement, as Atkinson's muscles screamed for mercy as he pulled the injured paramedic from a squat position.

"You're clear!"

He let go of the steering wheel and Zawadzki pulled the gurney through to the other side of the gathered cruisers. Atkinson shoved the paramedic toward two other officers, who helped the man toward one of the waiting ambulances. Atkinson crawled behind the nearest cruiser and collapsed on the ground, his shoulders and legs in agony.

Gunfire continued to tear through the night air.

"Who's firing?"

"Don't know. But a whole bunch of vehicles just pulled up over there and began firing on us and the gang bangers."

"Rival gang?"

"No idea, but we can't keep taking fire like this."

"Where the hell is SWAT!" yelled Atkinson to no one in particular.

"Two minutes out!"

"Make sure they have an update on the new arrivals, they're coming into a situation way hotter than they planned on."

Zawadzki dropped down beside Atkinson. "You okay?"

Zawadzki said nothing. Atkinson looked down at his partner of six years, then shook him. "Charlie!" he rolled him over and cried out as he saw the hole in the side of his face, penetrating the cheek bone and entering the brain.

Atkinson grabbed his partner, holding him to his chest, as tears filled his eyes. "No," he whispered. "No!" He lowered him gently to the ground, pulled his partner's gun from his hand, then jumped up, firing both weapons at the new arrivals, no longer caring if he lived or died.

Tonight, everyone dies.

Viale Vaticano
Rome, Italy

Dawson, Niner, Jimmy and Atlas, along with Reading and Chaney, stood in an alley across from the construction site at the North wall of the Vatican, waiting for the right moment. Dozens of police were in the area, but most had moved on after the rioters, leaving the immediate vicinity mostly empty, the police relying on the massive wall to protect the city. Unfortunately, due to the construction, there was a gap, and four officers stood there, talking amongst themselves.

"How are we going to get by them?"

"Red and his team will take them out."

"Non-lethally I hope?"

Dawson looked at Reading. "Of course."

The distinct sound of gunfire in the distance caused them all to freeze, then smile. Two of the four officers, along with most of the others scattered in the area, ran toward the sound of the gunshots, and within moments the area was almost entirely empty.

"Now would be a good—"

Reading didn't finish his sentence as both officers collapsed, then four men, all in black, race from the shadows and grab the two bodies, pulling them inside the city.

Dawson stepped out and casually walked across the street, with Atlas at his side. Jimmy and Niner followed, talking quietly amongst themselves. Reading and Chaney brought up the rear, about ten feet behind. To the casual onlooker, it might have appeared half a dozen tourists were out for a walk, if it weren't for the chaos from earlier. Dawson and Atlas reached the other side of the street, Jimmy and Niner only feet away from the curb when someone yelled.

All their heads spun toward the sound. It was a police officer who had just come from around the eastern wall. "Fermati!" he yelled.

"Let's go, gentlemen," said Dawson as he sprinted to the opening in the wall. He could hear the footfalls behind him as the rest of his crew followed.

"Fermati!"

This time there were two voices.

Dawson stopped when he reached Red, and turned, pushing Atlas, then Jimmy and Niner inside. He waved for Reading and Chaney, who had hesitated, but were now running toward the entrance. Dawson peaked around the corner and could see two officers racing toward their position. Reading then Chaney cleared, and Red hissed, "Follow me!" The new arrivals followed Red, with Stucco and Casey taking up the rear.

Within moments they reached a ladder that led to the old sewage line. Dawson sent Reading and Chaney down first, then Atlas and Niner.

"Fermati!"

The two officers had come through the wall, and were now pushing their way forward. Stucco and Casey each squeezed off a round, both officers dropping to the ground from the tranquilizer darts now embedded in their legs.

Dawson slid down the ladder, as did Stucco and Casey, and lastly Red. Red pulled the ladder down, placing it on the floor, then pointed at several duffel bags nearby. "Your gear's over there."

Dawson nodded, and he and the others quickly donned their equipment. Finished, Dawson tossed a vest to Reading, and one to Chaney. "Put these on, then grab whatever weapons you want from the bag."

Dawson stepped over to Red. "Situation?"

"I don't know where we're supposed to go from here. Our intel says this is the entrance to the hidden tunnel, but there's so much construction, that I don't know where to go."

Reading stepped up to the two men.

"Luckily for you blokes I'm here." He pointed at a newly bricked wall. "That, gentlemen, is the entrance. We need to knock that down, and we're in the tunnel."

Dawson motioned for Atlas and Stucco to get to work. Reading grabbed his arm, and lowered his voice.

"Listen, there's something you need to know about where you're going."

"What?"

"You'll see things in there that you'll want to look at, that you'll want to question. But you mustn't."

"What do you mean?"

"This is a top secret archive that only a handful of people alive on the planet today know about. If word got out, it could devastate the church. You must swear to never talk to anybody about anything you see in there."

Dawson didn't like it, but nodded. "Fine." *What the hell could be stored in this archive that was so secret?*

With only the second swing of a large mallet that had been left by the construction crew, Atlas was through the new wall. Niner walked over and peaked through, then looked at Atlas. "Why didn't you just run through it like in Somalia?"

Dawson chuckled at the memory of Atlas making an escape route by throwing himself against the mud walls of a room they had been cornered in during a hostage rescue. It had saved their hides, and had been fuel for dozens of jokes since.

Dawson stepped through the opening, then turned back to his men. "Anything you see in the next few minutes is top secret, never to be discussed, not amongst yourselves, your God, or your woman. Understood?"

"Yes, Sergeant!"

Dawson stepped into the darkness, flicking on his flashlight.

Just what the hell are we about to get into?

Outside the Southern Colonnade
Saint Peter's Basilica, Rome, Italy

DC Vitale rolled to the right and felt pieces of pavement, torn apart by the shots from above, rain upon his bullet proof vest. A volley of gun fire erupted from around him as he rolled onto his back, looking up at his would-be killer. But instead of a muzzle flash greeting him, he instead saw dozens of muzzle flashes from around him, at his level, aimed upward at the two gunmen, his fellow officers having regrouped enough to counterattack.

Both men were hit, and collapsed off the colonnade, and onto the road below. The officers rushed forward and grabbed the weapons before they could fall back into the hands of those pushing at the wall of reinforced polycarbonate. Someone stepped over and extended him a hand. Vitale grabbed it and was back on his feet.

"You okay, sir?"

Vitale nodded, rotating his shoulder. "Caught me in the vest."

"First time?"

Vitale shook his head. "I've been shot once, before vests were standard issue."

The officer smiled. "Hurts a lot less with the vest, I suppose?"

Vitale winced as he shrugged his shoulders. "I'll have to get back to you on that one." He pointed at the water cannon. "Get our comrade down from there, then put someone else on the cannon. We need that operational."

The man nodded and grabbed two other officers who climbed the vehicle. Vitale watched for a moment as the body was lowered, then surveyed the situation. The rioters had been forced down the southern bend, and once the water cannon was operational again, the crowds inside the southern colonnade shouldn't be a problem. He pointed to the roof of the colonnade as a group of armed officers rushed up. "Keep an eye up there for additional gunmen. Spread out and hold this area. Shoot anything that carries a firearm."

The commander of the unit nodded, and immediately ordered his men into position as Vitale turned the corner to follow the main body of the rioters. "Status?" he asked, raising his radio.

"Northern operation almost complete, barricades for the front gates and northern colonnade moving in now. Southern operation proceeding well now, the main mass has just been split into three. We'll begin moving in the southern colonnade barricades as soon as the main entrance is complete, over."

"Okay, let me know as soon as the barricades are in place, over and out."

Vitale jogged toward Piazza del Sant'Uffizio, where the split of the rioters was to have taken place, and arrived to find the square almost empty. As he looked in each direction, he could see the three groups pursuing their targets, and no signs of trouble, two of the groups still followed by water cannon that no longer appeared to be needed, their cannon silent.

He eyed a nearby concrete traffic barrier, and sat on it, resting for a moment. His eyes felt heavy, and closed for a moment as he said a silent prayer to Jesus, thanking him for a successful operation.

He opened his eyes, looking north at the southern colonnade of Saint Peter's Square, and sighed.

Ten thousand down, thirty thousand to go.

The Vault, Vatican City

"What the *fawk* is that?"

It was Niner. Reading grimaced. "Try not to look. Just keep moving forward."

"Are you fuckin' kidding me? I think I just saw ET!"

Atlas' deep voice boomed out across the massive complex, lost in the dark spoiled only by the narrow beams of their flashlights. "This is some freaky shit."

"BD, when we get outta here, I gotta take up praying."

Reading looked to where a flashlight bounced off a jar to his right and shuddered. *I'm definitely hitting a church when I get back to London.*

"What the hell?"

"Keep moving forward, keep your flashlights on the floor," ordered Dawson.

The flashlights immediately obeyed, and the comments stopped for a few moments.

"My God!" exclaimed Niner.

"Stow it, Sergeant," growled Dawson.

"Yes, Sergeant."

Reading pressed on a little faster. *It didn't seem this long last time.* But when he thought back on it, he was in a full tilt race, running on adrenaline, trying to save his friends. This time, there was no need to rush, except for the overly curious team of soldiers behind him.

He saw the beam of his flashlight reflect back off of stonework. He slowed down and ran the light across the wall, and soon found the opening to the stairs.

"Up the stairs gentlemen, then down a corridor, and we'll be at the exit and out of the rabbit hole."

"Niner, you take point."

"Roger," said Niner as he took the first step, his Glock in one hand, flashlight clasped tightly against it with the other. The rest of the team let him get ahead about ten steps then began to file in after him, leaving a similar gap.

Reading counted the flashlights then looked over at Dawson. "Why only eight?"

"Special assignment." Dawson flicked his flashlight. "You two go, I'll take up the rear."

Reading mounted the first step, and began to climb, Chaney close behind. The sound of so many boots echoing through the tight stairwell was almost claustrophobic. His heart began to beat faster, and his chest felt tight. *What the devil is happening? I never get claustrophobic.* But here he was. He focused his flashlight on the back of the man in front of him, who he believed to be Stucco, and stared at the bright patch as he tried to steady his breathing.

"You okay, gov?"

It was Chaney. "Yeah, just a little claustrophobic for some reason."

"You? Never thought you had that problem. Me, on the other hand. I'm 'bout ready to climb these bloody walls."

Reading chuckled. "We're almost there, just keep it together a few more minutes and we'll both be fine."

In fact, he was already feeling better. Just knowing he wasn't alone in his travails made him feel a little more at ease.

"I've reached the top," announced Niner from above. Several sighs of relief echoed through the narrow confines, including from Reading.

Another few twists of the spiral staircase and Reading too emerged to find the group spread out along the hall, with Niner at the end.

Reading and Dawson worked their way forward.

"What's on the other side," whispered Dawson.

"It should be an empty room."

"Okay, how do we open it?"

Reading paused, suddenly realizing that he had never gone through the wardrobe from this side before. And if he had, it would have been opened on the other side.

Dawson shone his flashlight at his own face. "You don't know?"

Reading returned the favor. "No, I've never come from this direction." He pointed at the wall. "On the other side is a wardrobe—"

"A what?"

"A wardrobe. Umm, big piece of furniture that acts like a closet, I think you Yanks call it."

"Continue."

"You climb inside, close the door, then push the clothes hook second from the left up, and it unlocks this hidden door."

"There must be a latch on this side," said Dawson, playing his flashlight along the wall.

"This is where Acton would come in handy," muttered Niner.

"Call him." It was Atlas.

"Huh?"

Stucco.

"Call him and ask what we should be looking for."

"Ignoring the fact that we probably can't get a signal in here, I've seen enough Indiana Jones movies to know we're looking for a lever to pull, or a stone to push," said Stucco. "Like that one." He pointed with his flashlight at a stone that was sticking out.

Dawson looked at Reading. "What do you think?"

"Well, as someone who has watched all four Indiana Jones movies on multiple occasions, including the fourth one with a new appreciation"—several chuckles broke out—"I would like to point out that while that stone may very well unlock the door, it may also cause the floor to fall out, the ceiling to begin to collapse, or a giant ball to come rolling down to crush us."

Dawson leaned forward and pushed the rock.

"Wait!" yelped Reading, but it was too late. The rock receded into the wall, and there was a clicking sound. The wall with the hidden door moved out slightly. Reading grabbed the now visible edge with his fingers, and pulled. The door swung open easily, revealing the inside of the wardrobe.

Dawson stepped in and pushed on the outer door.

"You have to close the secret door before you can open the outer," explained Reading.

"Lovely." Dawson looked around. "Okay, Jimmy, in here. Reading, you too since you know how to operate it." Jimmy climbed in, and Reading followed, pulling the door shut behind him. If he had felt claustrophobic before, this took the cake. Luckily the three flashlights had plenty to reflect off of. Dawson pushed on the outer door, and it swung open. He and Jimmy quickly exited, clearing the room.

Dawson stepped back in front of the door. "Okay, Agent, two at a time." He closed the door. Reading quickly shoved the hook up and the door clicked open. He pushed.

"Next two."

Chaney stepped in along with Niner. They pulled the door shut, then opened the outer door. The process was repeated for the rest of the team until at last Reading popped out after sharing the confines with Atlas. He sat on the lone bed, catching his breath, pointing at the wardrobe. "If we need to get out this way, go inside, close the door, push the second hook from the left up, then push the back after you hear the click."

He stood up, taking a deep breath.

Niner patted him on the back. "Thanks for the four-one-one, agent, but there's no effin' way I'm goin' back down there."

Chuckles filled the room, but they sounded almost as if they were chuckles of agreement to Reading.

"Now where?" It was Dawson.

"We're at the end of a hallway. If I remember correctly, we should be able to just walk down the hall, then hang a right. At the end of that is a stairwell that will take us to the main entrance."

"This is the Apostolic Palace, correct?"

Reading nodded. "Yes."

"Okay, once we get to the stairwell, I'll know exactly where we are." Dawson flicked the light switch, and everyone turned their flashlights off, sending the room into darkness. The door opened, and a sliver of light appeared that quickly widened as Dawson peered outside. "All clear. By two's, Red, you take point."

Red and Atlas took the lead, then Jimmy and Niner. Reading and Chaney followed, with Stucco and Casey, then Dawson and Spock bringing up the rear. At each branch in the hall, the team of two in the lead would check for hostiles, then the next two would take point. Reading began to wonder if he and Chaney were expected to take point, and prepared himself to do so when Jimmy and Niner took up position at the stairwell. Stucco and Casey slipped by, and Reading followed, with Chaney. Soon they were all slowly making their way down the spiral staircase.

Two muffled shots from below had them stop, the silenced weapons now carried by the team no longer non-lethal. Stucco waved everyone forward as he and Casey continued down the stairs. Two more muffled shots, then Stucco and Casey took up position at the foot of the stairs. Dawson and Spock rushed past Reading and Chaney, and turned right, toward what Reading remembered to be the rear exit. More muffled shots, including someone crying out, their call of warning cut short with a thudding sound, as if hit with a pillow.

Niner and Jimmy moved past Reading and Chaney, setting themselves up across the hall, their weapons aimed at the front entrance. Stucco urged the rest on, and within minutes they were all at the battle scarred rear entrance. Broken glass littered the marble floor, the large tiles that had stood for probably hundreds of years, torn to pieces from gunfire. Bodies lay about, including some of the defenders, but mostly the attackers.

Dawson led the team out the rear entrance, and they quickly tracked West toward a line of heavy trees.

If we can just reach those trees with no one seeing us.

Gunfire sprayed the grass in front of them as they all hit the ground.

I spoke too soon.

Ford Street
Dearborn, Michigan

"Lights! Lights! Lights!" whispered Lieutenant Jeffrey McKay. The driver leaned forward, killing the headlights, then McKay motioned for him to stop. "Lookey what we have here," he said, leaning forward. A few hundred feet away there was a line of hostiles firing steadily toward the mosque, hitting both sets of squad cars on either side of the building, and a mix of cars, most likely belonging to the original gangbangers. A line of vehicles, empty, sat behind the new arrivals. McKay ran a plate.

"Mohammad Kazi." He nodded as he read the long record. "Okay, we've got rival Muslim gangbangers, probably looking for revenge on the other guys for shooting up their mosque," said McKay into his radio. "Let's get out here, use their vehicles for cover."

The Lenco BearCat quickly emptied as McKay climbed out the passenger side. Silently his men rushed into position, lining up behind the row of Mercedes and BMWs belonging to the Muslim gang members.

"Everyone set," he whispered into his mike. A string of affirmatives, and he lifted a megaphone to his lips.

"This is the Dearborn Police Department. You are surrounded. Lay down your weapons, and raise your hands, and you will not be harmed."

They received the response he expected.

The gang members spun around and opened fire.

"Fire!" ordered McKay. Automatic weapons from either side of him opened fire for less than ten seconds, then stopped. McKay looked at the scene in front of him. All twenty plus of their opposition were down, some writhing on the ground, others not moving, likely to never move again.

Further beyond, in front of the mosque, hands were raised as those who had first arrived took the opportunity to surrender. They were swarmed from both sides by the original officers, as the SWAT unit moved in to secure the Muslim gang they had just engaged.

"All secured!" yelled one of his men. He raised his radio. "Send in the ambulances. And the coroner."

He strode toward the second scene as the last of the rival gang were handcuffed. "Situation?"

One of the men he recognized as Officer Mohammad Aman, walked up. "All secure now."

"Casualties?"

Aman frowned. "We managed to rescue Hasni. But Zawadzki and Atkinson are dead."

"Atkinson?"

"Yeah, he saved Hasni and a paramedic, then when Zawadzki bought it, he snapped and just jumped up, blazing away. He caught one in the neck after taking out a few of these bastards."

McKay frowned, shaking his head. "Such a waste of a good man."

Aman nodded, looking at the ground. "Yeah, well we had our differences, but when push came to shove, he did his job, and did it well."

McKay eyed Aman, then said, carefully, "I guess that's what ultimately matters. When the shit hits the fan, do you do the right thing?" Aman remained silent. "Where're the bodies?"

Aman pointed to a group of cruisers. "Back there. We haven't had time to move them yet."

McKay slapped the man on the shoulder, then strode across the pavement to the heavily damaged cruisers.

Christ, this was a war zone.

His mind flashed to the news, and the reports of chaos across America and the world.

And this is only the beginning.

Behind the House of the Gardener
Vatican City

Two single shots, separated by what seemed like a mere second, cracked the night air and the gunfire was silenced. Reading felt himself hauled to his feet as the team pressed forward to the tree cover.

"Thanks, Overseer, how's it look now?" Reading heard Dawson whisper.

Niner let go of Reading's vest and raced ahead before he had a chance to thank him. They all stood huddled behind several large trees for a moment, Reading catching his breath along with Chaney, the Bravo Team scanning the area with their night vision equipment.

Dawson hurried back to Reading. "Time for the door to be opened. We'll be there in two. Have them kill the lights if they can." Reading pulled out his phone and Dawson grabbed him by the hand before he could flip it open. He snapped his finger at Stucco who stood nearby.

"Cover."

Stucco nodded and pulled what looked like some sort of rain cover out of his utility belt, tightly folded. He tossed it to Dawson then returned his attention to watching their perimeter. Dawson unfolded the raingear rapidly. Reading took a knee, knowing exactly what was about to happen, and chastising himself for not realizing that the moment he flipped open his phone in this darkness, it would have been a beacon to all those around them.

The tarp was tossed over him, and he flipped open the phone, dialing Acton. It was answered immediately.

"Two minutes, try to kill the lights if you can."

"Confirmed two minutes, kill the lights if we can. See you soon, buddy."

He flipped the phone closed, then pushed the tarp aside, taking a deep breath as he freed himself from yet another claustrophobic situation.

What's happening to me?

Chaney grabbed the tarp and began quickly folding it up.

"Just in case," he whispered. Reading felt a slap on his back and noticed they were moving forward again. He followed Stucco, Chaney behind him, two more Bravo Team members covering their rear. They quickly raced forward, the trees providing excellent cover in the darkness. The team took a sharp turn to the left, and Reading followed, not sure where they were going, but hoping that the team knew. Within seconds they were huddled behind a stand of trees, looking at the back of the building Reading recognized as housing Giasson's security team.

And the lights were still on.

"You told him about the lights?" asked Dawson, shuffling over to Reading's position.

"Yes, maybe they don't have control?"

"Doubtful." Lights at one end of the building shut off. "Wait a minute." Another set shutdown, as if the building were shutting down one fuse at a time. Suddenly they were cloaked in darkness.

A single light, what Reading took for a flashlight, flashed on and off three times in a doorway across the rear parking area. Dawson raised his light and returned the signal.

"Let's go, low and fast."

They all jumped to their feet and raced across the parking lot. As they neared, the doors were thrown open, then a burst of gunfire from their right caused them all to turn. Two of the Bravo Team, Reading couldn't tell who, returned fire as they continued to run. Reading found himself slowing down, but a firm hand on the small of his back had him racing again. Two of the team entered the building, then Reading. He could still hear the gunfire outside, then it stopped. He turned to watch the rest of the team race in, then the doors were pulled shut and a team of Swiss Guards immediately set to securing the doors again.

"Welcome to the Vatican, gentlemen."

Reading smiled as he recognized Acton's voice.

"Jim! Glad to see you're okay."

"Isn't that supposed to my line? You're the one who just crossed half the city under fire."

Acton gave his friend a hearty handshake, then proceeded to greet Chaney and the Bravo Team he knew only too well.

"M. Giasson wishes he could have been here to greet you, but he was shot in the shoulder and is still quite weak. He'd like to discuss your exit strategy, and he has a request."

Dawson nodded.

"Lead the way."

Outside the Southern Colonnade
Saint Peter's Basilica, Rome, Italy

DC Vitale walked slowly toward the wall, watching the segments of ten foot high fencing pushed into place, secured together and to the existing waist-high fence already in place. The protesters were resisting, but continually pushed back with a blast of the water cannon. Vitale nodded with satisfaction, noting that everything was proceeding as per his orders, including the inclusion of small gaps large enough to squeeze a person through, every ten meters, now blocked by shield toting riot officers.

As he rounded the colonnade, he smiled, rotating his shoulder. The fencing along the exposed side of the square was almost in place, and two water cannons were keeping the crowds at bay until the work was completed. He continued to walk through the open area demarking the Italian/Vatican border, and rounded to the northern colonnade, inspecting the fencing.

With his hands on his hips, his shoulder still aching, his head bobbed.

"Very good, very good."

As he returned to the center of the square he raised his radio. "This is DC Vitale. Status?"

"Stand by."

Vitale's eyes narrowed. *Stand by?*

He felt a tap on his shoulder and he turned to see his second-in-command, Battista Riggio, standing beside him.

"What are you doing here?"

"I could ask you the same question."

Vitale smiled. "Getting a hands-on view?"

Riggio nodded. "Northern operation is complete and the officers not involved in transport have redeployed around the city. Southern operation is winding up, only a few hundred left, no real problems now. Two of our officers were wounded by gunfire, one dead, but you were there for that. Other than that incident, just a few injuries on both sides." Riggio motioned with his chin at the last piece of fencing being positioned. "What about them?"

"Set up the propaganda machines."

"Very Orwellian."

"But it might thin out the herd a bit."

"Speaking of—"

Vitale nodded. "Start the thinning out operation on the southern and northern colonnades now."

Riggio bowed slightly and stepped away, raising his radio. "This is Riggio. Bring in the screens, begin thinning out operations on north and south colonnades."

Vitale turned to see two flatbed trucks roar down Via della Conciliazione, toward the newly installed fence, then, about one hundred meters from the front gate, veer off to each side, the massive projection screens mounted on the flat beds already playing their pre-recorded messages, accompanied by loud speakers reading the messages, now exposed to the crowds.

"This is the Roma Polizia. All who surrender now, will be free to go home. Please approach any of the openings in the fencing, and an officer will assist you."

This message was repeated in Italian, Arabic and English, over and over. Vitale wasn't convinced it would work, but even if it influenced a few to cross the line, it was a few less they'd have to deal with later. As well, it allowed them to broadcast other messages. They were desperately trying to convince some of the Imams of the city to broadcast to those inside, and convince them to surrender.

This would take time.

Thirty thousand people, still fired up, will be hard to convince.

Corpo della Gendarmeria Office
Palazzo del Governatorato, Vatican City

"M. Giasson, good to meet you," said Burt Dawson, extending his hand. Acton noticed Giasson's returned handshake seemed weak, his hand falling limply to his lap after Dawson let go.

He looks like shit.

"Mario, are you okay?" asked Acton as he knelt in front of him, checking his IV bag. It was half full. "You're not getting enough fluids." Acton turned his head toward the door. "Medic!"

Seconds later the young medic they had met earlier darted in and rushed up to his boss. "You okay, sir?" he asked as he slid on his knees and opened his bag. He examined the IV bag, then the needle in Giasson's arm. "You pulled your needle out, sir." The medic reinserted the needle, and taped it in place more securely than last time. He held the bag up, looking for a place to hang it, when Niner grabbed a metal hanger off the coat stand in the corner, and unwrapped it. About a foot in he put a kink, then with his knife popped the top plug off the left side of the wheelchair's back. He stuck the hanger in the hole, then bent it at the top, making a hook. He took the bag from the young medic, and hooked it on the hanger.

"There you go, makeshift IV hanger, integrated in the patient's mode of transport, making it mobile," explained the seasoned warrior, in probably the most serious tone Acton could recall the man ever using.

The young medic looked at the MacGyvered rig, and nodded appreciatively. "Why didn't I think of that?"

"You were trained for peace, I was trained for war."

The man frowned, looking at the Delta team standing in and around the office. "It seems like we're in a war right now."

"We are," said Giasson, who already appeared to be getting a little color back.

"Agreed," said Dawson who sat in the only vacant chair, the others occupied by Acton, Laura and Reading, with Chaney sitting on the edge of the desk. Acton saw Giasson glance at him occasionally, apparently annoyed, but too weak to do battle.

"What do you need from us?" asked Dawson.

Acton answered, leaving Giasson to continue gathering strength. He held up the metal case. "We need to get this into the hands of His Holiness."

"Is that the scroll?"

Acton nodded.

"What's so significant about it, that all of"—Dawson paused, as if searching for words, then tossed his hands in the air—"*this* is necessary."

The archaeologist in Acton took over, and despite the horrors of the past day, he smiled. "It's an ancient scroll that we've carbon dated to within about a hundred years, overlapping the time Mohammad was alive."

"What, you're saying this was written by their prophet?"

Acton shook his head. "No, Mohammad was illiterate, couldn't read or write a word, which annoyed the angel Gabriel greatly if we're to believe Mohammad."

Dawson grunted.

"Okay, so what does it say?"

Acton opened the case and removed a file sitting on top of the sealed tube containing the scroll. "It says, 'And when the sacred months have passed, then kill the polytheists, but only the polytheists, wherever you find them and capture them and besiege them and sit in wait for them at every place of ambush. But if they should repent, establish prayer, and give zakah, let them go on their way. Indeed, Allah is Forgiving and Merciful.' And at the bottom, it says, 'As recited to me by the Prophet Mohammad, peace be upon him'."

Dawson's eyebrows had inched up his forehead.

"That's not right." It was Atlas' booming voice that interrupted the silence.

"What do you mean?" asked Niner.

"Well, I was raised Muslim, I guess I'm Muslim technically, but not a practicing Muslim. I've heard that verse many times, and what you read is wrong. It should be, 'kill the polytheists wherever you find them', not 'kill the polytheists, and only the polytheists, wherever you find them."

Acton smiled. "Very good, your Imam would be proud. You are exactly right. But as I'm sure you know, the Koran is thought to have actually been compiled *after* Mohammad's death. Many things at the time were transmitted orally, so errors could happen, others could change them when they wrote them down. What this seems to imply, is that the writer of this verse was in the presence of Mohammad at the time he wrote this, suggesting it is the accurate version of the verse."

"That's going to piss off a lot of Islamists," said Atlas.

"Why?" asked Niner.

"Because that verse has been used to justify Jihad against anybody who isn't a Muslim," explained Atlas.

"I don't want to sound like an idiot, but what's a polytheist?" asked Niner.

"Someone who believes in more than one God," said Laura. "Like the ancient Greeks or Romans."

Niner frowned. "I can just imagine what they think of me as a Buddhist." He turned back to Atlas. "So, why then the hatred of Christians and Jews? They're not polytheists."

Acton opened his mouth to answer, but closed it, extending his hand to let the one Muslim in the room answer. "There are additional verses in that same surah that refer to Christians and Jews, therefore the entire surah has been twisted to broaden the meaning of polytheists, and using that particular verse"—he pointed at the case—"as justification for killing." He rubbed his chin, then looked at Acton. "If this is indeed the original phrasing, then it changes the entire context of how that chapter has been interpreted, and would shut down a lot of the teachings that have come from it, that have been mostly violent."

Acton nodded. "Agreed. But first things first. We need to get this out of here and into the hands of the Pope so he can pass it over to someone respected in Islam."

"Why wasn't that done in the first place?" asked Dawson.

"Nobody wanted to touch it once they heard what it was."

A burst of air shot out from between Niner's lips. "Why the hell not?"

Giasson raised his finger but Dawson beat him to it. "Mind where you are, Sergeant."

Niner's brown skin reddened as his jaw dropped. "Oh shit! Sorry, I didn't mean any disrespect." He stopped then his eyes opened wider. "Oh Christ, I just swore again"—more horror—"oh shit! I don't know what I'm saying. Christ I can't—" He was cut off by Atlas' mammoth paw clamping over his mouth. A muffled, "thank you!" was heard, and the room turned back to the case.

"Nobody wanted to touch it probably from fear. Whoever has this will be a target. Look what happened with just word we had something that involved Mohammad."

Dawson nodded. "Okay, we'll get it out and into the proper hands. I assume you're coming with it?"

"I want these four out with you," said Giasson, sounding much better.

Dawson nodded. "Not a problem."

"But I need something else from you."

"What is it?"

Giasson suddenly trembled and paled. The medic checked him over, then looked at Niner, who pushed Atlas' hand away and moved to Giasson's side. After a quick check, he turned to Dawson. "This man needs a hospital, stat."

Dawson frowned. "Okay, we'll take him with us." He looked at Acton. "What was he about to say?"

"We have another situation."

"More important than this?" Dawson pointed at the case.

"Far more important."

Outside the Southern Colonnade
Saint Peter's Basilica, Rome, Italy

Marcello Primo was exhausted, but he knew there'd be no rest for him for hours. He had grabbed about thirty minutes shut-eye after the evacuation of the refugees, but now was back on duty, manning the southern colonnade. He could hear the loud speakers around the bend broadcasting their messages inviting those inside to surrender. Primo didn't think anybody would; peer pressure would keep everyone inside.

But sometimes, you just needed to make everyone else around you think you wanted to stay, even when you didn't. Primo looked at the opening in the gate, and saw just that in a set of eyes staring at him. The man was young, perhaps even a boy. His fist was pumping angrily in the air, but his eyes were desperate.

He wanted out.

He had managed to position himself at one of the two openings on the southern colonnade, but hadn't given any other indication he wanted out. Primo walked toward the opening, and motioned for a group of officers to accompany him. He gathered them around.

"Snatch and grab time. Let's pull as many out as we can, until they back away."

The men nodded, and Primo conveyed the same information into the ear of the man manning the shield. The crowd was loud, angry, but tiring. Their voices were not nearly as loud as earlier in the evening, and those at the fence seemed to be simply hanging on to it, rather than trying to push it down.

Primo turned to the dozen officers standing nonchalantly nearby. He lifted three fingers, then two, then one, then he spun, slapping the back of the officer manning the opening as the others rushed forward. The officer with the shield stepped aside, as Primo hit the right side of the opening, reaching in and grabbing the young man who he had noticed earlier. He pulled him out by his shirt, shoving him down the line of officers, half a dozen per side, and reached in, gripping another shirt.

He pulled, and experienced little resistance. *Apparently he wants out too.* He repeated this half a dozen times before the crowd backed off.

"Anybody else want out?" yelled Primo.

Angry fists.

Primo motioned to the officer with the shield, who repositioned himself. Walking over to the other opening, he motioned to the group of officers manning this opening and they repeated the process, the crowd dense enough, and loud enough, that the element of surprise worked again, and another half dozen were pulled through before the crowd could pull back.

This will take forever if we only get half a dozen at a time.

He looked at the dozen that had been pulled so far, huddled together, under guard, then had an idea. He knew his orders, but he hadn't been told exactly how to execute them, it was at his discretion. Extending his arm, he indicated that his officers form them into a line, then he motioned for the first one to step forward.

He didn't.

An officer pulled him by the arm to stand in front of Primo, both of whom were standing so the crowd could see them from the side. Primo pointed to the officer holding the gunshot residue test kits, and he trotted over. After swabbing the man's hands, a minute later they both watched to see if the liquid in the vial turned blue.

It didn't.

Primo shook the man's hand, pointed down the road exiting to the south where they had earlier pushed the rioters outside the square, and said, "You're free to go."

The man stared at him, a slight look of incredulity on his face.

Primo waited. *Does he not speak Italian?*

The man smiled and slowly backed away, toward the road, then turned and ran.

Primo motioned the next man over.

The process was repeated, but this one left immediately—no hesitation.

By the time the dozen were processed, and released, the attitude of the crowd had changed. Arms were shoved through the fencing, some pleading to be let go, and Primo smiled to himself. He knew the public display would work.

He raised his radio as he motioned for his men to set up for another batch.

"This is Primo, they're begging to come out from the Southern Colonnade after they saw the first batch we pulled out tested and let go, over."

"No takers on the North yet," said a voice he didn't recognize. "We pulled a few but tested them out of sight. We'll try your approach, over."

"We did the same thing at the East gates, and it's working. This is going to take a loooong time, over."

Primo smiled. What it showed to him was that the will of the crowd had been broken, at least in some of them. That implied hope. That implied an end.

He stepped forward, and motioned for the first crew to begin the next extraction.

Half a dozen at a time. We need something faster.

Corpo della Gendarmeria Office
Palazzo del Governatorato, Vatican City

Spock's eyebrow threatened to hide behind his hairline.

"Far more important?" repeated Dawson.

"Absolutely," mumbled Giasson.

"What is this other"—Dawson paused—"situation?"

Acton closed the case, patting it. "This is important to the Muslims, because it is something from the time of Mohammad. It is important to us since it might allow more moderate Muslims to preach against the extremists. But bottom line, it is of little importance to non-Muslims except for the chaos the Church's possession of it has caused.

"But what they're after"—he pointed at the security monitors on the far wall of the main security office, causing all heads to turn—"is something extremely important to the Church, and to all Catholics."

"Which is?"

"The bones of Saint Peter."

It was Dawson's turn to show a measured amount of surprise. "Excuse me?"

"Saint Peter was one of the disciples of Jesus, known as the Fisherman. He's the one Jesus said of, 'Upon this rock, I will build my church.'"

"I always wondered about that," said Stucco. "I didn't think Jesus ever made it to Rome, so if he never did, how did he indicate that this place"—he pointed at the floor, indicating the city itself—"should be where Peter was supposed to build the church?"

Acton smiled. "Excellent question, which I bet you most Catholics have no clue as to the answer. We think of him as Simon Peter. But back then, in ancient Aramaic, which would be what they spoke in Jesus' time and geographical location, his name was actually Shimeon Kaypha, and in Aramaic, Kaypha means 'Rock'. Jesus wasn't referring to a physical rock, but to Peter himself, and something he had done or represented. What that *something* was, is up for debate, but the 'rock' is not a place, it is a person, or something that person represented. In Catholicism, it is Peter, *Saint* Peter, the man who founded the church that would lead to the city we stand in now."

Dawson used his chin to motion at the monitors behind them. "And how is what they're doing link to the bones of Saint Peter?"

"They're digging through the church floor and into the Necropolis that lies underneath the basilica, where the bones, or what are believed to be the bones, are kept."

"Believed?"

"They *are*," said Giasson, with more energy than Acton had expected possible. But he said nothing else.

Acton continued. "There is some debate, but circumstantial evidence certainly suggests they are his bones."

"And you"—Acton raised a finger—"I mean *he*, wants us to risk our lives to save what *might* be the bones of Saint Peter," said Dawson.

"No, he wants you to prevent what is happening around the world tonight, from escalating. Can you imagine what would happen if Muslim extremists were to destroy or hold ransom the bones of one of the most revered men to over one billion Catholics?"

Dawson frowned, his head bobbing slowly.

"What we're seeing now play out around the world would be the tip of the iceberg. The tit for tat violence could quickly escalate out of control. *But*"—Acton paused for effect—"if we get this"—he patted the case—

"into *Islamic* hands, and prevent the bones from falling into *Islamists* hands, we have a chance of stopping this all today."

Dawson took a deep breath, then sighed. "Okay, so I'll take some of my men, and hold off ten thousand rioters in what I assume are cramped quarters."

"That's the spirit!" said Acton, grinning.

Dawson cracked half a smile, shaking his head.

"Care to join us?"

Acton's head jerked back in surprise at the question. There was no question he would. He looked at the case, conflicted.

"Don't worry, Professor, I was just kidding." Dawson pointed at the case. "In my opinion, *that's* more important."

Acton nodded.

"I guess you're right."

Dawson stood up.

"Okay, let's get this show on the road."

Chapel of the Sacrament, Saint Peter's Basilica, Vatican City

Pick axes, brought in earlier under the clothes of several of Hassan's men, were in full swing. The debris had been cleared and moved into the main hall of the infidels' church, and now "volunteers" took turns swinging at the hole in the ground. Unfortunately, they had no way to know how much further they had to go. It could be a foot. It could be ten feet.

If only they hadn't sealed the side entrance.

If they hadn't, Hassan would already have the bones, and would be broadcasting his demands to the world.

This thought caused Hassan to stop.

What are my demands?

He moved away from the crater, toward a far corner, his chin in his hand.

What are my demands?

He smiled. *Admission by the Catholic Church that Islam was the one true religion.* He chuckled. *That would never happen, and would be meaningless.* He rapped his forehead with his knuckles. *Think! You've nearly accomplished your goal, yet you have no clue what you want.*

He frowned. *Think politically.*

He pursed his lips. *Immediate withdrawal of all troops and financial support to Afghanistan and Iraq.*

That was easy. Perhaps even doable. The troops were out of Iraq, the American public were already questioning why they were still giving money to a country with trillions in oil reserves. And in Afghanistan, troops were already on their way out, and Catholics in the West wouldn't have a hard time making a pullout politically palatable since their lapdog, Hamid Karzai, had allowed the passage of a law that made it legal for men to rape their wives.

What else?

He grinned ear to ear. *Right of return for Palestinians.* He personally could care less about the Palestinians, an invented people, who none of the Arab states wanted. But, they were a thorn in the side of the Jews, and with there being millions of them in permanent refugee camps, their return to Israel would mean the eventual extinction of that country, by birthrate alone.

But, the Israeli's would never allow it under any circumstances. And there was nobody within Israel who cared about the bones he was about to possess.

Closing of Guantanamo?

His head bobbed. "That one's definitely possible," he muttered to himself.

"Sir!"

He frowned then turned on his heel.

"What?"

"Something's happening outside."

"What?"

"They've cleared everyone from outside the square—"

"So? We expected that."

"—and now hundreds are leaving, voluntarily."

"What?" Hassan strode toward the exit. "Voluntarily?"

"Yes, sir, through openings in the new fence they put up."

Hassan walked outside, and saw the crowd had moved to the ring formed by the colonnades, and the border between the Vatican and Italy.

This won't do.

He motioned for the others to join him.

"They"—he pointed at the crowd—"are our cover. We can't lose our cover." He thought for a moment then smiled. "Okay, here's what we'll do."

Rear Exit

Palazzo del Governatorato, Vatican City

Dawson stood at the door, cleared of the chains and sundry furniture that had been blocking it. He nodded to one of the Swiss Guards, who raised a radio.

"Now."

The lights began to shut off outside, and within moments, the entire complex was cloaked in darkness.

"Overseer, report."

"Hostiles converging on your location now. Several armed," said Mickey, today's Overseer with his new spotter, Jagger. Dawson couldn't help but smile at Niner's Mickey Jagger jokes, especially with Jagger's huge lips and Mickey's massive ears.

"We're exiting with fifteen, I repeat fifteen. Engage hostiles, report when clear."

"Engaging."

Dawson pushed the door open slightly, and could hear the footfalls outside echo between the building and the chapel behind the palace they now occupied. He flipped his night vision goggles down and immediately dozens of shapes, an eerie green, were racing toward him. He had visions of Zombie paintball, something he had recently tried with several of the guys.

It was a blast to say the least.

But this was real. Real guns. Real lives. And what he found disheartening, was that most of these men who were rioting, were normal, average guys, who yesterday were probably going about their daily lives at work, with their families and friends, but some strange twist of fate had them fired up into participating in something that may have never occurred to them to take part in if thought of without the emotion, the fervor, with which they were now gripped.

Mob mentality.

It was human inclination to run toward the crowd, to see what was going on, and once in the midst, to participate. Once the adrenaline began to flow, once the heart began to pump harder, it was difficult to not get caught up in the crowd. Even when the crowd turned violent, the average person, law abiding, pious to the core, could find themselves rushing forward, throwing rocks, screaming at the police, grappling with the riot squad, kicking the squad car, looting from the store.

It was primal.

It was human nature.

It was inexcusable.

But how many can honestly say they hadn't felt the surge at a football game. Hadn't wanted to punch in Apollo Creed's face, knock out Ivan Drago, and be Rambo as he killed an impossible number of Vietnamese and Soviet troops.

Once you were drawn into the narrative, whether it was fiction or real life, you wanted to be part of it, you wanted to participate, and sometimes it was beyond your control, and in the heat of the moment, sometimes it was extremely difficult to step back and ask yourself, "What am I doing? Why am I here?" And to make the even more difficult decision. "I'm leaving."

And tonight, many innocent people, caught up in a fervor, driven not only by the mob, but fueled with a religious dogma hammered into them since youth, would die. People who just yesterday might have served up a shawarma with a smile to the same Catholic they now wanted to kill, whose children might play with those of the Vatican staff. It was depressing.

And now more were about to die.

He spotted one with a weapon, probably a SIG SG 550 assault rifle taken from one of the security staff. Suddenly the target stopped racing forward, and blew backward, a bright green hole in the center of his chest. The body skidded across the pavement almost a dozen feet, then came to a rest.

His companions stopped. Another, armed, raised his weapon to fire at no one in particular, and he too was blasted from where he stood, and smeared against a wall behind him.

The rest scattered.

"Cleared for exit."

"Roger that."

Dawson looked back at the mass of people, all armed, all in body armor, but seven of which weren't his regular team. Two British cops, two archaeologists, two Swiss Guards, and one wounded civilian on a gurney. *This could turn into a real cluster fuck!*

He shoved the door open and stepped outside into the crisp night air, angry yells filling it from the south where the two armed hostiles had just been taken out. But there were yells coming from other directions as well. All directions in fact.

He ran across the parking lot, followed by Atlas, Jimmy, Niner and Spock, who each took knees, covering both directions in the center of the pavement. Stucco and Casey then exited, carrying the injured Giasson, with the professors, Swiss Guards, and Red bringing up the rear. Dawson scanned ahead, not concerned with the flanks, knowing his men would cover those. A controlled burst from one of the team behind him ricocheted off pavement, probably simply discouraging anybody from getting too close. He glanced behind him and saw the gurney clear the pavement, the door of the darkened building already closed behind them.

Everybody advanced to the side of Saint Martha's Chapel at the rear of the Governatorate Palace.

"How's it looking, Overseer?"

"Still looking good, proceed another—hold on, I've got something, your three o'clock."

Dawson looked, flipping his night vision back down. There was a group of men, about half a dozen, hiding behind an abandoned car, the engine long cold. Dawson pointed at his eyes, then toward the car. His men nodded in acknowledgement.

"Are they armed?"

"Absolutely three of them, not sure about the other two."

"Thin the herd."

"Roger that, thinning."

Dawson peered through the darkness at the green glows flitting in and out of sight behind the car. A cracking sound ripped through the night, and one of the men skidded out from behind the vehicle, and into plain sight, his weapon clattering on the ground, past him.

He wasn't moving, but a green glow rapidly spread across the pavement.

One of the men behind the car popped up and ran for the gun.

Dawson raised his weapon and fired a single shot.

The man dropped.

Another ripping sound, as if the end of a whip had snapped out across the darkness, sent another of their would-be attackers into the open, dead.

The remaining two jumped up and opened fire in their general direction. Bullets tore open the brick behind them as they all hit the ground. Dawson took aim and was about to squeeze the trigger when another shot from Overeer was fired, dropping both men in one shot.

"Nice shootin', Overseer."

"One for the books, BD."

"Are we clear?"

"Give me a second." Dawson waited. "Clear to proceed to next checkpoint."

"Roger that."

Everyone leapt to their feet, including a wincing Professor Palmer. She had been shot, just a graze, but had insisted on coming, and he hadn't heard a moment's complaint from her, and based upon his previous encounters, he never expected any. She was rock solid, dependable. *The kind of woman you need.* Dawson stowed the thought. He was a self-imposed bachelor. Many of the guys had wives, girlfriends, children, families, but not him. Sometimes it was lonely, but he never had to worry about anyone but his parents getting that visit from the Chaplain. *We regret to inform you that your son has died in a training accident.* What bullshit.

He rushed to a stand of thick trees, the same trees they had hid behind earlier, and within sight of the doors to the series of attached buildings leading to the Apostolic Palace, where their secret passageway would get them to safety.

A quick check behind him confirmed that the rest of the group had arrived safely, but as he looked at the rear doors they had exited earlier, his heart sank. There were dozens inside, apparently drawn by the gunfire.

"Looks like our exit is blocked," he said.

Red came up beside him. "How many?" he asked as he flipped down his night vision goggles.

"Looks like about thirty give or take."

"Hard to tell if they're armed."

"Some definitely are," came Overseer's voice over the comm. "At least six at my count, all mixed in with the others."

"We've seen it before," said Red. "When one with a weapon drops, another picks it up."

"Agreed," said Dawson. "We have to treat them all as armed hostiles."

"Sightseer, can you reposition to assist?"

"Already on our way, Bravo One," came Wings' voice over the comm. "ETA sixty seconds."

"Overseer, how's your field of fire?"

"I've got a clear view of the entrance with no obstructions."

"When Sightseer is repositioned, I want both of you to take out anybody armed. We'll advance on the position as soon as you've cleared some of them out. Proceed when ready."

"Roger that," said Overseer, echoed by Sightseer.

Dawson turned. "Atlas, Niner, Jimmy, you're with me. We're taking that entrance. Red, you hold this position until I signal the all clear. Fallback position is the Chapel, then the Governatorate Palace."

Red nodded and fell back to monitor the rear as Atlas, Jimmy and Niner crawled up beside Dawson.

"Sightseer in position and ready."

"Overseer ready."

"Proceed," said Dawson.

Glass shattered immediately, as two of the remaining windows were taken out, along with two targets inside. But it appeared the men inside were expecting this, and immediately began to spray the area with random fire, their attackers remaining unseen. Two more shots, and another two were down, and as Red had predicted, those unarmed quickly picked up the weapons, continuing to fire.

One of them pointed directly at the stand of trees they were hiding behind, and yelled something. Immediately the half dozen who were armed focused their fire on Dawson's position.

"Hit the dirt!" yelled Dawson as he looked back to see Acton throw himself over the injured Giasson, and pulling his fiancée down behind the two of them.

Now that's a brave man.

He, Atlas, Jimmy and Niner poured fire into the now windowless rear exit and into the marbled interior. Overseer and Sightseer continued firing from their most likely elevated positions, and within minutes, those that remained were on the run. Dawson watched as the last scrambled away, and he leapt to his feet.

"Let's move!"

The motley crew rushed toward the entrance.

"Still clear," said Overseer.

Dawson and Niner reached the entrance first, slamming a shoulder into either side of what was once a wall of windows. Jimmy and Atlas stepped inside, advancing through the hallways, toward the staircase they needed to take. The professors came next, on either side of the gurney carried by Stucco and Casey, then the two Vatican guards, followed by Red and Spock. Dawson entered the building, the marbled floor slick with blood and shattered glass, and rushed forward, toward the Apostolic Palace.

Moments later they entered the building and advanced on the staircase. As Acton began the climb, he grabbed Dawson's shoulder. "Good luck, Sergeant."

Dawson nodded. "You too, Professor."

He turned away and repositioned himself near the front entrance to the building. "Overseer, Sightseer, reposition for secondary operation."

"Roger that," they echoed.

Dawson looked over at the stairwell, and saw Red at the bottom. They exchanged a quick, informal, two fingered salute, noncommissioned officers not saluting each other formally, then Red turned, racing up the steps, leaving Dawson, Atlas, Jimmy, Niner and the two Swiss Guards, alone in the lobby.

"Out of the fryin' pan and into the fire?" asked Niner as he peered out the window.

"Let's hope not," replied Dawson.

But deep down, he had a strange feeling they all wouldn't be coming back from this one. The numbers were simply stacked too high against them.

Piazza Pio XII Square
Rome, Italy

DC Vitale watched with a smile as hundreds of former rioters streamed out the gates, desperate to end their ordeal. They were most likely tired, hungry, scared, and with the adrenaline of the moment wearing off, many were probably questioning why they were there in the first place.

"Sir!"

Vitale turned and saw one of his men approaching, accompanied by what he assumed to be an Imam in full regalia.

"Sir, this is Imam Farouk Wahhab. He has agreed to address the crowds."

Vitale extended his hand. "Thank you, sir, for agreeing to help us out."

The man accepted Vitale's hand, squeezing it tightly. "It is I who should thank you, for giving me an opportunity to correct a grave error I participated in."

Vitale loosened his grip but Imam Farouk held on.

"I don't understand," said Vitale.

"I was one of those who urged my followers here today, to demand that the scroll be returned to its rightful owners."

"I see," said Vitale.

"But I never intended"—the man paused, then let go Vitale's hand and opened his arms at the spectacle before him—"*this!* I don't think any of us expected *this*. A protest? Yes, absolutely, as is our right in a democratic society. But not a riot. Not wanton destruction. Not the occupation of a church, not worldwide violence."

Tears streamed down the man's cheeks, and Vitale felt his cold heart thaw a little. This was one of the men responsible for so many deaths, because he had let his hatred and dogma lead him to wield the weapon he controlled, those under his spiritual guidance. He may now regret his actions, but he had to bear some of the responsibility.

But that was for another day.

Today, if he could help quell the crowd inside, and to help bring the protest to a peaceful conclusion, then Vitale could see no reason not to let him speak. He led him to one of the vehicles with the audio setup, and a technician handed the man a microphone.

"Just press this button when you want to speak. Don't be shocked, it'll be loud."

Imam Farouk nodded, and stepped out from behind the truck, microphone in hand. He raised it to his lips when Vitale heard screams from the crowd. Gunfire tore holes in the cobblestone, each shot coming closer and closer to the Imam and the screens. Vitale watched in horror as the scene played out in slow motion before him. Each cobblestone hit turned into a powder, mini explosions seeming to erupt from the surface impossibly slow.

He felt himself move, the instinct to react kicking in his old bones, as he began to push forward, to do his duty. To his left the audio technician was turning, his body in the beginnings of a dive. The officer that had brought the Imam over had reacted slightly quicker, and was inches ahead of Vitale, as both shoved their feet against the stone surface, propelling their bodies forward, and into the danger that others were turning to flee from.

The Imam hadn't yet reacted, and in fact Vitale heard the distinct click as the button was pushed, and the intake of breath as it echoed across the stonework toward the crowd almost frozen in time.

Another shot tore a hole in the cobblestone at the Imam's feet. He began to spin, suddenly aware of what was happening. The microphone, still gripped in his hand, fell away as the man's arm dropped to his side, then extended out as he looked to jump away from the oncoming shots.

Vitale jumped. It was the only way he could think to reach the man in time, to do what he had been trained to do. To protect the innocent. Even if it meant sacrificing himself. Behind him he could hear the yells as his men began to react, but it wouldn't be in time, not if the path of these bullets were any indication.

His feet left the ground, he was now airborne, committed, with no way to adjust his direction. He saw the next bullet hit the Imam in the stomach, a bright crimson hole torn through his crisp white robes as the precious life giving fluid spilled forth.

He hit the ground hard, falling just short of the Imam, but the young officer, who had been ahead of him, squarely tackled the Imam, pushing him to the ground, the officer's back, replete with body armor, facing the enemy, shielding the Imam from the next shot.

Which did come.

It tore into the body armor, and from the look of shock on the young man's face, Vitale knew it had penetrated, the direct hit from a high powered weapon making quick work of the body armor never designed for such an impact.

Vitale scrambled toward the two, throwing his body over both of them as more shots rang out. The screens, mere cloth, were torn apart above his head, and the speakers were hit, the screeching sounds of the microphone hitting concrete, then rolling away, the button jammed in place, were cut off as the audio system was destroyed.

Vitale felt a fierce pain in his calf. He had been hit, he was sure of it. He raised his radio to his lips, huddling his body around that of the young officer and the Imam, neither of whom were moving at the moment.

"Do whatever it takes, but take out those shooters!" he yelled.

Gunfire from his men's positions replied, and he turned his head enough toward the gate to see what was happening. Dozens of bullets were now tearing at the ground, driving the crowd back, leaving two men exposed who continued to fire. The loud report of sniper rifles sliced through the din, and the two men dropped, causing the crowds to rush further back. Two more men rushed from the crowd, screaming a final prayer as they whipped their weapons back and forth, bullets spraying in all directions before they too were removed from the equation.

Then there was silence.

And pain.

Stairwell

Apostolic Palace, Vatican City

Acton gripped the case tightly in one hand, his weapon in the other, held out in front of him as he scanned the stairs ahead and behind them. Laura was on his six, covering him from behind, exactly like they had been trained. Two of the Bravo team were ahead of them, two were behind, with Reading and Chaney carrying Giasson.

They couldn't risk going up the steps too fast, otherwise they might run directly into a group of hostiles, but going too slow could leave them exposed from behind.

He exchanged a glance with Laura, who he could tell was thinking the same thing.

Let's move!

He heard two muffled shots from ahead, then a whispered, "Clear."

They continued slowly up the stairs, and Acton stepped around the bodies of two hostiles huddled against the railing, who had apparently hoped to surprise whoever was coming.

The Bravo team was quicker on the draw.

Another flight and they were at the floor with the passageway. They moved quicker now, the going easier with the stretcher, and they turned the corner toward the room at the end of the hall with the wardrobe that in this case would lead them to freedom rather than Narnia.

Something moved out of the corner of his eye.

Acton whipped around, raising his weapon, but before he could fire, he heard a shot from just behind him. The target dropped in a heap, and

Acton looked to see Laura's weapon raised and smoking. He breathed a sigh of relief, but Red slapped him on the back.

"Let's go, that's going to attract more of them."

Acton realized at that moment that Laura's shot, though probably lifesaving, wasn't silenced, or more accurately, muffled. And now anyone in the building would know they were there. They rushed down the hall, and Acton opened the door. He heard more muffled shots, along with other shots at full volume in reply. He yanked Laura into the room and Chaney and Reading turned through the doorway carrying Giasson.

Stucco and Casey entered, followed by Red and Spock, who continued to duck in and out of the room, exchanging fire with whoever was down the hall.

"We won't be able to hold this position for long," said Red.

Acton looked at Reading and Chaney. "You remember how it works?"

Both nodded.

Acton opened the doors. "Okay, get inside."

Reading and Chaney stepped inside, then Stucco and Acton lifted Giasson's limp form into the closet, followed by the stretcher. Acton slammed the door shut, hammering twice on the outside.

He heard the click of the hook, then some grunting, then the click again. "We're clear!" yelled a muffled voice.

Acton pointed at the window. "Laura, open the window, maybe they'll think we went out that way!" She nodded, rushing over to the window and throwing it open. Red stepped back into the room and pointed at Stucco and Casey. "Push that bed over here!"

The two men shouldered their weapons and grabbed hold of the bed, pushing it across the hardwood floor toward the door. Red and Spock stepped inside, shoving the door closed, then helped push the bed into position.

"That won't hold them long," said Laura.

"We just need a few seconds," said Red. He pointed at the closet. "Next three."

Acton opened it, helping Laura inside, then pointed at Stucco and Casey. "You two next, she knows how it works and where to go. I'll go out with them," he said, pointing at Red and Spock.

Thankfully the two men didn't argue, and both were in the closet with Laura within seconds. He closed the doors, and moments later heard the all clear.

He opened the doors. "Let's go, gentlemen." He climbed inside, with Spock and Red following. Acton closed the wardrobe doors just as they heard pounding on the door outside. He reached up, counting the hooks, then pushed the second hook from the left. The click sounded, and he pushed on the wall. He stepped through, followed by the others, just as the sound of the door outside splintering echoed through the stone passage. He pushed on the secret panel, closing it with a click, as he heard someone rattling on the handles of the wardrobe.

Everyone remained silent. They could hear the sounds of the doors releasing as the inner panel shut, then shouting in Italian and Arabic.

He heard Red whisper in his ear. "One of them just said they went out the window."

Acton didn't reply, already terrified that the hammering of his heart might give away their position. There was more shouting, some gunfire, then the sound of feet pounding on wood, then nothing.

"We're clear," said Red, still whispering.

Acton breathed a sigh of relief.

Flashlights flicked on, and Red slapped Acton on the back.

"Professor, you lead the way."

Acton recalled the last time he had led the way here, and wasn't too eager to comply.

But what are the chances they'll be here again?

Thinking back on his recent experiences, he wasn't sure he wanted to take that bet.

Main Floor

Apostolic Palace, Vatican City

Dawson looked up the staircase, resisting every fiber of his being from turning and assisting the rest of his team.

"What do we do?" asked Niner.

"We stay on mission."

Dawson activated his comm. "Bravo Two, Bravo One. Sit rep."

"Reached the room, beginning evac now, over."

"Do you need backup?"

"Negative. We're almost out, but a diversion from your end in sixty seconds will keep them from searching this room a little too closely, over."

"Confirmed. Diversion in sixty seconds. Out."

Dawson turned to Jimmy and pointed at the staircase. "Trip wire one flight up, then about six steps from the bottom."

Jimmy nodded, and rushed up the steps with Atlas. Dawson turned to one of the Swiss Guards. "Captain Denzler, wasn't it?" The man nodded. "Captain, what's the best way to get to the entrance to this Necropolis?"

"Out the way we came, then around the Sistine Chapel. That will lead us straight to the entrance. But we don't know how many of the rioters are there."

Jimmy and Atlas tore down the stairs, then set the second trip wire as Dawson led the team to the foot of the stairs. Jimmy rose, nodding.

"We're ready."

Dawson leaned into the stairs.

"Lieutenant, I think they went up the stairs!" he yelled, looking at Niner, pointing to the stairs winding below.

Niner grinned. "Negative, Sergeant, I think they went downstairs." He paused. "Follow me!"

Dawson then leaned in and sprayed a burst of gunfire at the wall, the least expensive thing he could find. Yelling from upstairs that began to get louder told him their diversion had worked. English voices, military, and gunfire. *Of course it was going to work.* Dawson then slapped the Captain on the back.

"Lead the way, Captain."

"Yes, sir."

Captain Denzler ran toward the exit they had just come through, followed by the rest of the team, and they soon found themselves traversing the same courtyard they had minutes before. This time, however, it was quiet.

An explosion from behind them caused them to all turn momentarily, then continue forward.

"Niner, just how big of a charge did you use?"

"Just half of what I had left."

"And the other half?"

There was another roaring explosion.

"Never mind." Dawson wondered how much damage had just been done to the ancient building. *Probably far less than the rioters have done.* They continued out of the courtyard, and were hugging a building to the left, which Dawson assumed was the Sistine Chapel. They rounded the building slowly, Niner and Jimmy now taking point, just in case they ran into any unwanted company.

Niner stopped, raising a fist. Dawson crept forward.

"Report."

"Six hostiles, at the end of this courtyard, I'm assuming standing at the entrance we need to get through."

Dawson motioned for Captain Denzler to join them.

"Are they in front of where we need to go?"

The Captain leaned forward.

"Yes."

Dawson frowned, and flipped down his night vision goggles. He took another look. "At least one of them is armed." *Damn.* He looked around. He'd prefer to have no witnesses to their entering the grottoes leading to the Necropolis below, but he couldn't see any way around it. Without killing them all.

Yells from behind them caused him to turn, looking at Atlas who was covering their six.

With hand signals, he indicated at least half a dozen hostiles were coming from the rear.

Shit!

He turned to the Captain. "Tell them to open the door in ten seconds."

The man nodded, raising his radio and relaying the order in a whisper.

Dawson charged forward, silently, his weapon raised, waiting for the first of those guarding the door to notice him. He could hear Niner and Jimmy on his flanks, only feet behind, the rest now running with him. He saw one of their jaws drop, and a finger point.

He squeezed the trigger, as did Niner and Jimmy, and within seconds all six were lifeless heaps. As they approached, Dawson heard gunfire from behind, but kept charging forward. The heavy security door protecting the entrance was slowly rising.

I hope that damned thing closes a lot faster than that.

He reached the entrance and climbed under, finding a regular door behind it, closed. He reached forward and turned the handle. It opened.

Thank God.

He stepped inside, then turned back, pulling the two Swiss Guards inside. Gunfire from his men's weapons continued, and they were answered by other types. This was definitely a firefight. Niner and Jimmy were laying down steady fire, most likely to let Atlas reach the door without having to look back.

Atlas's large frame suddenly appeared, and Dawson pulled him inside.

"Let's go!" yelled Dawson, and Niner and Jimmy stepped under the still rising door. More gunfire, this time exclusively from the enemy, sprayed at the doorway, and Dawson dove backward. "Captain, have them close the door!"

He heard the order go out over the radio, and suddenly the door dropped with a slam, the rattle of bullets uselessly bouncing off the thick metal surface indicating their mission secrecy had been compromised, but they were at least secure.

Dawson picked himself up off the floor, and turned to Captain Denzler. "Lead the way, Captain."

The man nodded, heading toward a staircase.

Dawson forced a deep breath out through his pursed lips slowly.

That was the easy part. Now for Mission Impossible.

Piazza Pio XII Square
Rome, Italy

DC Vitale rolled onto his back, his leg screaming in agony, as a contingent of officers, along with medics, rushed up to them. He reached down to grab his wound, and felt the wetness of blood as he tightened his grip.

"Sir, are you okay?" asked the first to arrive.

"Never mind me, check them out!" he winced.

He pushed himself away, gritting his teeth as he struggled not to cry out in pain. He knew the other two were worse off than him; he hadn't seen the young officer move yet, nor the Imam. The medics rolled the officer off the Imam, and he gasped.

"He's okay!" said one of the medics.

"No!" yelled Vitale. "He's been shot in the back, through the vest."

The medic rolled him back over and checked, then nodded. "He's been shot, through"—he paused and looked at his front—"and through." Examining the wounds with his gloved fingers, he looked at Vitale and smiled. "He'll be okay, it's a through and through, nothing major hit by the looks of it." They loaded him on a gurney, and pushed him inside a waiting ambulance within minutes.

The Imam though, was another story. A massive amount of blood stained his white robes, and Vitale, still gripping his leg, saw no signs of life, save for the fact the blood seemed to still pulse out of him, indicating a heartbeat. His view was blocked suddenly as a paramedic dropped in front of him.

"Where are you hit?"

"The leg." He moved his hand, and felt the paramedic go to work, cutting open his pants, then sock. A gurney was brought over, and he was lifted on to it.

"Wait!" he yelled. "What about the Imam?" He pushed aside the medic still blocking his view, and watched with a sinking heart as a sheet was lowered, covering his body.

"Sorry, sir, he didn't make it."

"What about my leg?"

"You've got a bullet in there, but judging from the damage, most likely a ricochet. We'll just patch you up and they can remove it at the hospital, and you'll probably be released within an hour or two."

Vitale pushed himself up. "If I'm not dying, then remove it here. I can't leave the scene."

"But, sir—"

Vitale pointed at his wound. "Fix it now, or I'm getting off this damned thing, and you can fix it later."

The man frowned, muttering something under his breath. "At least let me push you behind the ambulance, in case there's any more shooting."

Vitale nodded. "Good thinking."

He was pushed behind a nearby ambulance, then given a shot in the leg.

"What was that?"

"Tetanus," said the medic. He held up another needle. "This one's a local for the pain."

"But it doesn't hurt that much now."

"It will when I start digging for the bullet."

He felt the needle plunge into his calf before he had a chance to respond. A gentle warmness flowed through the area, numbing the pain. He lay back on the stretcher, looking around for someone to give him an update. Then he remembered his radio.

"This is Vitale. Report!"

"Barriers holding, crowd has dispersed further into the square on all sides."

"So no one is leaving anymore?"

"No, sir."

"Okay, have our sharpshooters keep an eye out for weapons. If they have clean shots, they can take them."

There was a pause.

"Do you need me to repeat that order?"

"N-no, sir, it's just that we've been ordered to hold our positions until our relief arrives, sir."

"Relief?" Vitale propped himself up on this elbow. "What the hell are you talking about?"

"We're to be replaced."

"By who?"

"The Army."

Vitale's chest tightened.

God help us all.

The Vault
Vatican City

Acton emerged from the stairwell, and turned to the left, directing his flashlight up. About fifty feet overhead his beam caught the bottom of the platform as it jerked its way down with its cargo, a stretcher bound Giasson, with Stucco and Casey at the controls, pulling in turns on the rope that lowered them a foot at a time.

Acton heard the others join him.

"Bloody hell, I think I'd rather have taken my chances in the stairwell," muttered Reading.

"He would have bled out," said Chaney, who Acton remembered had trained to be a doctor before deciding to become a cop. "His wound is only being held together by bandages."

"Do you think he'll make it?"

Chaney grunted. "I don't know. He's lost a lot of blood, and really should have been sedated and forced to lay down, with an IV drip, immediately."

"In ten minutes tops we're outside."

Acton looked up, urging the platform to go faster. It was only feet away, and each pull of the rope brought it that much closer, but it felt like an eternity.

Finally it hit the floor with a puff of dust and a clatter that echoed through the massive chamber.

Red pointed at Reading and Chaney with his flashlight. "You two take the Inspector General. Professors, you lead the way, we'll cover the rear."

Nobody said anything, they just carried out the orders. Reading and Chaney picked up the stretcher with Giasson, placing their flashlights beside either shoulder, providing Chaney an illuminated view of Reading's ass, and Reading the occasional hint of something ahead.

Acton smiled with a shake of his head, then took point with Laura at his side, both with flashlight and weapon extended in front of them. Within minutes they were clear of the Vault, and into the storm drain. Another eternity later, they approached the opening Atlas had knocked in earlier. They climbed through, then stood aside as the stretcher cleared, along with the rest of the team. Stucco and Casey scrambled up and out of the storm sewer.

Reading and Chaney pushed Giasson up the ladder, still on the stretcher, pushing on his feet to keep him from sliding, with Stucco reaching down and holding the moaning Giasson under his good shoulder. With a grunt from Reading, the stretcher cleared the ladder, and disappeared. The rest climbed the ladder with Red bringing up the rear.

Acton breathed a sigh of relief and looked at Laura.

"You were expecting to run into them again, weren't you?"

He nodded. "And you weren't"

She shook her head slightly. "I was convinced."

Red took one last look down the hole they had just exited, then at the team. "Okay, we'll go first, give the all clear, then you guys"—he pointed at Reading and Chaney—"then the professors."

He stepped through the opening in the wall from the construction with the rest of the Bravo team following. A whispered, "All clear!" was heard, and Acton motioned to Reading.

"Let's go!"

Reading climbed through the opening, followed by Chaney holding the other end of the stretcher, then Laura stepped through with Acton bringing up the rear.

"Fermati!"

Acton raised his hands. They were surrounded by police. He looked to see what Red and his team were doing, but they were nowhere to be found. *Where the hell'd they go?*

But he realized they weren't needed. This wasn't the enemy, these were the good guys. These were the guys they would have been looking for right now if they weren't already found. And an armed team of American special ops soldiers on Italian soil wasn't something that anybody wanted discovered.

He looked across the street where they had rallied earlier, and saw a face peeking out from the corner. It was Red. He gave a thumbs up, then disappeared. Acton smiled. *Mission accomplished, Sergeant.*

Reading was already lowering his gun to the ground, and calmly speaking. "Now, I'm just going to get my identification," he was saying. The officers continued to train their weapons on him, but Reading continued with his slow, deliberate motion. He unbuckled the body armor, and gently lowered it to the ground, then reached into his shirt pocket to retrieve his ID.

"Now here it is, I'm Agent Reading from INTERPOL. Here's my ID." Nobody reacted. "Is someone going to bloody look at it?"

Giasson moaned, then said something in Italian. One of the officers snapped his heels, and got on his radio as the others lowered their weapons. A hurried conversation in Italian was held, then a moment later an ambulance tore around the corner, spilling a gurney and two medics out as it arrived. Within minutes Giasson was in the back of the ambulance, being rushed to a hospital, leaving Acton, Laura, Reading and Chaney standing there, unsure of what to do.

The officer with the radio received additional instructions, then in broken English, said, "Follow me, please."

They climbed into a nearby squad car, two officers in the front, with Acton squeezed against the side, Laura in his lap, Chaney, shoulders rolled forward in the center, and Reading, knees in his face, tucked behind the passenger seat of the impossibly tiny car.

"Rapido, please," said Reading.

The officer they had been "dealing" with looked back and grinned. "Not long." They raced forward along the northern wall, then the car jerked to the right, along the front of the walled city, and moments later they passed the northern colonnade of Saint Peter's Square. As they rounded the massive structure, they skidded to a halt behind two flatbed trucks, and the doors were thrown open.

Everyone climbed out, with far too much grunting and moaning for the action heroes Acton felt like they were portraying, and they were led to a man lying on a gurney, his leg, by all appearances, being operated on in the middle of the piazza in front of Saint Peter's Square.

"Agent Reading, Detective Inspector Chaney," said the man on the gurney. "Forgive me if I don't get up to greet you." He laughed, then winced.

"Keep still!" yelled the medic who was in mid-stitch.

"Professors Palmer and Acton, this is Deputy Commissioner Vitale." Reading looked at the pale man. "Are you going to be okay?" asked Reading.

The medic raised his head. "This stubborn ass won't let me take him to the hospital." He shook the curved needle at Vitale, each shake yanking at the string, causing Vitale to pale a little bit more with each pull. "If you die from infection later, don't be blaming me."

"Just get on with it, dammit!"

The medic frowned, then turned his attention back to his sewing job.

"I understand you were inside?"

Reading nodded. "Retrieving this," he said, pointing at the case Acton still gripped tightly.

"What is it?"

"It's the scroll that caused all of this," said Laura, swinging her arms at the massive police operation.

"And what will you do with it now?"

"We're taking it to His Holiness," said Acton. "He's arranging a handover to Muslim authorities."

Vitale nodded. He motioned to the cops who had brought them here, saying something in Italian. Vitale turned back to Reading. "They will take you to the summer residence."

"In two cars," said Reading, holding up two fingers at the officers. They both smiled and laughed, then one of them trotted off to commandeer another vehicle.

Vitale reached over and grabbed Acton by the sleeve. He motioned with his eyes at the silver case.

"Get that damned thing out of my country."

Acton nodded.

"You can count on it."

Saint Peter's Basilica Façade
Vatican City

Hassan's heart pounded hard against his ribcage as he watched the crowds, screaming in fear, rush toward his vantage point at the front of the basilica. His plan had worked. The annoying appeal, repeating over and over, was gone. And the crowds, fleeing the return fire from the police, would never return to the gates. Unless he told them.

And that was not about to happen.

He raised his hands, stepping out of the shadows, as the crowd approached. He had no illusions that they were stopping out of respect for him, but more out of respect for the weapon he held in his hand.

The crowd stopped, and quieted down.

"My brothers! You have seen their treachery! You have heard their lies!" He pulled out his cellphone and held it up. "I have just heard what the infidels are doing! They are arresting our people as soon as they are out of sight. They are *not* letting them go as they would have us believe."

Angry mutterings began to permeate the crowd.

"Return to the gates, show them your courage, show them the power of Allah when it fills your heart, but don't trust the liar, for he cares not for you, but only for his craven idol"—he pointed at the church behind him—"built not to honor God, but to honor a man!"

He raised his fist in the air.

"Allahu Akbar!"

The crowd roared it in return.

"Now return to the gates, and show them the power of Islam!"

The crowd turned, and with a roar, rushed the gates again.

So easily manipulated.

Hassan heard a yelp of surprise from inside, then the pounding of sandals on marble.

"Hassan!"

It was Ziti, and he was excited.

Hassan's heart skipped a few beats as he realized there was only one thing that could have Ziti so excited. He turned with a smile, and was greeted with a grinning old man.

"Are we through?"

"We're through!"

Hassan ran inside, leaving Ziti skipping behind him, the old man giddy with excitement. Skidding to a halt at the edge of the crater, he peered over the edge, and into the center, where two men stood, pickaxes at their side, looking down a small, dark hole, maybe six inches across.

"Are we through?"

The men looked up and nodded, smiles on their faces at having been the ones to accomplish a goal they knew nothing of.

"Why have you stopped? Keep going, we need a hole big enough for a man!"

The men stepped back and began to swing in earnest, their pick axes slamming noisily against the rock, over and over, the rhythm intoxicating. *Any minute now!* Hassan sat on the edge of the crater, eagerly staring at the ever growing hole. It appeared to be a foot across now. A mighty swing from one of the men slipped slightly, and the pick axe disappeared inside the hole.

But it must have been a lucky blow, catching the underneath just right, for the entire section suddenly crumbled, and both men fell into the newly enlarged hole, and out of sight, with desperate pleas. A cloud of dust rolled from the hole, and Hassan held his shirt over his mouth and nose for several minutes as they waited for the dust to clear.

"Are you okay?" he called into the crater.

There was no answer.

Not even the sound of someone crying out.

Which wasn't right.

Unless.

Could they be dead?

He climbed gingerly deeper into the crater, and peered over the edge. Below, there was a pile of rubble, and the two men lay at the foot of it, unmoving, one, his head twisted at an unnatural angle, the other, his head out of sight.

He frowned. *Unfortunate, but they are in Jannah now, martyrs for the cause.* He wondered how he would earn his way into paradise. Would it be at the barrel of a gun, or by accident, like these two?

He prayed it was glorious, befitting a warrior of Allah.

"Rope!" he ordered, and a bundle was quickly tossed down. He wrapped it around his waist, then began to lower himself into the hole, several men holding the other end. Once his feet were clear and dangling underneath, he pushed himself away from the edge. "Keep going!" he called, and more slack was provided. Within seconds he was at the bottom, untying himself, and stepping down the rubble.

"Don't bother tying off, just come down!" he called, and those that remained of his team lowered themselves. Once inside, he surveyed their surroundings, orientating himself with where they were. He pointed. "The stairs to the Necropolis are over here."

Ziti looked at him. "I thought *this* was the Necropolis?" he said, pointing at the ground they stood on.

"No, these are the grottoes. The Necropolis is underneath."

Hassan walked about ten paces, then turned a corner, finding the narrow, steep stairs exactly where he expected them. He hurried down the steps, and turned the corner, adrenaline fueling him as his plan, less than two days in the making, was about to succeed. He paused for the others to catch up, then was about to continue forward when he heard something.

They weren't alone.

Castel Gandolfo, Papal Summer Residence
Outside Rome, Italy

Acton and Laura climbed out of the back of the police car as the second car occupied by Reading and Chaney pulled up behind them. Father Morris hurried down the steps to meet them.

"Come quickly, something is happening," he said with a quick bow. They followed him up the stairs and through a series of hallways, then into a large conference room. At the head of the table was His Holiness himself, who nodded at them, acknowledging their arrival with a smile, then he turned his head, his attention returning to the other end of the table.

Acton looked and saw three camera views. One was of the security headquarters he had come to know so well, and the other two appeared to be night vision helmet cam feeds.

He took a seat, the case still in his hand, unable to tear his eyes away from the screen.

"Is that the Necropolis?"

"Yes," whispered Father Morris, who sat to his left, Laura to his right.

One of the camera angles panned to the left, and Acton caught a glimpse of Dawson and Niner.

"Status?"

The voice wasn't from the room. It must have been somebody at security HQ.

"Unknown number of hostiles descending stairs, maintain communications silence from this point forward," whispered the voice. Acton could have sworn it was Dawson, and he gave Laura a quick look, who mouthed the same thought. He shrugged his shoulders, and turned back to the display.

The two views changed as the Swiss Guards providing it shifted, taking up positions behind the Bravo Team members lining both sides of the narrow passage, the only cover the openings leading to the various tombs located two levels below the massive basilica. There was a noise and Dawson's head spun around as he glared at the camera, even the grainy green image unable to hide his annoyance.

The flash of gunfire, followed by the static-laden sound of bullets ricocheting off the ancient walls, caused the entire room to gasp. Acton bit on his knuckle, as he thought of the history that was being destroyed.

Then he thought of the men who had become his friends.

And realized he couldn't see any of them.

Necropolis, Underneath Saint Peter's Basilica
Vatican City

Dawson hugged the wall of the tiny area they were crammed into, no more than a few feet wide at places, with occasional openings for the dozen or so tombs preserved here, but little else. *Like fish in a barrel.* The unmistakable sound, at least to Dawson, of the butt of a weapon scraping against stone, caused him to whip around, and silently chastise the Swiss Guard who had broken their cover.

But it was too late.

Immediately the confined area filled with the sound of gunfire and bullets. He raised his weapon, and let off several controlled bursts, as did the rest of his team. Within seconds the opposing fire stopped, their muzzle flashes disappearing, and Dawson raised his fist.

"Cease fire," he whispered.

Silence.

He heard a moan, then the scrape of a boot on stone. Footfalls on steps.

"Advance."

Dawson and Niner led the way, Jimmy and Atlas behind, as they quickly pushed through the tight passageway, toward the stairs. They stepped over several bodies before finding the tight, steep stairs leading to the grottoes above.

This is a sardine can.

They could just hold this position, keeping anyone else from coming down. But without knowing how well armed they were, he also knew that a single grenade, tossed down the steps, could end it for them all.

Shit!

He took a step up, looking back at the others.

"Spread out, one explosive and you're all gone."

Niner and Jimmy pushed the others back, and Dawson continued to climb, one step at a time, as quietly as he could, his weapon poking around the corner at the top.

Shots rang out and he jerked his head back.

"Status?"

What part of radio silence don't these guys understand?

He heard Niner's muffled voice over the comm.

"Radio silence!"

Another burst of gunfire, and Dawson knew his good karma was quickly being eaten up as the ricochets continued to miss, and "Allahu Akbar" repeated itself over and over with each burst of the weapon.

Time to end this.

He waited for the next burst to finish, then thrust himself around the bend, firing his weapon at the first thing that moved. The sustained burst continued until he had emptied his clip. He ejected it and seconds later already had a fresh clip loaded and ready.

But there was no point.

Through the night vision haze he could see his target was down, gasping for air as a chest wound sapped his strength. Dawson rushed forward, kicking the man's weapon away, then quickly scanned the area to make sure they were alone.

The man whispered, and Dawson leaned forward.

"What?"

"American?"

"Yes."

"What are *you* doing here?"

"Keeping the faith."

"What?"

Dawson's humor was apparently lost.

"You're dying. Is there anything you want me to tell your family?"

The man reached up and grabbed Dawson by the top of his body armor.

"Tell them I died a martyr. Tell them I died with honor. And tell them I will see them in Jannah."

Dawson was about to tell him there was no honor in what he had done, but was cut off by the death rattle of the man as the last gasps of life left him.

Then there was silence.

Dawson sat back on his haunches, then activated his comm.

"All clear."

Ataturk Airport
Istanbul, Turkey

"What the bloody hell are we waiting for?" boomed Reading. They had been sitting on the tarmac in Istanbul for over an hour. Fortunately Laura's G-V was air conditioned, whether in the air or not, and the thickly cushioned leather seats were comfortable with an obscene amount of legroom. With the size of the Vatican delegation, much of it hastily put together security, they had decided to take their own plane, arriving within minutes of the Vatican's, but according to the pilot, they didn't have approval to approach the terminal yet.

Chaney, who appeared to be having some fun with his old partner, pointed at another private jet. "Isn't that the Pope's plane?"

"You know bloody well it is."

"Well, it's moving."

"Huh?" Reading pressed his face against the window. "Brilliant! We're stuck here, and they're already leaving!"

Acton smiled at Laura, giving her hand a squeeze, and whispering, "If we don't get off this plane soon, I think Hugh's going to have a stroke."

She giggled and Reading looked at her.

"Don't make me arrest you, young lady."

"Oooh, young lady. I like that."

Reading blushed, and shook his head as he pushed himself deeper into the chair.

The overhead speakers crackled. "We've been cleared, folks. Just another couple of minutes."

Sighs of relief filled the cabin as the plane began to at last move, and true to his promise, the pilot had them in front of the charter terminal with the stairs lowered minutes later. As Acton stepped into the morning sunlight, several army vehicles raced around a corner toward them.

Acton held his hand behind him, stopping Laura from descending.

"What is it, Dear?"

"Possible trouble." He looked over his shoulder. "Hugh, want to bring that fancy ID of yours?"

"What is it?" his face replaced Laura's. "What the devil?"

Three vehicles screeched to a halt in front of the steps, two soldiers jumping out of each, then lining up in front of the plane. One of them, more ornately decorated than the others, was clearly in charge. He stepped forward and delivered a crisp salute.

"Captain Edmon Aslan of the Turkish Armed Forces. I am here to escort you to the press conference."

Acton let out a silent sigh of relief, and smiled broadly as he descended the few steps to the ground. He offered his hand and the man shook it firmly. Laura was next, and the man placed kisses on both her cheeks.

"Welcome to our country!" he said, clearly pleased with the situation. Apparently emboldened, he leaned in to give Reading a traditional kiss on each cheek, but Reading, long skilled in the art of avoiding this practice he found distasteful, extended both hands, his left hand planting itself firmly, but unobtrusively on the Captain's shoulder, and the other grasping the man's hand in a firm handshake. Kisses avoided, nobody offended.

"Thank you for providing us an escort, Captain," said Reading. "I assume His Holiness and party are already on their way?"

"Yes, under as much security as we can provide."

"Expecting trouble?"

The captain smiled. "I have been briefed, sir. And with what is being exchanged today, we would be foolish not to expect trouble."

Reading nodded in agreement, exchanging a quick glance with Acton.

"Let's just get there and get this over with," said Acton.

"Agreed."

Captain Aslan motioned to the rear of his vehicle, and Acton and Laura climbed in, while Reading and Chaney climbed in the rear of a second vehicle. Moments later they had left the airport, and were racing along a highway that had yet to see its morning rush hour begin, when a burst of smoke ahead of them caused their driver to slam on his brakes.

Dust and brake lights were all that could be seen. Acton's heart slammed in his chest as he put a protective arm in front of Laura, suddenly feeling very exposed in these Jeep style vehicles, the open top clearly not meant for security.

I hope they didn't put the Pope in one of these!

Captain Aslan jumped up and waved at the third vehicle to pull up beside them. He yelled something in Turkish and the vehicle sped ahead, into the now settling dust. A moment later a voice crackled over the radio, then what sounded like laughing. Aslan looked at his driver and burst out in laughter.

"What is it?"

The captain, still chuckling, sat back down in his seat and motioned for the driver to move on.

"It is nothing, just a broken down car that lost control and hit a lamppost."

They slowly moved forward, and a gust of wind cleared away the remaining dust, leaving a clear view of a car sitting on the side of the road, its front tie rod collapsed, the driver standing beside the car, slamming his fists into the roof over and over, yelling something.

"What's he saying?" asked Laura.

The Captain laughed. "He's saying, "I hate you, I hate you, I hate you!"

Acton heard a yell from behind them. He turned to look, and saw Reading standing in the back of his vehicle, pointing at the car, yelling something.

Acton cupped a hand around his ear.

"What?"

"It's a Jaguar!"

Acton burst out laughing and gave a thumbs up.

"What did he say?"

"He said it's a Jaguar."

Laura grinned, her head shaking. "Of course it is."

The Captain yelled something at the driver as they pulled past. This prompted the man to shake a fist at the Captain who roared with laughter, along with their own driver. He turned back to his guests. "I told him to replace it with something reliable, like a mule!"

They all laughed at the Captain's joke, and Acton began to feel slightly at ease for the first time since they had identified what the artifact was. He looked at Laura who had a beaming smile on her face, her eyes closed, as she enjoyed the wind in her hair.

Probably reminds her of driving her Porsche.

He leaned in and kissed her lips. She let out a little yelp of surprise, then began to return the kiss when she suddenly stopped and pushed him away.

"James, darling, we're in Turkey!"

Acton pulled back slightly. "So?"

"So." She dragged it out, motioning at the front seat with her eyes.

Acton winked and gave her a quick kiss, then sat back in his seat. They continued in silence, both of them with their eyes closed now, holding hands, simply enjoying the moment.

Acton began to think of the press conference. The plan was to have as many reporters there as possible. This meant it wasn't a secret handover. The thinking was that if it wasn't public, done by the Pope himself, too many might not believe it was the same scroll being handed over.

And it was supposed to be a quick handover. Short speeches, the opening of the case, some images of the unfurled scroll enlarged, then the handover. The Pope and entourage were then to return immediately to the airport, and return to Rome. If everything worked out according to plan, they should be here no more than ninety minutes.

Acton frowned. *Nothing ever goes according to plan.*

"We're here!" announced Captain Aslan.

Acton opened his eyes and gasped. The rear of the famed Sultan Ahmed Mosque, more popularly known as the Blue Mosque due to the blue tiles that adorned the interior, lay before them. The six minarets reached into the sky, controversial when first built four hundred years ago, as the common practice was four. It wasn't until a fifth minaret was added to the Grand Mosque in Mecca that the locals at last accepted it.

They pulled inside a parking lot, guarded by about a dozen Turkish police, the small force dismaying Acton. He leaned forward. "Captain, are you sure you have enough security?"

"This is all we could spare. We have had our own problems since the scroll was discovered, and our police are dealing with a massive riot. Not to worry, there is additional at the front."

Acton sat back in his seat as their Jeep pulled to a stop. He turned to Laura. "I don't have a good feeling about this."

She looked about for a moment then nodded. "I agree." She leaned in. "I wish I had my weapon."

Acton mouthed, "Me too," then climbed out of the Jeep. Reading and Chaney immediately joined them.

"This security is entirely inadequate," muttered Reading.

Acton nodded. "But what can we do?"

"Keep our eyes open." He pointed behind them. "Look, they haven't even closed the street." He stepped toward the Captain. "Captain, excuse me, but what can we do about closing this street? This poses a huge security risk."

The man shrugged his shoulders. "Nothing. Permits are necessary, and there was no time." He motioned at the security that was in place. "Even this was difficult to pull together, and is only because it is on private property." He leaned in. "Even in Turkey, people have rights."

Reading put a smile on his face. "Captain, I never meant to imply otherwise. I think you'd make a worthy addition to the European Union—"

"As do I."

"—but do you think you'll ever get in if the Pope is killed on your soil because you didn't take the most basic of precautions?"

Captain Aslan turned red, but nodded, then turned on his heel, yelling orders, and soon several vehicles roared from the parking area and to either end of the street. Reading turned and joined Acton, Laura and Chaney.

"That's a little better. Let's check out what the press conference security is like."

They rounded a set of trees and walked along a pathway, their current position actually behind the mosque. As they began along the northern side, Acton turned as he heard the distinctive sound of several motorcycle engines revving extremely high.

Then he gasped.

The police cordon had just begun, and as the rest of the group turned to watch, a tow truck with ramp raced up, slamming into the first vehicle, and grinding to a halt as the ramp extended to touch the road, apparently disengaged in the crash. The vehicle was quickly surrounded by security personnel, weapons pointed, but just as Acton was about to breathe a sigh of relief, the high pitched whine of the motorcycle engines spiked as a half dozen came into sight, each with a driver and passenger on the back.

Without hesitation they raced up the ramp and jumped over the tow truck and the army vehicle blocking the road. Acton counted six, and instinctively reached for his weapon, which wasn't there.

He and Reading looked at each other.

"The Pope!" they echoed.

Acton looked along the length of the massive mosque, and saw the Pope's entourage just turn the corner at the far end. They all began to sprint along the pathway as gunfire broke out behind them. Acton looked back and saw one of the motorcycles lying on the ground, but the surprised contingent of security personnel, already small due to lack of planning, were quickly overwhelmed.

Two motorcycles broke off and raced toward the same path that Acton was now on. "They're coming this way!" he yelled, causing all heads to turn and look. There was still a hundred feet to go to reach the end, and the two motorcycles were screaming toward them.

And nobody had a weapon.

Acton heard an engine gun and he looked behind to see the lead motorcycle screaming toward them, the passenger raising a weapon and aiming it directly at them.

"Look out!" The muzzle flashed as Acton dove toward Laura and his friends, both arms extended wide. He felt the impact as his chest hit Laura just below the shoulder blades, his left arm catching the rest of her as he pulled her in toward him so she wouldn't slip away. His other arm managed to catch Reading, but his bulk merely caused Acton to twist around. As he spun in the air, Laura still secure in his left arm, he could see the faces of Reading and Chaney as he sailed past them.

The younger Chaney reached out and grabbed Reading by the shoulder, yanking him off the path as the bullets tore open the stonework. Laura and Acton hit the ground, hard, and Acton rolled on top of her, covering her torso and head as best he could, desperately wishing he had the body armor on he had worn in the Vatican. He heard a thud beside them as Chaney and Reading hit the ground, then the distinct sound of bullets blasting over their heads as the whine of the motorcycles grew louder.

Acton heard the motorcycles downshift, and the whine of the engines easing off. "They're slowing down!" yelled Acton.

"That means only one thing!" said Reading.

Acton didn't need to hear it. He pushed himself up and whipped around, charging at the lead motorcycle. This appeared to catch the driver off guard as the front wheel wobbled slightly as he decided what to do. This caused his passenger to reach down and grab the driver's waist with both hands, leaving his weapon dangling to the side.

Acton rushed forward, closing the gap quickly, as the momentum of the motorcycle and his own legs pumped them closer and closer. The driver made a decision, gunning the engine and racing toward Acton, forcing his passenger to hold on even tighter.

Acton swung his right arm behind him then, with all the strength he could gather, whipped it forward just as the motorcycle reached him. His forearm caught the driver square in the chest, knocking him back into his passenger. Acton was jerked back, feeling the distinct pain of his shoulder dislocating, but as he flipped around and landed on his side, he saw the bike lose control and smash into the side of the mosque, spilling its two occupants onto the ground.

The second bike's engine screamed in protest, and raced past the scene, gunfire spraying wildly as the passenger fought for balance. Acton ducked, then jumped to his feet, sprinting toward the downed riders. The passenger was reaching for his weapon when Acton arrived. Stepping on the man's hand, he reached down with his left and pulled the gun from around the man's neck then raised it, aiming at the other motorcycle.

He squeezed the trigger, and the bullets went nowhere near where he wanted, this his wrong arm. Laura was now on her feet, running toward him, her arms extended in front of her. He tossed her the weapon and she caught it clean, spinning and opening fire. The passenger, who had twisted when they heard Acton's gunfire, jerked several times, then slumped backward, slightly exposing the driver. Laura continued to fire, lowering her aim, taking out the rear tire.

The motorcycle careened out of control.

"Don't be doing anything brave now."

Acton spun. It was Reading, standing over the driver, his foot on the man's weapon, a weapon Acton had failed to notice earlier.

"Is that all of them?" asked Chaney.

Acton shook his head then winced. "No, there were six motorcycles." As if to confirm the answer, the whine of the other motorcycles could be heard in the distance.

"They must be on the other side of the mosque," said Laura. She looked at his right shoulder. "Are you okay?"

Acton leaned against the mosque. "I think it's dislocated."

Chaney motioned for him to stand up. "Here, I'll fix that for you."

Acton didn't relish the idea, but knew it was the right thing to do. Chaney reached out and gently felt Acton's shoulder, but despite the care, it roared in pain as the endorphins shielding him from the shock wore off.

"Anterior dislocation, good, I can fix that here." Without looking at Acton, he asked, "First time?"

"Yup," wheezed Acton.

"Okay, lie down, arm to your side," directed Chaney.

Acton, gripping his shoulder, dropped to the ground, then lay down. Chaney bent Acton's elbow to a ninety degree angle, then rotated it over Acton's chest. He placed his hand on Acton's elbow, keeping the upper half of Acton's right arm stationary, then with his free hand, Chaney gently rotated Acton's lower arm away from his chest. A moment later Acton felt a slight jerk and an immediate wave of relief rushed through his body as the pain dropped dramatically. Chaney gently manipulated the arm several more times, then stood up, pulling Acton to his feet with the other arm.

"That'll be tender for a while, and when you get back home, have it scanned right away, just in case something else is wrong with it."

Acton nodded, gingerly rotating the arm, afraid it might pop out again.

Several screams reminded everyone of the situation.

"We need to get to the Pope!" yelled Acton. He pointed at the two on the motorcycle he had taken out. "Search them for weapons and ammo, then tie them up."

Reading and Chaney immediately went to work, expertly searching the prisoners as Acton turned and raced toward the other motorcycle with Laura. When they reached them it was clear both were dead. Acton reached down and grabbed the passenger's weapon, an AK-47, and two clips that had spilled onto the ground in the crash.

Gunfire from the other side of the wall sent his heart racing as he reloaded the weapon, all the while running toward the end of the massive wall. When Acton rounded the corner he nearly ground to a halt in shock. Three motorcycles had rounded the other side only moments before, and a steady stream of gunfire was directed from all three passengers at the limited security, the gathered journalists, and at the small stage that had been hastily erected.

A stage that had the Pope and the Imam standing on it, behind a small dais. As Acton ran toward the stage, he raised his weapon to fire at the terrorists attacking the event, but couldn't get a clean shot; there were simply too many people in the way. He pointed with his arm at what he assumed would be the escape route—the same way the attackers had come in—as most of the people present were rushing toward Acton's position, and would soon be blocking off any escape from that side.

"Cover their escape!" he yelled, looking back at Reading.

Reading nodded and raced across the courtyard in front of the massive mosque, followed by Chaney. Acton fought his way through the crowd, his eyes on the stage the entire time. He watched in horror as two of the Pope's security guards jumped in front of the bullets, mowed down in the prime of life, performing a task it was their honor to perform.

Then Acton came to a halt. "No!" he screamed, as he heard Laura cry out beside him. The first motorcycle had reached the stage and come to a halt. The passenger raised his weapon and opened fire. The Pope twisted his body, raising his robed arms out, forming a blind that hid the Imam. Now between the gunmen and the Imam, he stepped toward the elderly man and covered him with his body as several bullets slammed into his back, causing him to jerk and spasm in such a horrifically pathetic way, that Acton felt bile fill his mouth and tears burn his eyes.

Then he had a clear shot.

He raised his weapon and opened fire, as did Laura.

The bike was hit first, causing its two riders to turn to the new threat, then the shots found their marks, taking out both riders. The second and third motorcycles skidded to halts as the now cleared square provided them with little protection, most people either dead, lying on the ground in fear, or escaped by now.

Another burst of gunfire from their right. Acton took a quick glance and saw Reading and Chaney advancing along the wall, as Acton and Laura rushed forward, pouring bullets on their targets. It only took seconds, but it felt like an eternity to Acton, before the terrorists were neutralized, but Acton knew their mission had already been accomplished.

The Pope had been shot.

And there was no way he was going to survive, not with what Acton had seen. He jumped up on the platform, as did Chaney, as Reading and Laura covered them, making sure the terrorists were dead.

Acton dropped to his knees beside the body of the Pope, who lay atop the Imam. Three bullet holes were visible in the back of his robe, red circles highlighting their successful penetration of this man's armor of faith, an armor that had failed to protect him today, but had so many times just so few months ago.

Acton and Chaney rolled the old man off of the Imam. The pontiff gasped in pain. Suddenly a microphone was shoved in the old man's face, and Acton looked over his shoulder to see the press corps rushing back toward the stage, swarming it with their cameras and microphones.

The old man looked up at the camera pointed in his ashen face, and whispered, "My children, do not retaliate. Peace must once again reign." Reading and Laura, along with several of the surviving security, jumped on the stage and began to clear the press off. Acton paid no attention, focusing on the Pontiff he had been through so much with, when the old man reached up and pulled Acton closer to him. "Retrieve the skull. You know where it is."

Acton nodded with a smile. "Don't worry about it, Your Holiness. You're going to be okay."

The old man patted Acton's cheek. "Thank you, my child, but I feel God's warmth already enveloping me like a blanket. It is my time, I just pray that my death doesn't lead to more violence. Enough have died on my watch, that even if I prayed an eternity for forgiveness, I'm afraid it would not be enough."

He winced.

"Take it easy, sir."

The Imam, now on his knees, shuffled to the Pontiff's side.

"Do not worry my friend. We have the case, and your sacrifice will not go unnoticed." He rested a hand on the old man's forehead, and began to say a prayer in Turkish, the only word Acton understanding was the repeated use of Allah. He wondered for a moment if it was appropriate, but when he looked down at the Pontiff, he had a smile on his face, his eyes closed, and a look of serenity, as if he were one with his God, or his Allah, and prepared for whatever fate He had in store for him.

A last gasp, more of a sigh, then nothing. Chaney checked the old man's pulse. "Weak, but alive." He pointed at several of the surviving security entourage. "Get him inside." Acton bowed his head, and said a silent prayer, then he heard the squelch of a microphone, and opened his eyes. The Imam was standing in front of the dais. Acton looked over his shoulder and saw all the cameras and microphones aimed at the stage, as the old man cleared his throat.

Acton felt a hand on his shoulder. It was Laura. Her face was streaked with tears, and she fell onto his shoulder, hugging him as she sobbed. Acton himself felt his chest heave a few times, as the stress of the past days slowly released, and the frustration of it all, the futility of it all, was realized. After all they had been through, the Pope is gunned down for no reason other than hate. It was sickening.

The world would be better off without Islam.

He hated to think it, but it was a conclusion he was coming to. Were Christians perfect? By no means, Edison Cole and New Slate had proven that, but were they out actively trying to kill Muslims? No.

He sighed, and found himself listening to the Imam saying something impassioned in Arabic, then he paused.

"And now I will repeat what I have said in English. This man"—Acton looked up to see the Imam pointing at the Pontiff as he was carried inside the mosque, Chaney and Reading accompanying him—"represents the Catholic Church. He could have jumped off the platform and saved himself, leaving me to die, but instead, he threw himself in front of the bullets, allowing me to live another day.

"Would I have done the same for him? I would like to think yes, if the roles were reversed, perhaps I would have. But can I say it for certain? No. And what is that reason? Why am I uncertain? Is it because I am a Muslim, and he is a Christian? I am ashamed to say it may just be so. Is it because I am inferior, because I am a Muslim? Absolutely not, I don't believe that for an instant.

"Or is it because I feel I am superior, because I am a Muslim? That, I can't say with all honesty that I don't believe. For it is the way I was raised. It is the way I have raised my children, and it is the way I have taught many children. Islam is the way. Islam is the future. Islam is the one and true faith. All religions probably teach similar things, but there is a difference. While other religions may preach similar things, they don't preach intolerance as a principal. The Catholic Church was once a horribly intolerant, violent organization. But they had their enlightenment, their reformation, and now are peaceful.

"We Muslims are accused of being stuck in the dark ages. We were once leaders in the world, spreading knowledge and science. But now look at us. We are the poorest of the poor. And rather than try to improve ourselves, too many of us prefer to bring everyone else down to our level."

The old man took a deep breath and sighed as tears rolled down his cheeks.

"It breaks my heart to say what I am about to say." He squeezed his eyes shut and gasped out the words. "Too many of us hate." He gripped the edge of the dais, his knuckles turning white. "Too many of us hate. We hate the infidel. We hate what they represent. We hate their way of life. And we want to destroy that way of life.

"I could ask why, but I know why. Because too many of us are taught this way of thinking from the moment we are born. But the more important question to ask, is how? How will those who hate so much ever achieve their goals? There are over two billion Christians in the world. There are one and a half billion Muslims. On top of that, there are three and a half billion others on this planet that don't believe in Islam, and never will. What do you propose? To kill five and a half billion people, just to fulfill Allah's will? How could it possibly be Allah's will to kill five and a half billion people?"

He lowered his voice, staring out at the gathering crowd.

"Over the past days we have witnessed atrocities on both sides, around the world. These atrocities continue as I speak. They have occurred here"—he gestured toward the stage—"and they must stop. We have seen what hate and intolerance, on both sides, can accomplish—more hate, and more intolerance."

His voice began to rise, and Acton stood, with Laura, watching the Imam speak, Acton feeling the hair begin to stand on end as goose bumps spread across his body.

"The era of hate, the era of intolerance must come to an end. It is time for Islam's reformation. If Islam wishes to be great, it must learn to live within the world it finds itself. If Islam is indeed a religion of peace, then it must prove it by laying down its arms, and living in peace with those who don't believe as we do.

"It is time for the hate, the fear, the intolerance, all of it, to end. And to that end, I call on all my brothers and sisters around the world, and especially to those within the walls of Vatican City, to lay down their arms, and go home. Fill your heart with the love and joy that Allah demands, and go home. Clear your heads and your hearts of the hatred of the past, then go to your Mosque, and fill your empty cups with the word of Allah, the word of God, for they are one. We all believe in the same God, the same loving Allah who loves us all. And should your teacher, your Imam, continue to teach you to hate those who are different, those who don't believe, then rise up, and denounce him. Shake your fist in the air at *him*, not at your neighbor.

"It is time for those who hate, and those who preach it, to leave and lie down in the bed of snakes from which they came. It is time for us all to follow the example that this man, the Pope, showed us. He may yet die, having saved someone of a different religion, of a religion of which many of its adherents have demanded the death of his kind. And until each of us, Muslim and Christian alike, can say honestly to ourselves that we too would lay our lives down for our fellow man, no matter what their beliefs, than we are no better than those who would lay their lives down to kill someone who doesn't believe, like these wretched souls who lie before us today."

The cameras dipped to look at the bodies of the gunmen, before returning to the podium, but the old man had turned away, and now walked toward the mosque.

Acton and Laura followed in silence, laying their weapons on the ground as they entered the holy place, the doors closing behind them. Reading approached.

"They've taken him out the back, an ambulance is already on its way."

"Martin?" asked Laura.

"He went with them since he's the closest thing to a doctor here right now."

The Imam turned to face them, then shook each of their hands in turn.

"I thank you all for what you have done here today. Without you, I fear things could have been much worse."

"I can't see how," muttered Reading.

"Indeed. His Holiness being shot is a tragedy, and I pray he recovers. But these gunmen were after me, not him. They were here to kill the one who would cooperate with the Christian, who would accept delivery of the one thing they had finally found that might trigger the apocalypse, and the return of the Mahdi. Your Pope, His Holiness, may yet die a martyr, sacrificing himself on holy soil, to save a man who just yesterday wouldn't take his phone call, instead content to see the world descend into chaos to achieve my own selfish dreams of the Mahdi's return.

"But instead, here I stand, a changed man. I now realize my ways were wrong. Am I any less of a Muslim? No! I am even more of a Muslim, for now I actually realize what Islam is. It *is* a religion of peace, if one takes the struggle, the Jihad, within, and wrestles those demons that consume each of us; demons that belch forth hate and intolerance. Yesterday I could have cared less if this man had died, but today, I feel a great sadness. Should he die, I will mourn his passing, and I will rejoice in the fact he will take his place beside God in Heaven.

"And from this day forth, this changed man, will preach the true Islam. That of peace, of love, of tolerance. And hopefully the seed planted here today, will blossom the world over, taking its place not as a weed that must be eradicated, or must eradicate in order to survive, but as a flower, living in harmony with those other flowers on this wonderful planet of ours. Perhaps the Mahdi will return, with Jesus at his side, not after an Armageddon of war and pestilence brought on by the weapons of man, but after an internal war within ourselves. Perhaps each of us has his own Armageddon within, that we must fight, and win, and once won, we are then worthy of entrance to paradise. Perhaps paradise, Jannah as we call it,

Heaven as you call it, is gained through winning the battle within, rather than without. Wouldn't it be wonderful if Armageddon was merely a metaphor for a struggle within men, rather than between men?"

Acton eyed the case the Imam now held containing the scroll that had caused all of the days' chaos, and nodded.

Yes, wouldn't it.

In Front of Saint Peter's Square
Vatican City

Acton stepped out of the car the Vatican had sent to pick them up, then extended a hand to help Laura out. He had asked the driver to let them off in front of the square, rather than inside the grounds—he wanted to see for himself the damage.

But it was almost anticlimactic.

Though there was a heavy police presence still, they weren't in riot gear, and were mostly away from the main gate. Vatican security was heavy inside, but trying to keep as unobtrusive as possible. Gawkers lined the half-height fence, tourists denied access until the grounds were cleaned up. The police barricades were gone, no evidence remained they had ever been there. The blood and debris both within and out had been hosed down, forever forgotten in a storm sewer somewhere, or swept up and tossed in some mob run landfill, to someday find itself on eBay.

And the praying continued.

They had been in Turkey for two days after the attack, interviewed by various authorities since they had killed Turkish citizens, but after a strong word from the Vatican, Italian, British and American governments, they had all been released and flown on a chartered Alitalia plane to Rome.

During their "interviews", the Imam's speech had had a remarkable effect. People stayed home, and people went home. No more incidents had been reported, and the Vatican occupiers had lost their will to fight. The original text of the Surah had been released to the public, and it had been immediately denounced as fraudulent by many, but some were reserving judgment. Progress, perhaps. The Pope remained in hospital in Istanbul, too weak to move, his prognosis positive.

"Excuse me, sir, but would you mind taking our picture?"

Acton spun, recognizing the voice instantly, but when he saw the man holding out a camera, he decided to play dumb.

"Sure, no problem."

The man and his friend positioned themselves in front of the gates, with the dome of Saint Peter's Basilica in view behind them, and Acton held up the camera, taking several shots of the two very familiar men.

"What brings you to Rome?" asked Acton as the men approached for their camera.

"Just sightseeing. Unfortunate the timing, but it had been planned for months."

Dawson and Niner huddled on either side of Acton as he pretended to show them the photos he had taken.

"What are you two doing here?" he asked in a whisper.

"Just keeping an eye on things."

"I assume your mission was successful?"

"I like that one!" exclaimed Niner.

"Yes, we were able to preserve the bones and kill the instigators. Once they were dead, the crowd started to settle down, then leave."

"That's good. Mario will be relieved to hear that."

"You haven't heard?"

Acton felt a tightness in his chest.

"Heart what?"

"He's in a coma. They're not sure if he's going to make it."

Acton closed his eyes and let out a deep sigh.

"What is it, Dear?" asked Laura as she left a conversation she was having with Reading and Chaney. She smiled in surprise when she saw who

Acton was talking to, but kept quiet when they all gave her a look that was unmistakable.

Play along!

"Mario's in a coma, they're not sure he's going to make it," whispered Acton.

"Hi, nice to meet you," said Niner, extending his hand.

Laura blindly took it, her eyes clouded with tears.

"N-nice to meet you," she said.

"We analyzed some footage taken of the shooting of the Pope. What did he say to you?" asked Dawson.

"He asked me to retrieve the skull."

Dawson frowned. "That's what I thought he said." He shook Laura's hand. "And what do you intend to do?"

"I intend to do just that."

Whitechapel Road
London, England

Kirby Weeks, no longer fueled with pints of courage, marched toward the scene of his own personal crime, carrying a broom over one shoulder, and several garbage bags tucked into his belt. As he rounded the corner of Whitechapel, he stopped. There were dozens of men, unmistakably Muslim, their thick beards and garb dead giveaways.

Fear gripped him.

His legs wouldn't move, then he heard a voice echo inside his head, something the Imam had been overheard saying after his impassioned speech.

Wouldn't it be wonderful if Armageddon was merely a metaphor for a struggle within men, rather than between men?

He took a deep breath, and stepped forward. As he approached the men cleaning up the mess in front of their mosque, they all stopped to stare at him. He stopped a few feet from them, not sure what to say.

But he knew what to do.

He dropped the brush of his broom onto the ground, and began to push, to sweep away the hate he had felt, the hate he had helped manifest those few short days before.

And tears of shame, and hope, rolled down his cheeks.

The men continued to stare at him for a moment, then resumed their cleanup, with Kirby in their midst.

As one.

THE END

ACKNOWLEDGEMENTS

When I began to write *The Templar's Relic*, I had a vague idea of where I thought it was going. But, as often happens, it didn't go anywhere near where I expected, and instead I ended up with the novel you just finished, and still have that other story to write, with even more background built up around these characters I have grown to love.

How did I come up with the idea for an "invasion" of the Vatican? I was out for a drive, trying to think of what to write for my next scene. I had the protesters converging on the Vatican, with the plan being for them to remain outside, but for those who read my books, you know that's never enough for me.

For some reason the fall of Saigon popped into my head, the dramatic visual of helicopter after helicopter evacuating people, the panic and horror of the situation.

And then it hit me.

"What if the protesters rushed Saint Peter's Square?"

A smile spread across my face, my foot pressed on the accelerator a little harder, and when I got home, I began to type, and the fall of the Vatican was born.

As usual people need to be thanked. My wife and daughter, my parents, Rick Messina, David Brooklyn and Marcel Primeau (aka Marcello Primo!). And to the over fifty thousand who have helped make a dream come true, my humble gratitude endures.

J. ROBERT KENNEDY

ABOUT THE AUTHOR

J. Robert Kennedy wrote his first story when he was five.

Everyone in it died.

Things didn't get much better from there. After horrifying his teachers in creative writing classes he took an extended hiatus, returning to writing on a whim, haunted by the image of a woman standing in tall grass, the blades streaming through her fingers. The result was a short story, written in a single evening: *Does It Matter?*

And then he let it sit.

A couple of years later he let several friends read it and they encouraged him to try and get it published. He submitted it to *The Sink* and it was immediately accepted. Encouraged, he wrote a second story, *Loving the Ingredients*, and it too was accepted, along with a reprint of *Does It Matter?* by *The Writers Post Journal*.

With several publishing credits under his belt, he was ready for something bigger. A phone conversation with a best friend led to Robert writing his first novel, *The Protocol*. Lachesis Publishing, the first publisher he sent it to, agreed to publish it and cloud nine got a little more crowded.

This was followed by *Depraved Difference*, an international bestseller, and the re-release of *The Protocol*, and its sequels, *Brass Monkey* and *Broken Dove*, all international bestsellers. To date, all of Robert's books have been bestsellers in their categories.

Robert was born in Glace Bay, Nova Scotia, and grew up an Air Force brat, living in Halifax and Greenwood, Nova Scotia, Goose Bay, Labrador, Lahr and Baden, Germany, and finally Winnipeg and Portage la Prairie, Manitoba. After a brief stint at the University of Waterloo, like Bill Gates, he went into business for himself and settled in Ottawa, Ontario. Robert has a wife and daughter, and is hard at work on his next novel.

Visit Robert's website at www.jrobertkennedy.com for the latest news and contact information.

The Protocol

A James Acton Thriller

Book #1

For two thousand years the Triarii have protected us, influencing history from the crusades to the discovery of America. Descendent from the Roman Empire, they pervade every level of society, and are now in a race with our own government to retrieve an ancient artifact thought to have been lost forever.

Caught in the middle is archaeology professor James Acton, relentlessly hunted by the elite Delta Force, under orders to stop at nothing to possess what he has found, and the Triarii, equally determined to prevent the discovery from falling into the wrong hands.

With his students and friends dying around him, Acton flees to find the one person who might be able to help him, but little does he know he may actually be racing directly into the hands of an organization he knows nothing about...

J. ROBERT KENNEDY

Brass Monkey
A James Acton Thriller
Book #2

A nuclear missile, lost during the Cold War, is now in play--the most public spy swap in history, with a gorgeous agent the center of international attention, triggers the end-game of a corrupt Soviet Colonel's twenty five year plan. Pursued across the globe by the Russian authorities, including a brutal Spetsnaz unit, those involved will stop at nothing to deliver their weapon, and ensure their pay day, regardless of the terrifying consequences.

When Laura Palmer confronts a UNICEF group for trespassing on her Egyptian archaeological dig site, she unwittingly stumbles upon the ultimate weapons deal, and becomes entangled in an international conspiracy that sends her lover, archeology Professor James Acton, racing to Egypt with the most unlikely of allies, not only to rescue her, but to prevent the start of a holy war that could result in Islam and Christianity wiping each other out.

From the bestselling author of Depraved Difference and The Protocol comes Brass Monkey, a thriller international in scope, certain to offend some, and stimulate debate in others. Brass Monkey pulls no punches in confronting the conflict between two of the world's most powerful, and divergent, religions, and the terrifying possibilities the future may hold if left unchecked.

J. ROBERT KENNEDY

Broken Dove
A James Acton Thriller
Book #3

With the Triarii in control of the Roman Catholic Church, an organization founded by Saint Peter himself takes action, murdering one of the new Pope's operatives. Detective Chaney, called in by the Pope to investigate, disappears, and, to the horror of the Papal staff sent to inform His Holiness, they find him missing too, the only clue a secret chest, presented to each new pope on the eve of their election, since the beginning of the Church.

Interpol Agent Reading, determined to find his friend, calls Professors James Acton and Laura Palmer to Rome to examine the chest and its forbidden contents, but before they can arrive, they are intercepted by an organization older than the Church, demanding the professors retrieve an item stolen in ancient Judea in exchange for the lives of their friends.

All of your favorite characters from The Protocol return to solve the most infamous kidnapping in history, against the backdrop of a two thousand year old battle pitting ancient foes with diametrically opposed agendas.

THE TEMPLAR'S RELIC

From the internationally bestselling author of Depraved Difference and The Protocol comes Broken Dove, the third entry in the smash hit James Acton Thrillers series, where J. Robert Kennedy reveals a secret concealed by the Church for almost 1200 years, and a fascinating interpretation of what the real reason behind the denials might be.

J. ROBERT KENNEDY

Depraved Difference

A Detective Shakespeare Mystery

Book #1

Would you help, would you run, or would you just watch?

When a young woman is brutally assaulted by two men on the subway, her cries for help fall on the deaf ears of onlookers too terrified to get involved, her misery ended with the crushing stomp of a steel-toed boot. A cellphone video of her vicious murder, callously released on the Internet, its popularity a testament to today's depraved society, serves as a trigger, pulled a year later, for a killer.

Emailed a video documenting the final moments of a woman's life, entertainment reporter Aynslee Kai, rather than ask why the killer chose her to tell the story, decides to capitalize on the opportunity to further her career. Assigned to the case is Hayden Eldridge, a detective left to learn the ropes by a disgraced partner, and as videos continue to follow victims, he discovers they were all witnesses to the vicious subway murder a year earlier, proving sometimes just watching is fatal.

From the author of The Protocol and Brass Monkey, Depraved Difference is a fast-paced murder suspense novel with enough laughs, heartbreak, terror and twists to keep you on the edge of your seat, then

THE TEMPLAR'S RELIC

knock you flat on the floor with an ending so shocking, you'll read it again just to pick up the clues.

J. ROBERT KENNEDY

Tick Tock

A Detective Shakespeare Mystery

Book #2

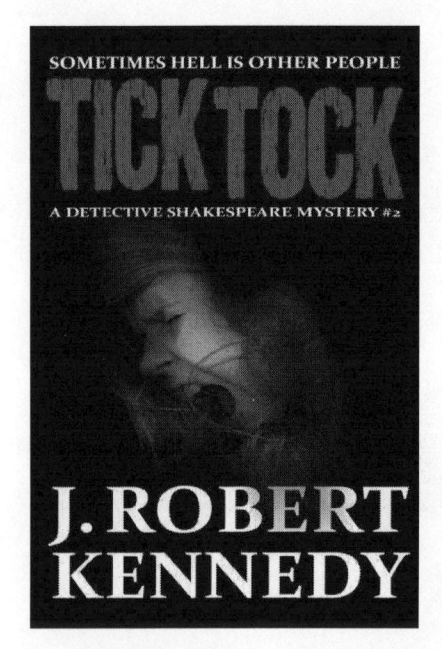

Crime Scene tech Frank Brata digs deep and finds the courage to ask his colleague, Sarah, out for coffee after work. Their good time turns into a nightmare when Frank wakes up the next morning covered in blood, with no recollection of what happened, and Sarah's body floating in the tub. Determined not to go to prison for a crime he's horrified he may have committed, he scrubs the crime scene clean, and, tormented by text messages from the real killer, begins a race against the clock to solve the murder before his own coworkers, his own friends, solve it first, and find him guilty.

Billionaire Richard Tate is the toast of the town, loved by everyone but his wife. His plans for a romantic weekend with his mistress ends in disaster, waking the next morning to find her murdered, floating in the tub. After fleeing in a panic, he returns to find the hotel room spotless, and no sign of the body. An envelope found at the scene contains not the expected blackmail note, but something far more sinister.

Two murders, with the same MO, targeting both the average working man, and the richest of society, sets a rejuvenated Detective Shakespeare, and his new reluctant partner, Amber Trace, after a murderer whose motivations are a mystery, and who appears to be aided by the very people they would least expect—their own.

Tick Tock, Book #2 in the internationally bestselling Detective Shakespeare Mysteries series, picks up right where Depraved Difference left off, and asks a simple question: What would you do? What would you do if you couldn't prove your innocence, but knew you weren't capable of murder? Would you hide the very evidence that might clear you, or would you turn yourself in and trust the system to work?

From the internationally bestselling author of The Protocol and Brass Monkey comes the highly anticipated sequel to the smash hit Depraved Difference, Tick Tock. Filled with heart pounding terror and suspense, along with a healthy dose of humor, Tick Tock's twists will keep you guessing right up to the terrifying end.

Printed in Great Britain
by Amazon.co.uk, Ltd.,
Marston Gate.